THE ROYAL COMPANION

TANYA BIRD

Copyright © Tanya Bird 2017

All rights reserved.
The right of Tanya Bird to be identified as the author of this work has been asserted by her in accordance with the Copyright, Designs and Patents Act 1988. No portion of this publication may be reproduced, stored in a retrieval system or transmitted in any form by any means, electronic, mechanical, recording, photocopying or otherwise with-out prior written permission of the above copyright holder.

www.tanyabird.com

❦ Created with Vellum

For Luke.

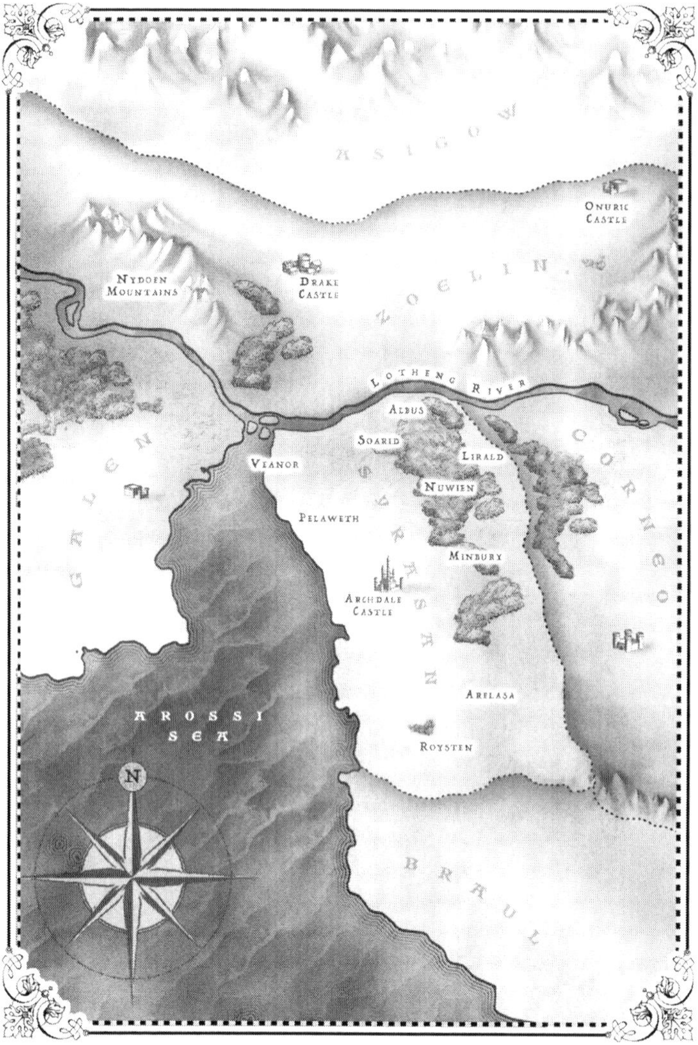

Asigow
Onuric Castle
Nydoen Mountains
Drake Castle
Zoglin
Lotheng River
Albus
Soarid
Lirald
Veanor
Nuwien
Pelaweth
Minbury
Archdale Castle
Arelasa
Roysten
Arossi Sea
N
Braul

PROLOGUE

They hanged the man outside of the church, in front of his family, his neighbours and a white-faced priest clutching the book of God. The body swung gently above the spectators, eyes bulging, head tilted at an unnatural angle. The only noise was the creak of the rope and the violent sobs of his widow.

Aldara wished she were back on the farm. She had never seen a man hanged to death. It was so rare in her village that the prince's men had been forced to construct the simple gallows just for the occasion. Noblemen rarely ventured this far south, leaving matters of the law in the hands of the local church. But one man from Roysten had sold Prince Pandarus a filly with an abscess, so Pandarus had made the journey from Archdale Castle to make a display of his intolerance of crime, which was a thinly veiled intolerance of the poor.

When Prince Pandarus spoke, there was a collective flinch among the crowd.

'Let us remember the kingdom that Syrasan is,' he said, seated on his horse next to the creaking gallows. The silk lining of his cloak flashed as he raised an arm to gesture. 'One of integrity.

Crimes against the people who are risking their lives every day to keep you safe will not be tolerated. Let this man remain here as a reminder.'

Blank, hungry faces stared up at him. But not the widow, whose eyes would not open. A tortured noise rang from her as she clutched the head of her son against her dress, trying to shield his view. Aldara swallowed down the lump forming in her throat and used the hood of her cloak to shield her own sight.

'We need to start moving,' Dahlia whispered. 'We cannot miss him.' She took hold of Aldara's laundered cloak and pulled her through the crowd as it began to disperse. The mud sucked at their boots as they moved out into the centre of the road, waiting for Pandarus to reach them. 'My lord,' she called, curtsying low as if standing on swept stone.

Aldara watched the hem of her mother's dress soak up the stagnant water around her feet. Pandarus did not slow his pace.

'I have nothing for you,' he said, increasing the distance between them and his grey mare.

Dahlia stood upright. 'I need nothing from you but a moment of your time, my lord. I wish to introduce you to my daughter before your departure.'

Pandarus reluctantly stopped his horse and looked at her. The two men flanking him stopped also, each with a hand on their sword. He pushed his thick cloak over his right shoulder, revealing a red 'S' on his arm, as though they needed reminding he was a member of the royal family. He turned his bored expression to Aldara. His hands loosened the reins a little.

Dahlia gestured for Aldara to step forward. She did as she was told, dropping into a small curtsy. Once she was upright, she removed the hood of her cloak as her mother had instructed. The cold air made her ears ache. Dahlia had forced her unruly hair into a low bun, and sections of it were blowing about her face in protest. She reached up and tucked them behind her ears.

Pandarus looked at the mud-splattered hem of her once blue

dress and then slowly moved his eyes up to her face. 'What is your name?'

'Aldara, my lord.'

'And what is your age, Aldara?'

'Fifteen, my lord.'

'Ah, not yet of age.'

Dahlia stepped forward. 'She will be sixteen in the warm season, my lord. And she reads and writes.'

Aldara stared at her mother, not recognising the tone of her voice. It was laced with desperation. Dahlia's pride usually kept her composed, even in the cold season when the food was gone. Having realised her own uncharacteristic behaviour, Dahlia collected herself, standing before Pandarus as though she was wearing something other than rags. Every hair was in place, released from its tight prison on wash days only. It was not even permitted time to dry.

Pandarus's eyes remained on Aldara. 'Have you seen a man hanged to his death before?'

She looked up at him and shook her head. 'No, my lord.'

'Was it difficult for you to watch?'

Aldara glanced down at his boots. She had never seen such clean boots, and wondered whether his horse had collected him from the front step of the castle. 'The grief of his family was very difficult to watch.'

Pandarus raised his eyebrows. 'Do you believe the punishment to be unjust?'

Aldara could feel her mother holding her breath. 'The real punishment is to his remaining family, who must now feed themselves and find a way to survive without him.'

He glanced back at one of his men with a smirk. 'Short-sighted criminals do not think through consequences of their crimes.'

'Hunger has a way of drowning logic.' She bit her lip to stop her mouth.

Pandarus looked back at Dahlia. 'I have met your daughter. What is it you want?'

Dahlia read him. Her time was up. 'She is intelligent and she is beautiful. I thought you may have use for her at Archdale.'

'I have no use for her personally.' He kicked his horse forward. 'However, write to me after her next birthday and we can reassess.'

The women curtsied, their eyes on the mud. They listened as the slush of hooves moved past them. When they rose, Dahlia narrowed her eyes on her daughter.

'Let's go,' she said.

CHAPTER 1

Aldara stood with Loda in the broken shade of a budding maple. Every few minutes the tall mare rubbed her sweaty head against Aldara, who struggled to maintain her footing against the weight of it. Loda. Her Loda. She would be left behind with the rest of them.

The family did not have the luxury of pets. Their animals had a use or they were eaten. Loda was the exception, a gift from her father on her tenth birthday. Her mother had been furious, insisting Isadore sell the thoroughbred for something that could be put to work. Much to everyone's surprise, the filly did not get sold. Six years later they stood together as old friends.

Her brother, Kadmus, was sowing barley on the other side of the fence. He had stripped down to a linen undershirt that clung to his wet body. A straw hat protected his face from the harsh midday sun. She remembered weaving the hat for him when she was twelve years old. It was full of mistakes, and he wore it every day of the warm season.

Kadmus had worked with a newfound intensity for the past two weeks, ever since Pandarus's men had visited. He had watched the men circle her, like a horse at the yards, inspecting her confirmation and commenting aloud as though the family was not in the room with them. They had instructed her to let out her hair and eyed her small breasts. They had asked her questions that made her father turn his eyes to the ground. Kadmus had left then. He had walked out of the small house and begun working. And he had not stopped since.

'Kadmus,' she called to her brother. 'Join me in the shade before you cook.'

'I need to finish this,' he said, without looking at her. He never looked at her anymore.

'Then you should have used the perfectly good harrow we have in the barn. You would have been finished days ago.'

'The horses mess up the field,' he said.

She rolled her eyes. Hitching up her dress, she took a handful of mane and swung her leg over Loda. She never used a saddle anymore, and Dahlia was forever scolding her for it. 'Ladies don't ride bareback.' It was no secret her mother wanted her to grow up.

Before she had even gathered the reins, the mare lurched into a canter. Aldara did not bother with the gate. She cleared the fence in one smooth stride and landed with minimal disruption to the freshly sewn seed. Within a few paces she reached Kadmus and bent low to snatch the rake from his hands. She came to a stop a few yards away from him. He stared at the hoof prints in front of him and the upturned seeds. She had ruined his perfect rows. He glanced up at her and squinted against the bright sun.

'Don't you think I have enough to do around here? How about helping instead of creating more work before you leave?'

At least he was talking.

'How about you stop punishing me as if my leaving is my choice?' She threw the rake at his feet. 'I don't want to go!'

Kadmus bent over and rested his hands on his knees. He was still out of breath from his work efforts. The defiant expression faded from her face, and her eyes welled up. She looked away then.

'Do you think I want to be sold off like the livestock? I don't want to go,' she repeated. Her voice was softer then.

Kadmus retrieved the rake off the ground and continued working. He was not angry with her. He was angry at his mother for selling his sister, and his father for letting her. He was angry because even though they needed the gold, he knew it was not only about the gold. Dahlia had conspired this uncertain future for her only daughter for years, and he could not fathom why.

'Father lets her do as she pleases,' he said, covering the exposed seeds with the toe of his boot. 'He could have said no.'

Aldara studied him. The neck of his shirt was yellow and frayed. He needed new clothing, and without the gold from her sale, he would not get it. The kingdom was still at war, and even if their crop was successful, they would not be guaranteed a sale.

'No one says no to our mother,' she said. 'And perhaps she knows something we don't.'

'That woman knows everything. It's terrifying. If you had been born a boy, we would have had two more years.'

'If I had been born a boy, I would have been considered useful and not been sold at all.'

'You're as useful as any man when you actually work.'

He leant on the rake and looked at her for a long moment. There was more he could say, but Isadore was walking towards them with a pail of seed.

'What are you two plotting?' he asked, handing the pail to Kadmus. 'On second thought, I don't want to know.' He gave Loda a rough pat on the neck.

'It's too hot for sowing,' Aldara said. 'We want to go for a swim.'

Isadore laughed. 'You're only here a few more weeks and you're still trying to weasel out of work.'

'It's not appropriate for ladies to swim. You better get used to fanning yourself at the castle,' Kadmus said.

He enjoyed baiting her and always made a point of not smiling. Isadore's eyes went to his feet. Any mention of Archdale had that effect on him.

'It's not appropriate for you to swim naked, but we can't keep clothes on you,' Aldara replied, keeping the conversation moving.

'Why don't you put that useless mare back in the stable and bring back a horse that can work,' Kadmus said. 'And the harrow.'

'Good idea,' Isadore said, looking up again. 'When the work is done, we will swim.'

Aldara smiled to herself as she turned Loda towards the barn. She rode along the fence line, so as not to disturb any more seed. The sun poured down on her, its warmth stinging her skin beneath her threadbare dress. But she did not wish it away, for soon enough the cold would arrive and leech the warmth from her bones.

CHAPTER 2

Aldara dismounted. She could feel the heat of her mother's fury. Dahlia stood with her hands clasped tightly and her eyebrows fused. She had removed her apron and put on her good dress, which had once been a vibrant green. Aldara was not sure if it was a sign of respect for the guards or if she was trying to pretend she was not poor. She may have been able to hide the calluses on her hands, but there was no hiding their poverty.

Aldara glanced over at the guards waiting in the nearby shade, suffocated by their embroidered tunics and knee-high boots. They showed little interest in their surroundings. It was not a social visit after all. She walked towards Dahlia, Loda trailing behind her, using her spare hand to brush horse hair from her dress. There was no sign of her father. The man who usually managed to be everywhere at once was suddenly nowhere to be found. Perhaps he could not witness the sale of his only daughter.

Her eyes flicked to the bare paddocks behind the barn where their failed barley crop had just been cleared. Too much rain, and then nothing. She could taste the dust that the breeze carried. Kadmus crossed in front of her, carrying cups of water for the guards. He tried to smile at her, but it was an uncomfortable lie for both of them. She recalled his words from earlier that morning; he had said no to their parents as if the decision was his. He had told them he would find more work, even though he barely slept as it was. They all knew there was no more work. Families found other ways to survive, like selling their least useful members.

Dahlia did not see it as a sacrifice. She told them it was an opportunity. She spoke of Aldara's life at Archdale as if it would be a better life, an easier life. She seemed sure of it. Isadore had said nothing as he stared into his thin soup. Dahlia reminded them that the gold would ensure they ate in the cold season when the rest of the village was starving.

'Aldara will have more food than she will know what to do with,' she had said before fleeing the room.

'You smell of horse,' Dahlia said, once Aldara was close enough to hear. She snatched the reins from her daughter's hand.

Aldara kept her eyes on Loda. 'I am sure they have baths at Archdale.'

The guards were shifting their weight from foot to foot, looking at the sun to gauge how much daylight they had left. She was delaying them. Dahlia reached down for the small hemp bag by her feet. It contained all of Aldara's belongings, none of which would be of any use to her at Archdale. There was a clean dress, some undergarments, and a wooden hair comb that struggled to contain her hair. It was the one thing she wanted to take. There had been a woman selling them in the Roysten marketplace, and her father had seen her slow down to look at them. They had all kept walking without saying a word, knowing there was no money for such things. A few weeks later Isadore had found her cleaning tack in the barn and handed her the replica he had made by hand. She had wrapped herself around him as though she were ten years old again.

'Kadmus will ride with you,' Dahlia said, pulling Aldara from the memory. She was holding the bag out for her to take.

Aldara took the reins back from her mother. 'Then I shall ride also.'

Dahlia snatched them back from her. 'You will ride in the cart with the guards. There will be no more discussion about the horse.'

Kadmus walked over to Dahlia and gently pried the reins from her hands. '*I* will ride Loda to the castle. We need to build up her stamina and prepare her for work,' he lied.

Aldara reluctantly took the bag from her mother and looked at her properly for the first time that day. She searched her face for signs of grief. All she saw were blackened eyes and creased skin, a result of little sleep and too much outdoor labouring. She appeared much older than her thirty-eight years. Isadore often reminded Aldara that she looked just like her mother did when he first met her. He would smile as he described her. Aldara could not picture a youthful version of her mother.

'Will I be allowed to write?' she asked, forcing Dahlia to meet her eyes.

Her mother reached out and began tucking stray strands of hair behind Aldara's ears. She was not gentle.

'The castle staff will instruct you on those matters. Now off you go. Your father needs help, and you have delayed the king's men for long enough.'

'Where is he?' She glanced at the barn again.

'Trying to keep us fed.'

Aldara could turn and walk away from her mother, but she did not know how to leave her father. Of course there was no choice in the matter. She moved her feet, one in front of the other. Her legs felt as though they were shackled and weighted. There was still opportunity for Isadore to appear, shouting he had changed his mind and could not see it through. He could tell Dahlia he would not let her go with strangers, that it was better to have nothing and be with people you love. But there was no shouting, only the slow shuffle of footsteps on the crusted earth, and the heavy thud from her chest.

The guards were waiting by the cart. One of them took hold of her arm as she climbed in. She pulled free from his grip. The offer of a hand was good manners; anything else was farm-handling.

The cart differed from theirs. It was not stained green with manure or littered with barley. The wood did not hold small tufts of wool pulled from the backs of sheep. She made a seat from her bag and watched Loda shift sideways as Kadmus mounted her. The mare was rarely ridden by anyone other than her. They eyed one another through the bars of her small prison. Kadmus handled the mare without difficulty. He was a strong rider, a requirement of farm life, but also attributed to sibling competitiveness. They had spent their entire childhoods trying to prove they were faster and more skilled than the other. The challenges they set themselves had been met with disapproval from their mother and became a constant source of amusement for their father, who was often called upon to settle disputes between them.

One of the guards reached inside his tunic and pulled out a few pieces of gold, which he handed to Dahlia. Aldara had expected a pouch. A few pieces did not seem enough for handing over one of your children. But what did she know. Dahlia's hand closed tightly around the gold as she thanked him. Aldara looked at the house where she spotted her father leaning against the outside stone wall. His head was slumped forward, and she could see his shoulders shaking. She moved onto her knees, holding the rails of the cart. She wanted to call out to him but was afraid of what she might say. His eyes went to her, but he did not move. The guards climbed onto the front of the cart, and it lurched forward, swaying above the uneven ground. Kadmus trotted silently alongside her, pretending not to see the breaking of hearts. Aldara watched the farmhouse, and her mother's back, shrink behind a rising cloud of dust. Her father blended into the shadows. The cart seemed much smaller. For years she had watched lambs leave the farm the same way.

'What was my worth in gold?'

The guards did not respond.

'It doesn't matter,' Kadmus said quietly. 'What is the correct amount for such a thing?' He kept his eyes ahead also.

Archdale was north of Roysten. A half-day's ride with fit horses and no stops. A few hours into their journey Aldara glanced up at the sun and realised they were moving east. She asked the men why they were travelling east, and once again they did not respond. When she looked at Kadmus he shook his head and continued to follow without comment.

By mid-afternoon they arrived in Arelasa, a large village known for its food market and high theft rate. They came across a frail man walking in the middle of the road. When the guards stopped to ask for directions, a flea-infested dog with all of its ribs on display emitted a low growl of warning at them. The man pointed a deformed finger as he spoke, his breath so vile with infection that when the smell reached Aldara she had to resist the urge to cover her nose and mouth. He was still talking as the cart pulled away.

The guards, in search of the baker's house, followed the partial directions until they were met by the smell of warm bread. The mouth-watering scent led them to a small wattle and daub house close to the road. It was bursting with half-dressed, barefoot children. They filled the small vegetable garden at the front of the house. 'They're here!' one screamed before running inside.

A girl wrapped in a yellow dress, and the legs of a small girl, came outside to see. 'Do not let mother catch you trampling her potatoes,' she said, waving the children off the vegetables. She gently placed the clinging girl down and picked up a bag sitting in the doorway. It looked just like Aldara's. The children gathered around her then, all speaking at once. Six girls, two boys. She bent down and hugged each of them before planting noisy kisses on their dirty faces. When she reached the smallest girl, she closed her eyes and buried her face in her hair as though inhaling her scent.

'Will you come visit us when you are a princess?' the girl asked.

Nobody said anything. More kisses. Her parents stood behind a border of children, barely composed. One of the guards coughed and gestured towards the cart. Gold was handed over. Gold in a pouch. Aldara felt like she was intruding, so she turned towards Kadmus. He was letting Loda drink from the trough while he stared at the road in front of him.

A few minutes later the arm-grabbing guard helped the curvy girl into the back of the cart. She placed herself opposite Aldara. 'Good thinking,' she said, sliding her bag beneath her as a seat. Fresh tears remained on her cheeks. She brushed them aside before smoothing down her stained dress as though creases were the issue with it. It was probably her best dress. It was probably her mother's best dress before that, a familiar story of the poor. Aldara looked down at her own dress, which had been rehemmed more times than she could remember. It had once been her mother's best dress. She remembered holding onto fistfuls of vibrant blue material as a child. She also remembered being regularly shooed from her mother's skirts. The blue cotton had faded with the memory. And now it was covered in horse hair.

'Don't cry,' the girl called to her mother as the cart pulled away. 'You'll start the children off again.'

The youngest was already wailing. The sound could still be heard as they turned the corner and headed out of the village.

'I was selected by Prince Pandarus himself,' the girl said as if answering a question.

Aldara felt herself jump. She looked at the girl and said nothing.

'He bought bread from me at the market. My sister stood by, besotted, while he asked me about the bread's quality and taste. I barely breathed through the entire transaction.' She laughed at the memory of it. 'A few minutes later he made a request to my father for me. The prince himself,' she repeated. 'My youngest sister thinks I am going to the castle to become a princess.' Her face reddened and her eyes went to her lap.

'And what are you going for?'

The guards exchanged a laugh between them. Kadmus was still staring at the road. The girl glanced at them before looking back at Aldara. 'To be his Companion of course.' She seemed confused by the question.

'How do you know he did not buy you to serve?'

The girl laughed. 'Maids are paid a wage and are free to leave.'

Aldara looked at Kadmus, who knew very well she was looking at him. 'Prince Pandarus did not even notice me until mother used me as a road block. Why did he buy me?'

'Your wit perhaps,' he said.

No one said anything further.

When the sun was low in the sky and the road began to widen, Archdale rose like a mountain on the horizon. Kadmus moved Loda a few paces ahead of the cart to take in the sight of it. Isadore had promised to take Aldara when they were not so busy on the farm, but they were always busy. There were no leisure days for farmers. She still remembered the stories they told her when she was younger, of castle walls touching the sky. She could not comprehend such a thing when she had barely travelled outside of Roysten, and she struggled to fathom how men could build a curtain wall so high when each bluestone brick weighed more than her.

They came to a stop in front of the portcullis, sitting in a queue of riders and a cart loaded with pigs. Every person had to explain the purpose of their visit before they were permitted entry. The girls watched as the portcullis was raised and lowered ahead of them. When they finally reached the two guards, sweltering in direct sun, they were immediately waved through the gaping mouth of Archdale. As the cart rolled under the arch, Aldara felt a surge of panic. She turned around in search of Kadmus. When he went to ride through after her one of the guards blocked him.

'That's far enough for you,' he warned, hand on his sword.

Loda raised her head, and her front legs came off the ground. She did not like people in her way.

Aldara turned to the guards driving the cart. 'Stop. I need to speak with my brother.'

They ignored her, so she crawled to the back of the cart and unlatched the door just as the portcullis began to lower behind them. Kadmus watched her, unable to do anything else. He stared through the gaps in the iron as she jumped from the back of the moving cart and stumbled towards him. But there was nowhere for her to go. One of the soldiers had her back in the cart before it had even stopped moving. She was on her hands and knees, panting, at the feet of the girl. Her head hung inches from the floor while tears landed by her hands. When she looked up, the girl was watching her with pity, the excitement in her eyes gone.

'I did not get to say goodbye to my brother,' Aldara said to the backs of the guards.

No response.

She sat up and pressed the back of her head against the wall of the cart. Only then did she feel the heat of tears on her face.

CHAPTER 3

Fedora stood in front of the two girls with the straightest back Aldara had ever seen. Her thick hair was pulled back, held together by a spray of pearls that contrasted her dark skin and fierce green eyes. Her silk dress exposed her shoulders and wrapped her throat. When she spoke, nothing moved above the mouth.

'What is your age, Aldara?' Fedora said.

She seemed to already disapprove of the answer. Aldara wondered if it was perhaps the smell of horse she disapproved of.

'Sixteen, my lady.'

'And what is your age, Hali?' she said, turning to the other girl.

'Nineteen, my lady.' Hali replied with a nervous smile.

Fedora looked at her with suspicion. 'Nineteen and not wed?'

'No, my lady.'

'Are you a virgin?' There was a long silence before she spoke again. 'There is no point in lying. You will both be examined by the physician.'

'Yes, my lady.' She was kneading the fabric of her dress between her fingers.

'Let go of your dress, Hali. Your mind should not be available for all to see.' Fedora waited for her to look up. 'Follow me,' she said, turning and walking from them. The tail of her silk dress slid along the polished floor, and her jewelled shoes made a delicate clicking noise against the marble. The filtered light from the corridor windows reflected off them, making light dance around her.

Aldara watched her own worn boots slap the ground. She glanced behind her to ensure she was not leaving a trail of dirt. When she looked forward again, she almost walked into Fedora, who had stopped walking and was watching her with unblinking eyes. They had arrived at a door.

'I will organise some duties to see you through the next season. You will not be socialising until your age is less apparent.'

Aldara shook her head. 'I am sixteen. Many women are wed at this age.'

'You may well be. However, you appear younger than your sixteen years. While men are attracted to youthful women, it will be difficult for you to fulfil your role in its entirety if they view you as a child. There are things we can do to age you, but time is what you need right now.' Her eyes flicked down to Aldara's breasts.

Aldara took the opportunity to ask the one question no one seemed to want to answer. 'Can I ask what role I am to fulfil when you feel I am ready?'

Fedora's expression suggested she preferred to share information on her terms rather than be questioned. 'You are a gift between brothers. This is not an appropriate discussion for a public space. In the future you are to keep your questions for the privacy of the Companions' quarters.'

'Which brother?' she persisted.

Fedora looked both ways down the corridor, and when she was sure there was no one around, she spoke in a lowered voice. 'Were you told nothing?'

Aldara shook her head. 'Nothing.'

'I am not sure why that would be, as it is not a secret. You were purchased by Prince Pandarus as a Companion for his brother, Prince Tyron. You will be working towards this role beginning today.'

Aldara shook her head again. 'Purchased *for* him? I have never met him. Wouldn't he want to choose a Companion for himself?'

Fedora crossed her bare arms elegantly in front of her. 'It is not your place to question decisions made by the princes. Scrutiny is reserved for those with power—wealthy men. As you are neither wealthy nor a male, you can hold your questions. Am I understood?'

Aldara nodded.

'*Yes, my lady,*' Fedora said slowly.

'Yes, my lady.'

Aldara knew little of Prince Tyron other than he was known as the Prince of Mercy. Kadmus had once told her the story of how the prince had pardoned a man who had been caught stealing grain from the royal supply. The hollow-faced wife of the thief had brought their children to the castle gate and requested an audience with whoever would see her. Prince Tyron had appeared, and after seeing the pinched faces and wasting limbs of her children, he had agreed to hear her out. She had fallen to her knees and begged for the life of her husband, their only provider, to be spared. The man was released that afternoon. Her favourite part of the story was he had also given the family a side of pig and two loaves of bread to take home with them.

Aldara knew little of the youngest prince, Stamitos, and even less of Princess Cora. She had heard only the gushing descriptions of her beauty from a clearly besotted Kadmus. 'Have you ever heard of a princess that was not beautiful?' she had asked him when he finally fell silent. 'With enough food, gold and servants, anyone can be made beautiful.' He had accused her of being jealous. She *was* jealous, but not of her beauty, rather the fact she could eat to bursting without worrying about where her next meal would come from.

Fedora gave a small clap of her hands and raised a perfectly arched eyebrow. 'Can we proceed, or do you need a moment?' Her tone was not friendly.

Aldara was finding it difficult to process everything at the speed required of her. 'Sorry, my lady.'

Fedora led them through the arched doorway into a small room with an uneven stone floor and a lit fireplace. Fireplaces were becoming common in noble houses throughout Syrasan. The rest of the kingdom relied on warmth from the stoves that cooked their soups and baked their breads. In the warm season many cooked in open fires outdoors to keep indoor temperatures bearable. The heavy stone walls at Archdale seemed to repel the heat.

'Ladies,' Fedora said. 'I want to introduce you to Violeta, Panthea, and Rhea. They are Companions to some of Archdale's most important guests.'

Aldara looked at the three women seated in armchairs with books in their ironed laps. Blemish-free, expressionless faces, rehearsed in Fedora's technique of not having your inner-thoughts on display.

'This is Hali and Aldara,' Fedora said, gesturing towards them.

The women's eyes swept over them. They nodded and said something courteous that did not match their tones. Then they returned their disinterested faces to their books.

Fedora exited through a different door, signalling for the girls to follow her. They entered the sleeping quarters where there were two rows of beds dressed in white linen. Aldara thought of her bed at the farmhouse, which had been dressed in exactly two blankets, one which provided warmth, and the other so worn it was pointless. She did not know any farming family who could afford to use linen on their beds. When they could afford linen, it was used for undergarments and shirts. Dahlia used the scraps to make aprons and pillows.

Aldara thought back to the cold season Kadmus had lost one of his blankets to their plough horse. The horse became sick with heaves, and the thought of losing the horse had Dahlia in a silent panic. Kadmus was wished the horse a quick recovery, or death, whichever got the blanket back the quickest. The horse recovered, but inconvenienced him by taking weeks to do so. They had been fortunate enough to have mattresses stuffed with wool from their own sheep, which provided more warmth than the straw used by most people.

'You will sleep here,' Fedora said, pointing to the two closest beds.

Hali took a few steps forward and placed her bag next to one of the beds. She ran her hand across it, enjoying the luxurious feel of it beneath her hand. Aldara resisted the temptation to do the same.

'Meals are served in the front room where we entered,' Fedora continued. 'If your duties cause you to miss a meal, you can eat in the kitchen downstairs. The kitchen maids are very accommodating as they understand the unpredictable nature of your duties. You are not, however, permitted to eat in the hall, unless you are invited to do so by a member of the royal family or one of their guests. Usually, such an invitation will come through me. I suggest you limit your time outside of these quarters for now. Wandering about can be problematic for those who are still learning.' She paused to make sure the girls understood. 'Herbal tea will be provided with your meals. All Companions are required to drink it, regardless of their duties.' Another, much longer pause. 'There are robes at the end of your beds. Take them with you to the bathing room, which is through that door. When you are done, meet me in the dressing room. I will find something appropriate for you to wear for your chores.'

Hali looked up. 'Chores, my lady?'

It was the first time Aldara had seen Fedora blink. It was done with perfect restraint.

'Yes, Hali. Everyone contributes in their spare time, and you will have plenty.'

Hali could not hide her disappointment. 'But we are Companions, not maids.'

Fedora's eyes glowed a little brighter, but the rest of her remained perfectly still. 'At the moment you are nothing. An uneducated commoner, unworthy of even serving food to guests. Do not confuse Archdale with the whorehouse in your village. You will have to work hard for the privilege of keeping company with Prince Pandarus. Only once you meet, or exceed, the high standards set by your fellow Companions will you have the opportunity to prove your worth. Until then, I suggest you get to work.' Hali turned her burning face to the floor. Before she could respond, Fedora spoke again. 'There is no shortage of prostitutes in the kingdom, and there are many women who would not charge for the opportunity.'

Aldara could see Hali's embarrassment growing. 'Surely you can forgive Hali for her confusion. She was bought by a prince who showed little interest in her education when he met her at a bread stall.' The words just came out. It was not uncommon for her mouth to get ahead of her good sense.

Fedora's expression did not change. 'You have much to learn, child. Let us hope you are a fast learner, or you will spend the rest of your youth cleaning the prince's fireplace and fetching water for the women in his bed.'

Aldara failed to see the downside in that threat but dared not say as much.

'You will both attend church in the mornings,' Fedora said, moving the conversation along. 'You will be discreet at all times and stay within your designated area.'

'Is that compulsory?' Aldara asked.

Fedora looked taken aback for the first time. 'Which part?'

'Church attendance, my lady.'

'Are you too busy for God?'

'I don't believe in God.' There was an unnerving silence while Fedora waited for her to elaborate. 'I once saw a six-year-old girl sitting on the side of the road, holding her baby sister. Her sister would have been no more than two years old. It was snowing, and it was far too cold for either of them to be outdoors, but they were hungry and begging for food. I had nothing with me, so I told them I would bring them something on my return trip. When I returned, I found them both dead. Someone had stolen the cloaks off their bodies.' She could still see them slumped together. Their blue, open mouths. 'I have doubted God's existence since that day.'

'God is not to blame—the girl's parents are,' Fedora replied, unmoved by the story. 'You will need to find a way to believe. Your faith is not negotiable here.' She left them alone with the vision of two dead girls.

Hali sat on the bed and pressed the soft robe against her chest. She raised her shiny eyes to Aldara. 'Perhaps God took the girls someplace warm.'

Aldara gave her a small smile. Her stomach felt tight, and she was swallowing down waves of nausea. She could see her own fear reflected in Hali's face, and all they could do was move, begin. 'Let's go wash,' she whispered.

They followed the scent of flowers to a small, steamy room with four wooden tubs. Water was draining from one of the tubs, running across the sloped floor and through a gap at the bottom of the far wall. Two women sat by the stove where a pot of water was bubbling away. Their hair was still wet from bathing. They stopped their quiet conversation and looked curiously at the new arrivals. Aldara swallowed again and checked each tub to see if any were filled. One was. She placed her hand into it to check the temperature of the water and then looked back at the stove where the water continued to boil.

'Help yourselves,' said one of the women, gesturing towards the pot.

Aldara tried to be discreet as she came between them, but they were watching her closely. 'Thank you,' she said, to no one in particular. She added the hot water to the tub and signalled for Hali to climb in before refilling the pot.

'That one is for Pandarus,' said the redhead, nodding at Hali.

The other woman laughed. Aldara pretended not to hear. When it was her turn to bathe, she covered her breasts with one arm as she climbed in. She took soap from the nearby table and smelt it before scrubbing her entire body and lathering up her hair. Two bottles of oil sat next to the soap. She lifted one and sniffed it. It was a familiar flower she could not place. She added a few drops to the water and then used the ceramic jug to rinse herself. When she stood, she felt three sets of eyes on her. She retrieved her robe and secured it tightly around her body. She had never bathed in front of anyone other than her family.

Hali applied both oils to various parts of her body. The smell took over the air and made Aldara cough.

'Those oils are meant to enhance your natural scent, not drown it,' said the redhead. She stood up and took them from Hali's hands. Hali wiped her wrists against her robe. 'My name is Astra.'

'I'm Hali. And this is Aldara.'

Aldara gave a nod and watched as Astra gently tipped the oil and barely touched it to her wrist. She pressed her wrists together before opening her robe and lightly touching her collar bone. Aldara looked away then. Astra noticed and laughed. She turned to the other woman. 'She's shy,' she said, in a teasing voice.

The other woman did not join in the laughter, but there was amusement in her eyes. 'Leave the poor girl alone, Astra.' She stood up then. 'My name is Idalia. You can be forgiven for finding Astra intimidating. She is Pandarus's little prize.'

Astra waved a hand. 'What Idalia always fails to mention is

she is the *king's* Companion. She has been his only prize for almost five years. Pandarus has had many *prizes* in that time. They are frequently updated,' she added, looking at Hali. Her playful tone did not match her expression. 'And what about you?' she asked Aldara. 'You are not his type. I am guessing you are a coming of age present for Stamitos.'

Aldara shook her head. 'I am a gift, my lady, but for Prince Tyron.'

Astra smiled, revealing straight, white teeth. Her lips matched the colour of her hair. 'You can call me Astra. Save the formalities for Fedora.'

Aldara realised how ridiculous she must appear to such beautiful women. Their bodies were long and lean and their skin radiant. Idalia's eyelashes kissed the tops of her cheeks whenever she looked down, but it was her confidence that held Aldara's attention.

'What can we expect to see from you ladies?' asked Astra. 'Pandarus maintains high standards for his Companions. Anything interesting we should know about?'

'Interesting?' Aldara said.

'Yes. Aside from your obvious traits, what were you bought for?' Her chin lifted a little, showing off her perfect jaw structure.

Idalia could see they did not understand. 'Astra plays the harp like she was born with it in her hands. The king's most distinguished guests often request that she play for them. I dance, but only if the king is present.' She began to comb her hair. 'Companions are not the kingdom's most beautiful, we are a collection of the most talented, educated, and desired. We are the best parts of all women.'

'Of course being beautiful is part of being desired,' added Astra. 'You will not see any talented and educated women here with horse-like teeth and eleven fingers. Let's not mislead them completely.'

Hali looked nervous. 'Does baking count?' Aldara smiled. The others just blinked. When no one spoke she continued. 'I make sweet breads that taste so good, people travel from other villages to buy them. I use preserved quince. Not many people are familiar with quince. They are shipped from Galen when the weather cools.'

Aldara wanted to hug her. The castle had the best cooks in the kingdom. Though it did explain her full curves while the rest of the South were covered only by their clothes.

Before another word could be spoken Fedora entered the room at a brisk pace. 'Idalia, the king has returned and is requesting your company before his evening meal.'

Idalia secured her robe and left them.

'You are to assist Idalia,' Fedora said to Aldara before turning to leave.

Aldara had no idea what that entailed. She glanced at Hali before following after them. When they arrived at the dressing room, Aldara stopped in the doorway. The explosion of colour made her breath catch. An endless rainbow of dresses, hanging, folded in neat piles, and draped over purple velvet chairs. To the right there were rolls of luxurious fabrics and a timber stand with rows of shoes. High leather boots weaved with fine leather laces, jewelled slippers, and suede ankle boots with shiny brass buckles.

'Breathe,' Idalia said, as she made herself comfortable in a chair. She smiled at Aldara in the mirror.

Aldara exhaled and stepped inside. Fedora searched through one of the piles and selected a blue cotton dress with long fitted sleeves. She handed it to Aldara.

'Put this on and fix your hair. There are clean undergarments in a trunk over there,' she said, pointing.

Aldara took the dress and ran her thumb across the soft fabric. The stitching was faultless. She carefully lifted it so that it fell open and held it at arm's length by the shoulders. The bust and waist were gathered, and the cuffs trimmed with cream lace. 'I wear this for chores?'

Idalia glanced at her. 'Something needs to set you apart from the maids.'

Aldara laid the dress over a chair while she retrieved some undergarments. They were diffcrent from anything she had previously owned. She held each piece up as she tried to figure out how they might be worn. Fedora saw her struggling and walked over.

'That is a breast band,' she said. She picked up what appeared to be shortened pants and handed them to her. 'We do not wear loin clothes here. These should fit you.'

Aldara was studying the frill around the leg when she realised that Fedora was waiting for her to dress.

'Are you able to fix hair? Paint faces?' Fedora asked as she corrected the undergarments and helped her into the dress.

'I can do hair. I have never painted a face,' Aldara replied, pressing her lips together.

'Children do that with their lips when they are shy or nervous. You will need to learn better ways of dealing with nerves.'

Aldara relaxed her lips. 'Yes, my lady.'

By that stage Idalia had slipped into a light green silk dress that gathered at the shoulders. The neck was lined with small emeralds, and the back was open, revealing her creamy skin.

'Fix her hair, and I'll come back and show you how to paint faces,' Fedora said.

Aldara stood with her hands at her side, looking at the mass of chestnut hair. Idalia caught her eye in the mirror and signalled for her to come closer.

'Fedora may seem hard, but the lessons she teaches are essential to your success here,' she said, handing Aldara a comb. 'She was the king's Companion before me, and she has been at Archdale since she was fourteen years old. There is no better teacher for this life.'

Aldara began to twist Idalia's hair into a bun. 'Why is she no longer his Companion?'

Idalia handed her a jewelled comb. 'Look around you. I am the oldest Companion here. The novelty does not last long for men who have women at their disposal. Youth does not last. The lucky ones stay on to mentor, but even that cannot last.'

'Why not?'

'Because of what they represent.'

Aldara thought for a moment. 'And what of the unlucky ones?'

Idalia looked at her in the mirror. 'It would be uncomfortable for all to have former Companions running about the castle doing laundry and serving food. Companions have one purpose, and when they are past that purpose, they go.'

'Go where?' Her eyes did not leave the mirror.

Idalia shrugged. 'Some place where beauty and talent go to die.'

Fedora walked back into the room and picked up paints from the table. 'Watch and remember,' she said to Aldara.

Aldara knew she needed to learn more than she needed to breathe. She did not want to disappear. The only talents she had brought with her were farming and horse related, and she was certain her fence repairing skills would impress no one.

Fedora finished applying final touches of paint to Idalia's lips and took a step back to inspect her work. 'You will accompany Idalia to the king's quarters and return as soon as she is accepted by the king's guard. You will speak to no one. When you return, you and Hali will assist some of the others to prepare for a gathering tonight. Am I understood?'

'Yes, my lady.'

Aldara had no idea where she was going. She followed Idalia

and made mental maps in her head so she could find her way back. She struggled to focus with all the distractions. The coloured glass windows in the corridors depicted graphic images she would have to look at on the walk back. Idalia did not speak one word to her. With her head high, she floated, green silk sweeping the floor behind her. They arrived at a guarded double wooden door. The guard opened it without speaking. He nodded at Idalia and then glanced at Aldara. She kept her eyes on the ground in front of her.

'Thank you, Aldara. You can return to your quarters,' Idalia said, passing the guard.

Aldara gave a small curtsy and turned as the doors closed behind her. She paused for a moment and looked both ways down the corridor. Breathe. The sound of approaching footsteps made her hold her breath again. When she looked to her right, she saw four women walking towards her. The woman at the front had a gold crown weaved through her honey hair. Aldara's eyes went to her slim, youthful face with its well-proportioned features and vibrant green eyes. Those eyes were looking directly at her, filled with disapproval. The giant corridor did not seem wide enough suddenly. She backed up against the door in a panic, but the guard pushed her forward again. Princess Cora's eyes were locked on hers. She stopped walking, and the other ladies immediately stopped behind her.

'Where is your decency? How dare you not curtsy before the Princess of Syrasan?'

Her venomous tone did not match her appearance. Aldara's gaze moved down her embroidered dress before settling on the floor. 'Forgive me, my lady,' she said, dropping into a curtsy. She remained there, hoping the princess would move on. No such luck. Before she had a chance to stand, she heard footsteps approaching on her left. She glanced up just as Fedora came to a stop next to her.

'I apologise, my lady,' Fedora said, lowering into a curtsy next to her. 'The girl is a peasant and has just arrived at Archdale today.'

Cora's eyes remained on Aldara as she returned upright. 'Perhaps you could keep the whores on a shorter leash and out of my way. We cannot have them lingering outside the king's quarters, cheapening our home, can we?'

Aldara felt as though her lungs were being pressed together. She watched Fedora lower into a curtsy once again as Princess Cora continued past her, flanked by her ladies whose icy gazes made her shudder. Fedora said nothing. She turned and began walking away. Aldara followed out of fear of being separated. Only when they had reached the Companions' quarters did Fedora turn and look at her. Her expression was a mixture of anger and concern.

'Princess Cora…' She considered her words for a moment. 'Her ladyship has little patience for…many things, but the Companions most of all.'

'I am sorry.' Aldara's voice was barely audible.

Fedora did not care for apologies. 'The princess has a lot of power over many aspects of castle life. So unless you want to be scrubbing floors in the kitchen, I suggest you stay out of her way.'

'I wasn't ready. I couldn't remember my way back. Why did you send me?'

'Because your lessons start now. If you encounter a member of the royal family, you move out of their way and you curtsy until they have passed.' Her shoulders dropped a little. 'You will not forget it now. Go and help Hali in the dressing room, and then you can both return here for the evening meal.'

Aldara's feet did not move. Fedora read her expression.

'What is it?'

She pushed some loose hair back from her eye. 'I'm not like the others. I am not sure I can do it. Any of it.'

'You are not the first common girl to find your way behind

these walls, and as you can see, the Companions here are anything but common. Each is extraordinary. It is a process.'

Aldara should have felt comforted by those words, but she did not. Watching Fedora walk away only reinforced just how common she was.

CHAPTER 4

Tyron rode his horse alongside a pile of twisted bodies, looking at each face. Typhoid had taken them before the Corneon army could. He was all too familiar with the devastating effects of the disease and knew how fast it could spread in the conditions of war. He stopped his horse to study a boy the same age as Stamitos, a boy who had probably spent his youth waiting to come of age so he could fight alongside his older brothers. Every mother dreaded the arrival of her son's eighteenth year, knowing the dangers that awaited him. That boy's mother would soon learn of her son's death, validating every fear she held.

Tyron turned to face the clearing where eighty-foot pines had stood three months earlier. His men had sawed through their thick trunks and used horses to tear the stubborn roots from the ground. They had needed space for the men to sleep, eat, and kill, a visual border for their enemy, an enemy that did not care for borders. Now it was a festering grave, thick with flies and crows. His remaining men were still sifting through the dead, faces wrapped with cotton to block the smell of so many open wounds.

They searched for Syrasan men who deserved something more than to rot beneath their enemy.

Little grew in the East during the warm season, and nothing seemed to survive the cold. The need for food was forcing the Corneons west onto more fertile land, Syrasan land. Food shortages were a problem everywhere, and survival instincts were making good men do desperate things, like transforming a dense forest into a mass graveyard. During battle these men had collapsed at his feet while he moved about them in an automated state, his technique flawless, his mind closed. He did not hesitate as he drove his sword through the chests and necks of Corneon men, but a small piece of him died alongside each of them. Afterwards, he had crouched on the bloodied earth, panting, listening to the groans and final breaths of the dying. Some of his men fought out of obligation, many out of loyalty to his father. Some of them were knights, a few of them his friends. When the Corneons finally retreated, packing up the few horses that would last the journey and disappearing into the tree line, he was forced reflect on his losses. And he could not bear the sight of it.

Leksi rode up beside him then, a handkerchief over his mouth. 'We should leave.' He was terrified of dying from disease; he wanted to die fighting.

'We should bury the dead,' Tyron said.

'There are plenty of men to bury the dead. Your fight is over. The risk of typhoid is too great. You cannot survive three months of fighting only to die of typhoid upon your return. You will be laughed at. Mothers will use you as an example every time their children don't wash their hands properly. Don't embarrass me.'

Tyron had no idea where Leksi found the energy for humour. He seemed to thrive in the conditions of war, growing stronger while the rest of them wilted. Food and sleep were optional for him. He also happened to be the most skilled knight that Tyron had ever encountered. Tyron's men often joked that Leksi was his guardian angel. It would have been funny had it not been so close to the truth. His friend since birth had saved his life more times than he cared to admit.

The dead remained in the sun awaiting their burial. Tyron and Leksi rode their wasting horses east through the parched villages. Women lined the roads to pay their respects to the prince, but their gazes went to the empty road behind him. They were waiting for their husbands and sons. Tyron could barely raise his eyes to them.

'I could eat an entire deer,' Leksi said, as they exited the small village of Minbury. 'That will be the first of many requests when we reach Archdale. Deer have the good sense to flee large groups of armed men. I did not see one the entire time we were there. Not sure where the meat came from that we were eating, but it didn't taste familiar.'

'Only you would complain about the quality of food during a war. And I am fairly certain it was horse we were eating.'

'Well-bred I hope.'

Tyron's hunger was secondary to his need for sleep. He also wanted a wash with hot water. Wash, sleep, and then some steaming soup and fresh bread in the quiet of his quarters. But he knew better. King Zenas would throw a feast to celebrate his return and their shallow victory. There would be too much food, too much wine, more guests than he could handle, and little sleep. His father would talk at him, his mother would fret, Cora would complain, and Stamitos would hound him for battle details he was not prepared to share. And then there was Pandarus, whose shame would see him drink himself into a stupor. He would make inappropriate jokes in front of guests, some of who might be mourning. They would likely quarrel over something trivial and then avoid each other for a number of weeks.

'And real women,' Leksi said, pulling him out of his thoughts. 'Tonight we will be dining with Syrasan's finest blooms.'

'Yes, and most of them belonging to Pandarus.'

Leksi mulled that over for a moment. 'Tradition supports his right to keep Companions.'

'Companion. Singular. One Companion.'

'He enjoys new things.'

'When he is bored,' Tyron replied, glancing at Leksi. 'The Noble Companions are a collection of his previous impulses. When the novelty wears off, they are handed down to desperate guests like yourself.'

'Pride has its place, and inside the walls of Archdale is not that place. I have been secretly waiting for Astra to join the Noble Companions.'

'It's no secret. You have always had a thing for redheads.'

'Surely he's done with her by now.'

Tyron smiled. 'I wouldn't hold my breath, though the drunker he is, the more generous he becomes with them. You will not be alone in your bed tonight.'

'I know. I'll be with Violeta.'

Violeta had been Pandarus's first Companion. She was experienced. The perfect post-war treat for a man like him. A lady in all regards, but never in bed. It had been a long three months sleeping in an empty bed with only men for company.

Archdale appeared before them, and they stopped their horses to absorb the vision. Behind those walls was every comfort a man could dream of, and yet Tyron hesitated. He knew the comforts would not be enough to stop him spiralling.

'How long do you suppose until I will have to come to your chambers and drag you from your bed?' Leksi said, reading his thoughts.

Tyron said nothing. Last time it had taken months. Leksi had come every morning and sat by the untouched food in the darkened room, talking about horses, hunting, weather, and women. He would lay out clothes on the bed while he talked, and they would remain there until his squire arrived with his evening meal and packed them away. Then one day Leksi had arrived and found Tyron already dressed. He did not come the next day. The need had passed.

Leksi kicked his horse into a trot and led them up the wide dirt road to the already opening portcullis. It was Tyron's horse that decided to follow. Soon the previous three months would become just another story told to young aspiring knights. Another great defeat of Corneo.

Tyron was greeted outside of his quarters by Pero, his relieved and eager squire whom he had sent back to Archdale at the first confirmation of typhoid.

'Welcome home, my lord. Shall I send for some food?'

Pero understood that his master was not one for pointless conversation. Tyron patted his arm as he passed. 'Hot water first. Good to see you well.'

Once inside his chambers, he leant against the heavy wooden door, willing away the threat of visitors. The room looked unfamiliar. Someone had redecorated in his absence, no doubt his well-meaning mother, who always insisted that a change of scenery was the best thing for his mind. An oil painting hung above his bed. It was of a place he had never seen. The bed curtains tied to the posts were red velvet. What he actually needed was something familiar to take hold of. How was he meant to sleep surrounded by the colour of blood? He walked over to the curtains and pulled at them until they came down. He kicked them to the corner of the room and looked back at the bed, which was dressed in white linen. The air returned to his lungs.

~

IT WAS his mother who reached him first. He had just finished washing when she burst through the door, unannounced. Pero rushed in after her and a gestured apologetically to him. Tyron dismissed him with a shake of his head. There was no point fighting it. Pero left, closing the door behind him.

'My dear son,' Eldoris said, her eyes shiny. She stepped up to him and held him. But not too long because she knew better.

Tyron watched his mother harness her emotions. Those moments reminded him she was a queen as well as his mother.

'We have prayed every day for you. The priest is sick of the sight of me. Here you are at last. And a hero.'

'Not a hero,' he said, stepping back from her.

'This was your victory.'

'A generous term for what it was.'

She took a breath before speaking. 'Our borders are safe for now.'

He looked at her. 'At what cost?'

She nodded and walked over to the small window, taking a seat on the cushioned armchair, an armchair that had also been introduced in his absence.

Tyron leant against the wall on the other side of the room, resisting the urge to lie on the bed. 'What is news here? Make it good news.'

Her gaze went to the window so he would not see the worry on her face. 'Stamitos is suddenly a man. He has so much to give the Syrasan people when he comes of age next season. However...his...enthusiasm concerns me.'

She was a queen, but she was a mother first, fiercely protective of her children. A Galen trait. Family was everything to the Galens. Eldoris and her two sisters had been raised by their mother, Queen Kaiya of Galen. The role of governesses was purely educational. Lessons of life and love were taught by family. One year after her marriage to King Zenas, the new queen of Syrasan had given birth to Pandarus. She had caused great confusion in the castle when she insisted on nursing him herself for the first two years of his life. She attended to him throughout the night and allowed him to sleep in her arms during the day. When Tyron was born two years later, Zenas let her do as she pleased, making no comment on the nursing. And when he took his first Companion, shortly after Tyron's birth, despite promising before God to be faithful to her, she did not say a word. Two more children came along. And other Companions.

'Perhaps Pandarus will learn something from his youngest sibling,' Tyron said, rubbing at his eyes to fight off sleep.

Eldoris looked at him, disapproval etched on her face. 'I was hoping you would leave the fight at the border. Pandarus has been of great help to your father in your absence. He has been liaising with King Jayr. A challenging man,' she added.

'God help the Zoelin people with him on the throne. He was unbearable as a prince. Now he is gagged by no one.'

'There has been talk of an alliance.'

'God help us all then.'

Eldoris waited for him to look at her, but his eyes were heavy and closing. 'Someone needs to ensure we have allies while you take care of our enemies. We are not all born great soldiers, my love.'

The door swung open and Cora appeared in the doorway. She stepped into the room, uninvited, and took in the sight of her brother. 'Thank goodness you are alive,' she said, her tone filled with drama. 'Now everyone can stop mourning you as if you are dead.' She made herself comfortable on the edge of the bed.

'Where is my squire?' asked Tyron, glancing at the door. If there was one person he needed announced, it was his sister.

'Probably still pressed up against the wall, shaking,' she replied.

Tyron exhaled. 'What did you do to him? He is terrified of you.'

Cora pretended to be offended by the accusation. 'Nothing. Shall we have him beheaded for his incompetence?'

'Careful, you sound just like Pandarus.'

She looked around the room. 'Did you bring me anything?'

Tyron shook his head and glanced at his mother. 'I have been fighting a war, not taking a pleasure journey.'

'Why on earth were you gone so long? I hope you at least won.'

Eldoris rose from her chair and walked towards the door. 'Honestly, Cora, let your brother be. He fights so that you can continue to enjoy your privileged life here.'

Cora turned her pouty face up to the ceiling. 'Is that what I am doing here? I thought I was waiting to be married off.'

Eldoris ignored her, eyes on Tyron. 'Please get some rest, my love.'

'That was my plan.'

Once Eldoris had left the room, Cora looked at Tyron. 'Have you seen Pandarus yet?'

Tyron noted the flicker of mischief in her tone. He never played Cora's games. She loved to make trouble and had spent most of her youth developing her abilities. Her siblings had learned their own unique defence skills in the process. 'Why do you ask?'

'I heard he bought you a whore,' she said, with exaggerated delight. 'One of your very own. Though no doubt you will share her with Leksi, like you do most things.'

For as long as he could remember, Cora had wanted Leksi. And for as long as he could remember, Leksi had shown little interest in her beyond the usual impulses of a young boy. Leksi was aware of her feelings, however, and he enjoyed the small amount of power that gave him. It was never a question of beauty. She was without question the most beautiful princess Syrasan had ever produced. It was her appalling manners and blatant self-interest that had noblemen fleeing. Tyron had suggested to her once that if she did not open her mouth, men might actually want to marry her instead of just admire her.

Her eyes had burned through him.

'You think I should shut my mouth and be beautiful? You are just like all the other men,' she had said before walking away.

It was the first time Tyron could remember seeing something different in her face. Something painful. Something human. While he acknowledged that there were aspects of her life over which she had no control, in all other aspects, she was highly manipulative in getting the things she wanted. Leksi presented a unique challenge for her.

'Is that your way of checking if Leksi returned with me?' he said.

Cora rose from the bed and placed a delicate hand on her hip as she walked towards the door. 'I look forward to this evening. We can all celebrate your return and raise our cups to Syrasan's heroes.'

'I will be impressed if you make it to the toast. Usually your ladies have to carry you to your quarters before then.'

She stopped and looked at him. 'The attention *is* exhausting.'

'I think we can safely credit the wine.'

She glanced at the pile of velvet in the corner of the room. 'I see our redecorating efforts were much appreciated. Honestly, brother, where is your gratitude?' She left the room before he could respond.

Tyron shut the door behind her and leant against it once again. He used his remaining energy to walk to his bed, which he was asleep on within moments. All too soon he would have to wake and pretend to celebrate their controversial victory. While the guests stood with smiles on their faces, he would see only the faces of the dead who remained at the Corneon border, wide-eyed and open-mouthed, falcons hovering in the skies above them. He would not forget their faces. They would appear whenever he closed his eyes and still be vivid when he woke drenched in sweat. Eventually he would find a place in his mind for them, along with all the others. If only he could sleep for longer.

CHAPTER 5

Aldara was just about finished with Hali's hair when Hali leapt from her stool and vomited into a nearby jug. Aldara filled a cup of water from one of the clean jugs and sank down onto the floor next to her. They looked at each other in the mirror.

'What if he is utterly disappointed?' Hali asked, face pale.

Aldara turned towards her and pinned loose threads of hair. 'He won't be,' she whispered.

'I have nothing else to offer him. You heard Fedora, she actually said that.'

Aldara kept her eyes on the hair. 'He does not need anything else from you. He has Astra for those things and did not buy you for your musical talents.'

Hali's shoulders dropped a little. In the two months they had been at Archdale, they had discovered only that she spoke too much. She had no other talents. Pandarus had grown impatient with Fedora's insistence she was not ready to socialise and had eventually demanded she be present at the feast to celebrate the return of his brother. He wanted both new purchases on display.

'Aldara's age is too evident,' Fedora had said to him.

'She is a gift for Tyron. What is the point of her if she is not available to give?'

Fedora had been dealing with Pandarus since his coming of age nine years ago. She was not unnerved by his tantrums.

'I assure you she will be an absolute prize when the time is right.'

He did not care for waiting, and he left her without pleasantries.

Fedora had worked tirelessly with the new arrivals, teaching etiquette, languages, history, and politics. Outside of books, they were average singers, poor dancers, and useless with musical instruments of all kinds. She focused on languages, which they were picking up rather quickly. She provided them with charcoal, ink, and coloured paints, hoping to find alternative talents to offer the princes. Neither could draw, and their colour mixing almost always resulted in murky shades of brown.

When Fedora walked into the dressing room, she paused as the smell hit her. 'Dear God, who is ill?' She spotted Hali on the floor clutching the jug and forced herself forward. 'You do not get to be sick this evening. You have been requested, the invitation already accepted. Now you must attend. Please go do something about your breath and find a smile. It is a feast, not a wake.'

Hali scurried away. Fedora met Aldara's eyes in the mirror.

'She is as ready as she will ever be, so there is no point indulging her. I will ensure she receives some wine with dinner to relax her for the evening.'

Aldara nodded. 'Yes, my lady.' She stood, picking up the dirty jug that remained next to her on the floor. 'What would you like me to do this evening?'

'Stay here. And pray Hali does not return until the morning.'

Aldara was the only Companion that did not socialise. She knew Tyron had returned, but because she was not ready to meet him, no one spoke of it. She felt like a child tucked up in her bed while the adults played. Time alone also meant time to think, something she tried to avoid. Her mind always wondered to Kadmus, his resigned face as the portcullis had lowered between them. She saw it over and over. Then she would remember her broken father amid the shadows of the farmhouse and the indifferent face of her mother. These visions consumed her. She tried to focus instead on the feel of the linen against her bare feet. The clean smell of her nightgown. But the dark room and silence permitted her mind to run freely. It was the early hours of morning when she fell into a reluctant sleep. When she opened her eyes, she looked over to the empty bed next to hers and smiled.

Only Astra and Rhea joined Aldara for the morning meal. They stared into their bowls, pushing vegetables around with their spoons. No one mentioned Hali's absence or asked Rhea why she had returned early. Aldara had learned that everything that needed to be said was said to Fedora. While the women were happy to share shoes, clothing, soap and jewellery, intricate details of their social lives remained theirs.

That morning Fedora kept to her usual lesson plan, focusing on conversation etiquette. One hour into the lesson, Aldara realised the social rules being taught applied only to the Companions. They were expected to remain neutral on most topics, a strategy which minimised the chance of offending anyone at all.

'Rhea, what if a Zoelin guest asked your opinion on the recent Corneo war?' Fedora said, pacing in front of the empty fireplace.

'I would say what a great Syrasan victory it was. I would use the opportunity to discuss the strength of the Syrasan army and remark on how reassuring that must be to our allies.'

Fedora nodded her approval. 'Do you have anything to add, Aldara?'

Aldara glanced at Rhea, already sensing her hostility. 'I would refer to previous victories to highlight our enduring strength, despite being a relatively new kingdom.' Fedora nodded her approval, but she was not done. 'Of course if I were having an honest conversation, with unrehearsed answers, I might comment on the high number lives lost of both sides. I might mention the devastation Corneo faces with its ongoing food shortages.'

Rhea shook her head. 'Must you always do this? Your opinion does not matter to these men. It does not matter to anyone.'

Fedora's lips pressed together. 'Thank you, Rhea,' she said, quietening her. She looked back at Aldara. 'It is your role to guide the conversation in a direction that benefits the king you serve, not offer opinion. But you already know that.'

Aldara blinked. 'A far safer option would be to ask the guest's opinion, agree with it, and remember my place.'

'Enough,' Fedora said. 'You forget that these lessons are for your own protection. You never know who these men are and what influences they may have. Your job is to strengthen alliances, not start quarrels.'

Aldara swallowed and looked down. Before she had a chance to apologise, Hali entered the room, hair dishevelled, with traces of paint around her eyes and lips. Fedora walked over to her and touched her arm, the way a mother would.

'Wash and then go to the kitchen for some food,' she said, before removing her hand. 'Drink your herbs. I will speak with you after you have slept.'

Hali nodded. 'Yes, my lady.' She glanced at Aldara as she passed her.

'The rest of you are free to read,' Fedora said, concluding the lesson.

Astra stood up, her chair screeching along the floor. No one said a word as she hurried from the room. Fedora selected a book from the shelf next to the fireplace and handed it to Aldara.

'You can brush up on your Galen history.'

Aldara stood up and took the book from her, but she did not move.

'What is it?' Fedora asked, sensing a question.

'It's about the herbs. I have not bled since I started taking them.' She kept her voice low so the others would not hear.

'A sign of their effectiveness. Their purpose is no secret. They reduce the chance of pregnancy.' She did not lower her voice. 'Companions are not like other women. They are eternally virtuous in a sense. Men want their wives fertile, not their Companions.'

Aldara watched Rhea step away from the table and settle into an armchair. Then she turned back to Fedora. 'You say they *reduce* the risk. Have there been Companions where the herbs have not been effective?'

'None that have ever remained here. Drink the herbs. The day-to-day life of a Companion is already uncertain. We control the things we can. Now go assist Hali,' she said, taking the book back from her. 'You can continue with your reading afterwards.'

They both knew Hali needed no assistance. It was either a gesture of kindness or a clever means to end the discussion.

Aldara found Hali in the bath, face lit with excitement. She walked over to the tub and took both of Hali's wet hands in hers. 'I am glad you are happy.'

'I need not have worried. He was visibly pleased with his choice,' Hali said. She did not need prompting for more details. 'I had heard such nasty things about him, but he was charming and funny. And clear about his wishes,' she said, a flush of red coming to her face. 'Do you know that you bleed the first time? Lucky Fedora warned me or I may have embarrassed myself.'

Aldara shook her head. 'I didn't know, but there is no need for me to know. Did he mind a woman bleeding on his bed?'

'He seemed pleased by it, murmuring into my ear about virtue and God's gifts to great men.'

'I suppose it's a sport for a man like him.'

Hali pouted. 'What do you mean a man like him? I am telling you he is not the man people paint him to be.'

'On the contrary, your story proves he is that man.'

Hali sunk back into the water. 'Well, you didn't know he was funny, did you?'

Aldara realised she had ruined Hali's good mood. She forced a smile. 'No, I didn't. I'm sorry. I'm actually very pleased for you.'

She heard more about the evening than she had been prepared for. Hali discussed in detail all of her *talents* that had been unearthed within the walls of Pandarus's chambers. They were likely not the talents Fedora had in mind, but Pandarus's opinion would count for more in the end.

'What of the feast?' Aldara asked, changing the subject.

New energy came to Hali's face. 'It was like nothing I have ever attended. I ate pork so tender it fell apart in my mouth before I had even chewed. I have an unquenchable thirst from all the salted fish I ate. Or perhaps it was the wine.' She regathered her thoughts. 'All of it served to us as if we were noble guests.' She looked down at the water as she ran her finger over its surface. 'We danced, and then Idalia danced. No one noticed the other Companions after that. I wish you could have seen her come alive before the king.' She took hold of Aldara's hands again. 'I saw him, you know. Your prince.'

Aldara rolled her eyes and pulled her hands away. 'My prince? He does not even know of my existence.'

'Of course he does. To be honest, he was quite dull. He barely left his seat. Perhaps it is better you do not have to suffer through his company yet.'

Aldara stood up and wiped her hands on Hali's robe. 'He has just returned from war. I think he can be forgiven for seeming a little indifferent.' She gestured for Hali to stand and wrapped the robe around her.

'What's wrong with you? You're moping.'

'I'm not moping.' She thought for a moment and then shrugged. 'Maybe a little. I think I just need to get outdoors. I honestly do not care if I never meet him as long as I am not kept inside forever.'

'Careful, you sound like a farm girl.'

'I am a farm girl.' Aldara reached down, scooped up a handful of water, and poured it down Hali's back. Hali squealed.

A few minutes later the two girls were on their hands and knees, using towels to soak up the water on the floor. Their game had ended with jugs, and now Aldara needed to change her dress.

'Perhaps he will not want me at all and Fedora will send me out to be a stable hand,' Aldara said.

Hali sat back on her feet and looked at her. 'Be careful what you wish for. You just might find yourself wearing men's clothing, shovelling manure all day.'

Aldara shrugged and glanced down at her soaked dress. 'Sounds like my old life.'

Hali flicked water at her before continuing to clean.

Over the following weeks, Hali spent more nights with Pandarus than not. She would return in the mornings exhausted. Wash, eat, sleep, and then be requested again in the evening. Aldara thought Fedora would be more pleased, but she said nothing aside from quiet whispers with the servants. While it was clear Pandarus was enjoying himself, Fedora appeared to be bracing for something.

One afternoon while Aldara was being privately tutored on Zoelin history, she decided to raise the topic with Fedora. She was seated opposite her at the table, with paper and ink spread before her. There were no books, just Fedora's bottomless pool of knowledge. Aldara glanced over to where Panthea and Rhea were reading before leaning forward so she would not need to raise her voice.

'Will Hali be all right?'

Fedora gave a brief look of disapproval before answering.

'The Syrasan tradition for royal men has always been a single Companion. It is common for that Companion to change; however, Prince Pandarus is the first prince to keep multiple Companions at one time. This is new territory for everyone, and the women struggle with the uncertainty it creates.'

Aldara returned the quill to the inkhorn in front of her. 'Astra is unmatched in talent and beauty, so we have to assume she is safe. Will he dispose of Hali when he is bored with her?'

Fedora raised her eyebrows. 'That is very perceptive for a girl of your age. He keeps Astra because she is desired by all of his peers. She is safe for as long as this is true.'

'The pregnant and the old disappear. What happens to the young and beautiful when they are no longer of use?'

Fedora glanced at the women by the fireplace. 'The fortunate ones stay on to entertain noble acquaintances. That does not always work of course. It can be uncomfortable for men to see their former Companions with others. Most disappear like the pregnant and the old. Where do you think one could go from this life? Other households do not keep Companions. And noble men do not marry unvirtuous women. Use that perception of yours, Aldara. These are questions you already know the answers to.'

Panthea looked up from her book, and they both fell silent for a moment.

'Fetch your paints,' Fedora said, standing up. 'I want you to paint a scene from this very room. The women seated before you speak a minimum of three languages, fluently. Capture their brilliance.'

Aldara was a terrible artist. Panthea and Rhea paid no attention to her as she sketched and painted. They had come to view her as a maid, doing nothing for themselves when she was around to do it for them. She was always fetching their dresses, collecting garments from the seamstresses, and bringing them food from the kitchen. Aldara went along with it because it felt like a much safer existence. Even at sixteen she had become mindful of her expiry date.

After a few hours she stopped and studied the disproportionate painting of two faceless women. She felt a cold panic as she realised her sloppy depiction of them might one day be the only evidence they had been there at all.

CHAPTER 6

The air at Archdale began to thin. The sun lost its sting and took a little longer to thaw the walls. Evenings crept closer. An extra woollen blanket appeared on the women's beds. Their softness and thickness were all Hali could talk about. Aldara said little, but at night she moved her toes against the linen, enjoying the extra weight.

Aldara preferred to do her chores early while the rest of the castle slept. It was the only time she was alone for the day. She enjoyed the silence and the relaxed way she could move about the castle. She often loitered in the corridors where the sun spilled through the windows, piecing together Syrasan's history from the stories told on the walls and windows.

One morning she stood with a pile of fresh towels pressed against her chest, strolling between the stained-glass windows depicting different battles in their history. She stopped in front of a red glass panel with horses, twisted and bleeding at the feet of their riders. She stepped closer and pushed up onto the tips of her toes so she could see the wounds of the men.

'Syrasan's first battle with Corneo in 1478,' a voice came behind her.

Aldara's feet dropped, and she swung around to find a man standing a few feet away. He was looking past her to the window. She followed his eyes back to it.

'Just two years after Corneo was divided,' he continued. 'They were trying to avoid civil war.'

Aldara gazed at the painful scene. 'If only they could have foreseen that the real fight was in front of them.'

He was silent for a moment, and when he spoke it was almost a whisper. 'Yes.'

Aldara glanced over her shoulder, eyes moving to his bare feet. She was trying to guess his position from his clothing. His untucked shirt was high-quality for a servant. Her eyes flicked up to his face. He appeared as though he had not yet slept. 'I remember my father telling me the story,' she said, her eyes returning to the window. 'The Syrasan army had not been ready. Many of the soldiers were young and inexperienced, and their loyalty to their new king did not make up for this.'

'But they fought hard to defend their new life.'

'And lost.'

He looked at her then, as if noticing her for the first time. 'Yes. But later they would win it all back.'

'And the Corneon people would starve. That is why this scene is so confronting. It is not just their deaths you see, but their hunger.'

When he did not reply she turned to face him. But he was no longer there.

CHAPTER 7

The day before Aldara's seventeenth birthday, Pandarus sent for Fedora to meet with him in his chambers.

'I will be hosting a hunt tomorrow,' he said, leaning back in his chair.

'What is the occasion, my lord?'

He folded his hands in front of him. 'Must I need an occasion?'

He was frequently agitated with her these days. Fedora knew better than to indulge him. She waited for him to continue.

'I am fending off boredom and inviting others to join me before the snow arrives and traps us all indoors.'

Fedora bowed her head. 'I will help in any way I can, my lord. Are there any particular requests for the event?'

Pandarus tapped the boot resting on his other knee. 'Yes. I want every Companion in attendance. Now that Tyron has emerged from his cave of self-pity, I want the girl introduced. I want him to enjoy himself so the mood is not completely destroyed by his presence.'

Fedora curtsied. 'As you wish, my lord. Will His Majesty be in attendance?'

He shook his head. 'He prefers to leave the hunting to the young and save his energy for the feasting.'

The disrespect did not go unnoticed by Fedora.

'Idalia will need to remain behind. However, there is no reason why all the other Companions cannot attend.'

He stopped tapping his boot. 'You usually make up reasons.'

She blinked. 'My recommendations are made with your best interests in mind. I aim to protect the reputation of your family and the standard of the women I mentor.'

'Yes, yes,' he said, waving his hand dismissively. 'You sound like my old governess. That is all.'

She curtsied and left him. When she was back in the Companions' quarters, she gathered the women in the front room. Idalia and Astra took two of the arm chairs while the others sat at the table. Astra's book occupied the third armchair. She did not offer to move it, and no one asked her to. These opportunities served as reminders to the others of her rank.

'Prince Pandarus is hosting a hunt tomorrow,' Fedora began. 'The guests will be received at the stables in the early morning. You are expected to attend and socialise with them prior to their departure. Idalia, the king will not be taking part in the hunt, so you will remain here. There will be around twelve guests plus the three princes.'

Idalia looked relieved. She had been unwell for a few days and appeared not to have fully recovered.

'Aldara, I trust you can find something suitable to wear. Consider the type of event you are attending whilst keeping in mind it will be your first introduction to his lordship, Prince Tyron.'

All eyes were on Aldara then. She looked only at Fedora, waiting for more, but nothing more was offered.

'What would you like me to do at the event?'

'Everything you have been taught since your arrival six months ago,' Fedora said.

Panthea was the first to lose patience with the conversation. 'Must everything be so difficult with you?' she said, standing.

Fedora silenced Panthea with a glance before returning to Aldara. 'You know what is expected. Do not lose confidence simply because the time has come for you to put it into practice.'

Rhea and Violeta exchanged a smirk.

∼

ALDARA RESISTED the urge to look at the others for fear she would see Hali's face reflecting her own terror. She had been mentally sorting the cloaks and gloves for the women. Outdoor events required far more planning. Now she had to include herself in the equation.

The Noble Companions followed Fedora out of the room. Astra stood slowly, eyes on Hali. She spoke to her while she was walking away, a disrespectful act according to Fedora law.

'I am surprised you have been requested for daytime socialising. Whatever will you do with yourself in the light of day with no wine to fuel you?'

Hali kept her eyes on Aldara until Astra had left the room. 'She makes a valid point,' she said, her eyes welling.

Idalia laughed and stood. 'Oh, Hali, do not listen to her. Astra needs you to fail. You are her biggest threat at this point in time. You cannot blame her. She does not want to end up seated at the table with the other bitter, used-up Companions or find herself exiled from Archdale in the early hours of morning.'

'Where do they disappear to?' Aldara asked. She noticed that Idalia's face was flushed, assumedly from being so close to the fireplace.

Idalia shook her head and glanced about the room. 'I would imagine they become governesses of sorts. Lonely, barren governesses who are occasionally bedded by the lords who own them.' She paused for a moment. 'Imagine how hated they must be by the lady of the house.'

'Why not return them to their families?'

Idalia looked at her as though the suggestion was ridiculous. 'Because we are commodities, bought and sold. By the time a Companion is sold she is worth around six times the gold that was paid for her. We are the highest educated, most socially refined women in the kingdom. Could your family afford to buy you back? Even if they could and did, what would they do with you?' She paused for a moment so Aldara could think about it. 'You would be a ruined woman with no marriage prospects. You would waste away at your family's farm until your death.'

Aldara did not want to think about it and wished she had not asked the question.

'But why would they want to profit off us?' said Hali. 'These men care for our wellbeing in some capacity. We share their beds, after all.'

Idalia tilted her head. 'Have you learned nothing in your time here? Ours are not love stories. They would sell us to brothels if that produced the best financial outcome for them.' She left them then, seemingly exhausted from the conversation.

Once they were alone, Hali reached over and took Aldara's hand, interlacing her fingers. 'Make sure you don't start tending to the horses tomorrow,' she whispered. 'I need you here with me.'

Aldara squeezed her hand. 'I was thinking I would join the hunt.'

Hali forced a smile. They were both pretending they were not afraid.

'Fedora believes you are ready,' she said. 'That is all the reassurance you need. All of those awful paintings you keep bringing back to our sleeping quarters have led to this moment.'

'Awful? You are attacking my *only* talent.'

'If that is the talent you are leaning on then we should probably say our goodbyes now.' Hali smiled. 'I believe we are yet to uncover your talent.'

'I hope you are right. My family cannot afford to buy me back, even at half price.'

Hali stood up. 'Let's go and choose you a dress that sets you apart from the stable hands. Tomorrow you finally meet your prince.'

In the morning, Aldara woke before the others. She sat in her nightgown in front of the mirror in the dressing room, staring at the girl, trying to see the woman. She was seventeen that day. Although coming of age for a Syrasan woman was sixteen, she still felt trapped in her adolescence. If she had been on the farm, her brother would have woken her before dawn to go riding before their chores began. They would have returned to the house as the sun was climbing and gulped down a hot morning meal of broth and bread, reluctantly served up by their mother, who would complain the entire time they were eating. 'We'll be hungry tonight,' she would say, ruining the mood for everyone. Her father would smile with his eyes only and wink at her. Later he would help her with her chores so she could spend the afternoon as she pleased.

Aldara looked away from the mirror and swallowed down the choking feeling rising in her throat. The moment of self-pity was interrupted by Hali bursting into the room and planting an excited kiss on her cheek. 'Put on the dress. I want to see you in it,' she said. 'You will have the attention of every man today.'

Aldara watched in the mirror as Hali laid out the garments. 'With Astra in attendance I cannot imagine anyone will even notice I am there.'

Hali glanced at the door to make sure no one was coming. 'She rarely visits his bed, you know. He may flaunt her in front his guests, but those angelic hands of hers do not venture further than her harp these days.'

Aldara stood and walked over to the dresses hanging along

the wall. She pulled a cream coloured dress from its hanger and held it against herself. 'He has you for his bed.'

A worried expression settled on Hali's face. 'Yes, but there is a reason she is not off entertaining his friends with the other *retired* Companions. He needs the best. And she is still the best in the terms that matter.'

Aldara looked at her, unsure what to say.

'It's all right,' Hali reassured her. 'I may not be the smartest Companion here, but I can figure out the basics.' She took the dress from Aldara's hands. 'Put that away. We already decided on this one.' She held up the deep blue silk dress with short sleeves and plunging neckline. 'You won't be able to wear anything underneath from the waist up.'

The dress had a thin belt that wrapped underneath the bust, designed to give a fuller appearance. Hali had helpfully pointed out that Aldara needed such a feature.

After Aldara had slipped into the dress, she stared at the mirror. Initially, she thought she appeared older, but the longer she looked, the more she felt like a child playing dress-up.

'Sit,' Hali instructed. 'I will do your hair and face so that the next time you look into the mirror you smile at what you see.'

Aldara had never seen Hali concentrate so intensely on a task. She spent most of her time painting Aldara's eyes and left the rest of her face natural. She combed her hair to the side and did a braid before fixing a silver hair piece behind her ear. When Aldara looked back at the mirror, her breathing slowed. The blue paint around her bright eyes made them a startling highlight. She stood up and studied her reflection. She felt far less ridiculous and almost seemed like one of them.

Hali could not stand around admiring Aldara since she had to get herself ready as well. The room was filling with women. They said nothing as Aldara painted their faces, fitted their dresses and picked out their jewels. Most of the women had chosen velvet for its warmth, but when Astra saw Aldara, she went and changed into a silk gown.

Fedora came to check on the women before their departure. She circled the room, casting a critical eye over each of them. Her face gave little away. She paused next to Aldara for a moment. 'Lovely,' she said, before walking on. 'It is cold outside. Do not return to me ill. Most of you will be requested this evening, and I do not want to have to explain to our lords that you are not well enough to attend.'

The women moved around Aldara like a flock of startled birds. Colour swirled about her while her own feet remained anchored to the hardwood floor. Hali stopped in the doorway to wait for her, but Aldara waved her on. Finally, she was alone with her mirrored reflection once again. She lifted her dress off the ground to see her silk shoes.

'I wore that dress once,' came a voice from the doorway.

She looked up to see Idalia leaning against the wooden frame. Her hair was out, and her face scrubbed clean. She wore a simple cotton dress and had a blanket draped around her shoulders.

'It was years ago, but I will never forget the way the king watched me that day.' A faint smile came to her face. 'That is the right dress for you today.'

Aldara pressed her hands against the belt. 'I imagine you filled it much better than I do.'

Idalia laughed. 'Your youthful appearance will one day work in your favour. Do not wish it away. Men never do the math, but most see clearly.' She pulled the blanket tighter around herself.

'Are you still unwell?'

Idalia shook her head. 'Just tired.' She pushed herself off the doorframe and walked off towards the bedroom.

It was time for Aldara to catch up to the others. She did not look back at the mirror, instead envisioning Idalia in the same dress, standing boldly before a besotted king. Success meant survival. That is what moved Aldara's feet forward.

CHAPTER 8

Tyron had never been one for riding without a destination, but now he rode aimlessly for long periods, and sometimes at ungodly hours. He had just returned from a ride when his brothers walked into the stables with a tangle of excited dogs at their feet. He dismounted, and a groom rushed forward to take his horse.

'Have someone check him over,' he said to the young boy. 'He feels lame.'

Pandarus and Stamitos joined him, whistling at the dogs in an attempt to calm them. Stamitos put a hand on Tyron's shoulder and squeezed it. Pandarus folded his arms in front of him.

'I thought that gelding of yours was unbreakable,' Stamitos said.

Tyron watched the horse walk away. When it was out of sight he looked at Stamitos. He was taller than Pandarus now, but a childish smile flickered on his face, a reminder he was still a boy despite his recent coming of age. Tyron thought of Pandarus at that age, ruler of his younger siblings, barking orders at them as though he were already king.

'Perhaps today you could retire your old warhorse and make

use of some of the other mounts wasting away here. These are the finest horses in Syrasan,' Pandarus said, looking about. 'They are not here for show.'

Tyron could not have disagreed more. 'Then stop buying them,' he said. 'Let us put the gold to better use.' His eyes remained on Stamitos. 'The gelding has a lot of fight left in him. Don't feed him to the dogs just yet.'

Pandarus's gaze remained on Tyron. He did not like to be reprimanded by anyone, but especially Tyron. 'Will you be joining the hunt today? It will be a large group, and I am sure the men will feel honoured by your participation.'

Tyron glanced at him tiredly. The sarcastic tone reminded him of Cora. Hunts hosted by Pandarus were an excuse to display his horses, his dogs, his riding abilities, and his women. He liked to prove he could handle a bow, to make up for his inability to use a sword with any skill. Half the guests would come to hunt; the other half would come for the women. It was exactly the type of gathering Tyron tried to avoid. Stamitos enjoyed them because he was starving for action in any form he could get it. Hunting deer and boar was his only option for now.

'The guests will be arriving shortly, so I suggest you select a horse that can stay upright,' Pandarus said, losing patience. 'Also, do you recall that during your absence I organised a gift for your return?'

Tyron remembered—he remembered thinking he would have preferred a horse. Pandarus was the last person he trusted to make that choice for him. Tyron had socialised with his entire collection of women and often had difficulty deciphering between them. Aside from a few varying physical attributes, he found them eerily similar. There was a reason Tyron did not have a formal Companion. He preferred to keep them as far away from Fedora as possible. 'I recall I was appreciative of the gesture,' he said.

'Appreciative of the gesture?' Pandarus said, gaping at him.

'You have yet to meet the girl, let alone bed her. I would have been better off giving her to Stamitos or putting her to work in the kitchen.'

'Wait a minute,' Stamitos said, folding his arms and puffing his chest. 'While I am not as fussy as Tyron, I do have a type.'

'Since when?' Pandarus said.

Tyron suppressed a smile. 'Don't you remember when he got into the wine cellar a few years back and announced to a room full of guests he "prefers them tough more than pretty"?'

Pandarus nodded. 'I remember he was sick on my boots. I threw them out.'

'It is no secret I prefer a woman who can handle herself,' Stamitos said.

The warmth of the moment was enough to make Tyron agree to the hunt. 'I'm going to change before the others arrive.' He glanced at Pandarus. 'Do not start without me.'

Tyron left the smell of grain and manure and walked up the gravel path towards the castle. Pero was following a few paces behind, always respectful of his need for space and quiet. Tyron was watching the gravel crunch beneath his feet until he heard the crunch of footsteps ahead of him. He looked up and saw the Companions moving towards him like a shifting rainbow. There they were, the kingdom's most beautiful, the majority hand selected by his spoiled brother who insisted on the best of everything.

As he neared them, he nodded in their direction. They stopped and curtsied before him.

'Good morning, my lord,' they murmured, maintaining their positions as he passed.

All but one, that is. She was far behind with her face tilted up towards the sun, enjoying its warmth. She was oblivious to what was in front of her, arms swinging, creamy skin flashing beneath her blue cloak. Her golden hair was braided to one side, exposing her neck. Tyron's eyes remained on that neck for longer than they should have. He forced them up to her face, and seeing she was not going to stop, he paused to watch her collide with the woman in front of her. She stumbled back and looked around, an expression of panic on her face as she tried to read the situation. When she noticed him standing there, he could tell that she did not know who he was. Her eyes took in his attire and locked onto his arm where the royal symbol was secured. She immediately fell into a curtsy and turned her eyes to the ground in front of her.

'Good morning, my lord.' She was barely audible.

Tyron was suddenly aware that he had stopped walking, which meant the other women were still lowered in a curtsy. He was about to walk on when the girl returned to a standing position prematurely. He could not help but enjoy her expression as she realised her mistake. She seemed to be trying to decide whether to return to a curtsy. To save her any further embarrassment, and release the women from their long-held positions, he nodded once in her direction and continued up the path.

∽

ALDARA WAS DROWNING in the disapproving stares from the other women. Hali held an expression of pity, which was worse. She had just disrespected a prince and made a fool of herself in the process. Fedora would not be pleased with that first impression.

The women took a moment to collect themselves before continuing. This time Aldara remained alert as she followed behind. When they stepped off the path onto the paved yard, Aldara and Hali stopped to take in the sight of the tethered thoroughbreds and overdressed men.

'Watch,' Hali whispered.

All the men ceased talking, inspecting the women as they approached.

'Fedora is always stressing the importance of discretion, and yet the men have none.' Hali sniffed the air. 'All I can smell is manure.'

Aldara could only smell horse and leather. It calmed her. She watched as the other women slipped into the setting, positioning themselves among the guests as though they were about to have their portraits painted. Astra was first to greet Prince Pandarus, who Aldara recognised from the day of the hanging in Roysten. He had the same expression of self-importance, and the same spotless boots. She had to admit that he looked twice the man with Astra standing at his side. It was as though the sun was rising next to him. Her tangerine dress spilled onto the ground beneath her long cloak, and her gold earrings swung as she spoke. Aldara noted the convincing smile on her face, her modest body language, and the way she turned into him when he offered to take her cloak. She was his in that moment.

'She will be freezing in five minutes,' Hali said. 'When she is done pouring herself over him, I will give you a formal introduction.'

Aldara spotted the third prince a few feet away. He was broad shouldered with laughing eyes. His clean-shaven face and sandy coloured hair were different from his siblings. A sinking feeling came to her stomach as she watched him.

'That was Prince Tyron, wasn't it?' She looked at Hali. 'On the path?'

Hali nodded, keeping her face neutral for those around them. 'I warned you about his demeanour.' She glanced at Aldara. 'Don't worry, when he returns you can start fresh. Introduce yourself formerly and make a good impression.'

'You only get one first impression.'

'He probably won't even make the earlier connection.'

Aldara was doubtful of that, but it was not the time or place to debate the topic. The men were swarming about the other women like children around sweetbread. 'We should socialise,' she said, finding her smile.

The kitchen servants had arrived and were serving refreshments from a small wooden table dressed in red linen. They kicked the dogs sniffing around their feet, waiting for food to fall. A harp and chair, carried by servants, was being positioned next to the table. A handful of guests applauded, a show of encouragement for Astra, who placed a modest hand on her chest and excused herself from Pandarus's shadow. She made her way through the middle of the adoring men and made herself comfortable on the chair. She spent a few moments positioning her dress in a way that enhanced her angelic appearance. Her head rolled in towards the harp, and her eyes closed as her fingers touched the strings. The silver cuff on her left arm was reflecting the morning sun. She appeared to be radiating light. From that moment on, she seemed oblivious to the stares of the men. While Aldara had seen her practice many times, she had never seen such a sensual performance. She was almost fooled by it.

'Let's go before the other women get their claws into him,' Hali whispered, removing her cloak and shivering against the cold air.

One of Hali's many talents was her ability to show cleavage regardless of the style of dress she wore. Her physique could not be harnessed. The removal of the cloak must have had the desired effect because Pandarus was suddenly walking towards them with his eyes fixed on Hali's breasts.

'Ah, there you are,' he said, placing a hand at the base of Hali's back.

A childish smile came to Hali's face as she curtsied before him, nice and low so he had a clear view down her dress. 'Good morning, my lord,' she said. 'Allow me to formally introduce you to Aldara. I believe you met her in the village of Roysten awhile back.'

Her tone had a purr to it Aldara had never heard before.

Pandarus looked at Aldara, beginning at her face and working his way down her body with no discretion.

'My lord,' she said, lowering into a curtsy. Even with her cloak on she felt exposed.

'Fedora has kept you well-hidden,' he said. 'I was quite nervous on my brother's behalf.'

Aldara continued to smile. 'Fedora has high standards for all the ladies, my lord. She wants only to please you and your family.'

'You sound just like her,' he said, glancing at her chest. 'I remember you in Roysten. You were knee-deep in mud when I met you.'

He was trying to embarrass her. 'It would not have been appropriate to approach you on horseback, my lord.'

Pandarus lost his playful expression and studied her face. 'And what has kept you busy with Fedora for so many months?'

She felt like she was being sold all over again, her worth continually being weighed up. 'I have been very fortunate in receiving a broad education. I am learning to speak the native Zoelin language at present.'

'Aldara loves history,' Hali added. 'She stays up most nights devouring books she has already read.'

Pandarus looked away. 'Perhaps you and Tyron are suited after all. His tastes are vastly different from mine, and his standards much lower.'

He turned his entire body away from her then. Aldara stared at his back for a moment. It seemed their conversation had ended. Hali gave her an apologetic glance. She curtsied, excused herself with no response from him, and slipped into the shadows of the stalls.

She leant against the wall, heart pounding, trying to slow her breathing using a technique Fedora had taught her. 'Great women remain poised at all times,' she had told them. 'Have you ever seen a flustered queen?' Remaining composed under pressure was essential because falling apart was not an option for a Companion. Emotion was a private luxury.

As she remained hidden, listening to the hum of rehearsed conversation, a groom led a grey destrier gelding past her. Another man came and stood in front of the horse, observing his gait before moving to the side to watch from a different angle. Aldara could see the gelding's stride was short. The man walked over and lifted the right front hoof, examined it, and then let go. He said something to the groom who then tied the horse up before leaving to get tack.

Aldara emerged from her hiding place and walked over to the gelding. He stood with his eyes blinking as he dozed. His back foot rested lazily while he flicked his tail at lingering flies. She stepped forward and held her hand out for him to sniff. When the horse realised that she was not offering food, he lost interest and continued to doze. There were scars streaked across his chest and head. She reached up and touched the one above his eye, tracing it up to his ear. He enjoyed her touch and moved his head towards her. She rubbed his forelock for a moment, and he leant into it. Her hand moved down his neck and over his right shoulder. She could feel heat coming from it. Using both of her thumbs, she gently pushed downwards. The gelding raised his head and stepped away from her. Placing both of her hands around the top of his leg, she ran them all the way down to his hoof. A moment later she felt the warmth of his muzzle on her back. 'I am not sure that is entirely appropriate,' she said, standing upright.

At that moment she noticed a figure standing ten feet away, watching her. It was Prince Tyron. Her hands fell to her side, but then remembering how unsanitary they would be, she clasped them behind her back. They looked at each other for a moment. Aldara knew she needed to introduce herself, but he was an awkward distance from her and she did not want to yell or make a sudden move towards him. Tyron helped by taking a few steps towards her.

'He is an old war horse,' he said, explaining the scars. 'I don't have the heart to replace him. I owe him my life. He has saved it enough times.'

The distance between them still seemed too great for polite conversation, so Aldara stepped closer to him. She had forgotten to curtsy, and now it was too late. The gelding let out a bored sigh, and they both glanced at him.

'Good horses cannot be replaced,' she said. 'You are lucky. My mare would abandon me at the front line at first sight of the enemy. She could not be trusted to return me safely from berry picking.'

A smile flickered on Tyron's face. 'Spirited mare?'

'My father said we were well suited.'

She was not meant to speak of her previous life unless asked directly about it. Thankfully he did not seem to mind. She glanced at him. His dark hair reached down to his green eyes, and she wondered how he tolerated it at that length. Syrasan men traditionally kept their hair short. Many in her village kept theirs shaved to prevent lice.

'You are too well dressed to be a groom,' he said.

She laughed without meaning to. 'Apologies, my lord. My name is Aldara. We almost met on the path earlier when I miraculously saved myself from falling at your feet.'

He seemed amused. 'Some light entertainment on an otherwise dull walk.'

He had the straightest teeth she had ever seen on a man. Their brightness contrasted his short beard, another unusual feature on a prince.

'Fedora will be pleased to hear you were entertained,' she said. 'I must remember to mention that later when I am being reprimanded.'

The sound of Hali's laughter made them both turn their

heads. She was standing with Pandarus by the refreshment table, and whatever he was whispering into her ear was causing her to blush and squirm next to him.

'Do you think he is able to hunt?' Tyron said, looking back at her.

Her eyes returned to the gelding. 'I am not trained in such things, my lord. However, he appears to have a shoulder injury.'

Applause broke out among the guests. Astra stood up and stepped away from the harp. She gave a small curtsy to her admirers. At that point Pandarus moved away from Hali and walked among the men, basking in the praise of her, as though it were praise of him. Astra smiled appreciatively and waited for Pandarus to reach her so he could take her hand and display her like a well-bred dog. It was not until the applause subsided that Pandarus noticed Tyron and Aldara standing together in the stables. He let go of Astra's hand and began walking towards them.

Aldara thought Tyron tensed up as much as she did. They both seemed to be bracing for his arrival.

∽

Tyron cursed inwardly as his brother joined them.

'Is this our new horse marshal, brother?' Pandarus said, keeping his eyes on Aldara. His voice was loud and drew the attention of nearby grooms.

'It appears I will need another horse for the hunt. Mine is lame.'

Pandarus continued to stare at Aldara. 'Is he? Was this your diagnosis?'

Tyron could tell immediately from his brother's tone that he did not like Aldara. This made little sense to him as Pandarus had made the purchase himself. There were only two possible explanations: she had injured his pride in some way or he did not like the idea of Tyron having something he did not.

His brother's persistent gaze was making Aldara nervous. She barely had the courage to look up at him, but she did because respectful conversation demanded eye contact.

'Only an observation, my lord.'

'Does this knowledge of yours come from years of farming, or do we need to have words with Fedora about her lesson plans?'

And there it was again.

'Call it instinct,' she said.

Tyron realised at that moment that the dislike was mutual. Pandarus would not like that from a woman one bit. They normally fell at his feet. Tyron stepped between them and untied his horse. He had hoped to shut the conversation down, but instead, Pandarus stepped closer to Aldara and placed a hand her back.

'I imagine you probably have some hunting experience also?' he said. 'Any tips for my brother.'

Tyron glanced at the hand on her back trying to figure out his game. He could tell Aldara wanted to step away, but she had not been taught not to.

'I hunted for potatoes only, my lord,' she said, remaining still. 'And with varying success.'

Tyron did not look at her as he suppressed a grin.

Aldara curtsied extra low to ensure that Pandarus's hand left her. 'I wish you both luck today. I will leave you to prepare. Please excuse me.'

The men watched as she walked over to where Hali was standing with an older gentleman. Tyron had a theory that all of the Companions eventually became the same person. They arrived as individuals, with unique personalities and histories, but these traits were erased during their transformation into well-spoken seductresses, conveniently fluent in the languages of their received guests. He had no doubt Fedora would strip Aldara of herself and he would one day see only what had been created for him.

'I've had women like her,' Pandarus said, still watching her. 'And I tire of them quickly.'

Tyron shook his head. 'You tire of all of them quickly. If I recall correctly, you said the same thing about Idalia a few years ago. What you mean to say is that you do not like *unattainable* women.'

'Nonsense. I have a unique interest in unattainable women. I have bedded as many married women as I have unmarried.'

'Because they were attainable.'

'They are all attainable. I could have that farm girl sent to my room tonight.'

'And she would come out of obligation. That is not the same thing and you know it.' He handed the lead over to a groom and walked into the stable to begin his search for a horse.

Pandarus, not done with the conversation, followed him. 'I have high standards; that is why she was given to you. It seems I have to make all the decisions around here. You should take the young filly at the end if you want something that will last the day.'

Tyron kept walking. 'I really hope you are talking about a horse now.'

Pandarus ignored the joke. 'You're defending her. That means you are fond of her.'

'I am not defending her. I am commenting on you.'

'Don't get defensive. I am pleased you like her. You know I hate to waste gold.'

'Your collection of horses suggests otherwise.'

Pandarus disregarded that comment. 'I just hope the little virgin prude does not prove a disappointment in your bed.'

She had definitely hurt his pride. Tyron kept his eyes on the filly in front of him. She was lean and tall for her breed. 'We have barely spoken two words to each other.'

'What has conversation got to do with anything? I only hope she loses her frigid demeanour. Exciting at the beginning, I agree, but you will soon tire of it.'

Tyron said nothing.

'I should warn you, she will not age well. I have met her mother. A true labourer's face.'

Tyron signalled to the groom to saddle the horse. His eyes drifted to where Aldara stood among men twice her size and three times her age. He could not imagine her working on a farm. Perhaps that was why her mother sold her. 'Why are you warning me off the gift you gave?'

'I'm doing no such thing. I'm simply managing your expectations,' Pandarus replied, turning to leave. 'I will request she attend the feast tonight. You can make up your own mind about her in the morning.'

'No,' Tyron said. He blurted it, without knowing why.

Pandarus turned back and looked at him, waiting for an explanation.

'Tell Fedora she is not ready.'

Pandarus shook his head. 'Ready for what?'

A room of drunken men, Tyron thought. 'To socialise.'

'I have no idea what goes on inside your mind.'

A horn sounded. The dogs barked excitedly, making conversation impossible. Pandarus left to find his mount. The groom handed Tyron the reins of the mare, who was dancing about with excitement, and took hold of the bridle to steady her while he mounted. In the mounting yard, the Companions had gathered to wish the riders luck as they climbed into their saddles. Aldara stood at the back, using a hand to shield her eyes from the sun. The others stood with their hands folded in front of them, backs as straight as their manners. Tyron let his horse circle the group rather than fight to keep her still. He found his eyes wandering to where Aldara was patting the heads of the dogs that passed her. Occasionally she looked in his direction. A second horn sounded.

The dogs raced out of the yard ahead of the horses. Tyron's horse lunged into a canter, desperate to lead them.

Within moments the men, horses, and dogs had disappeared, leaving the stables quiet.

∼

THE WOMEN STOOD amid settling dust, waving the dirt away from their faces. They left the smitten grooms and the tired kitchen servants and made their way back up the path to the castle.

Astra was the first to bathe; Aldara was the last. That was the pecking order. Aldara added some boiled water to the tub before peeling off her robe. She buried her face in her hands to relish the smell of horse before it was washed away. When she finally sunk down into the water and closed her eyes, she saw tired, green eyes with locks of dark hair falling over them. She opened her eyes to see Fedora standing next to the tub. One look at her face told her she had not come to praise.

'When you are dressed, you can assist the others with their preparations for the evening. They will all be attending. You will not.'

Aldara sat forward and covered her breasts with her hands. 'Prince Tyron did not request I attend?'

Idalia walked in and stopped a few feet from them, waiting for their conversation to finish.

'You are not ready,' Fedora said.

'You said I was.'

'And I stand by that. However, it is not my opinion that matters in the end. Your situation is unique in that the prince did not select you for himself. He may reject you for those reasons alone.'

'And I will disappear.'

'Not necessarily. Your virtue is an asset for as long as you keep it though you should prepare yourself for the possibility of entertaining noble guests in the future. I will wait for Prince Tyron's wishes to be made clear before discussing this with you further. I am yet to speak with him directly.' She turned to Idalia. 'Yes?'

'The king has requested to see me, my lady.'

Fedora nodded. 'I will have Hali help you prepare.'

Aldara sank back down into the cooling water. She was a child among beautiful women. She had fooled no one with her grown-up dress and barely rehearsed manners. It took her a moment to realise Idalia was still standing by the door.

'I will make a terrible governess,' she said to her.

Idalia did not laugh. 'You are young and still learning. It is difficult at your age to comprehend what is expected of you.'

Aldara had almost forgotten she did not want to be a part of their world, a world where women were bought like prostitutes and disguised as something more. 'How old were you when you arrived here?'

'Fifteen,' Idalia said, crossing her arms in front of her. 'I had not even come of age. The daughter of a blacksmith who drank all that he earned and then hated us for his failures.' She was silent for a moment. 'My mother sold me to protect me. I cried for her every night for the first season I was here.' She glanced at Aldara. 'You don't cry, so you are already doing better than me.'

'You would not cry for my mother either.' She smiled and stared at the water. 'When did you begin socialising?'

'I was sixteen, but that is not the question you should be asking.'

'What question should I be asking?'

Idalia unfolded her arms and combed her hair with her fingers. 'When did I become the king's Companion?'

Aldara watched her fingers move gracefully through her thick hair. 'All right, when did you become the king's Companion?'

There was another silence as Idalia revisited the memory privately before saying it aloud. 'It was two days after my nineteenth birthday. It had been a long and difficult four years. Three of those had been spent entertaining the king's guests. Then one night the king invited me to his chambers, and as far as I am aware, there has not been another Companion in his bed since. Some say not even the queen.'

Aldara shook her head. 'Why then?'

'He could have had me at any point during that time. I danced myself to the point of injury for years, determined to be seen by him.'

'So what changed?'

'I grew up. I felt good in my skin suddenly. Men paid attention, not just to the pretty face, but to the woman I had become. One night I walked into the great hall and realised all eyes were on me. Men, women, servants. Even the queen saw it. I was the most desired woman in the room. When he saw that, he saw me.'

'And what of his Companion at the time? Did she…disappear?' She almost did not want to hear the answer.

Idalia shook her head. 'No. She is our mentor. And one day I hope to replace her again.'

CHAPTER 9

The following morning, Aldara was woken by Hali climbing into her bed. She smelt of wine and sweat. Her mouth and gown were stained red. Aldara used her fingers to comb the sticky hair back from her face. 'Long night?'

Hali's body was heavy and still. 'It was Prince Tyron, you know.' she said, already falling asleep.

Aldara stroked her hair. 'What was Prince Tyron?'

'He told Pandarus you were not ready to entertain.' Her eyes were closed and her body twitched as sleep took over.

Aldara lay there thinking about what a disappointing gift she must have been. When she was sure Hali was asleep, she slipped from the bed and crept past Astra, who was fast asleep beneath a pile of blankets taken from the empty beds. She washed her hands and face and twisted her hair into a high bun. It was too early for the morning meal, so she ate some of yesterday's bread that was sitting by a jug of water on the table and then began her chores.

The goal of the day was complete distraction. She could not let her mind stop. If she had been on the farm, she could have thrown herself into some real labour. Hanging dresses did not have the same effect as ploughing a field by hand or hammering a fence post, but she gathered all the dresses and undergarments that needed washing and walked down to the servants' quarters, where she asked a startled maid for some lye and a washing bat. With all she needed, she walked through the small door to the washing area outside where she washed rung and hung everything herself, leaving only the mending for those with some skill. When she went to collect yesterday's laundry, the maid looked at her tiredly and told her it was still being pressed and she would bring them up later. Aldara offered to help but was told no, so she took a seat and waited, watching the process so she could do it herself next time. The maid did not appreciate the audience.

Aldara climbed the stone steps with a basket of dresses and undergarments resting on her hip just as the air was warming. She stepped into an empty corridor and strolled along it, relishing the silence. As she neared the great hall, she heard voices. Prince Tyron was standing at the entrance, talking quietly to his squire. She stopped walking and considered turning around, then rationalised that perhaps it was that sort of childish behaviour that was hindering her. Instead, she lifted her head and quickened her pace.

Tyron stopped talking when he saw her. His eyes moved over her as she hitched the heavy basket higher onto her hip and walked, unblinking, towards him. When she was closer, she dropped into a curtsy.

'Good morning, my lord.'

Tyron took in her long-sleeved cotton dress and unbrushed hair piled high on her head. Her face was scrubbed clean, making her appear younger than when he had last seen her.

'That seems too heavy for you,' he said as she rose.

That was all he said, yet his eyes remained on her and his feet did not move. She would have kept walking had he not been looking at her as if he was about to say something more.

'How is your horse this morning?' she asked, filling the silence.

A smile formed on his face. 'I was just wondering the same thing. Would you care to join me for the inspection?'

He looked away, and she suspected the question had fallen out of him and he was trying to think of a graceful exit from it. She glanced down at the basket, thinking through the logistics of his offer.

'My squire will let Fedora know of your whereabouts. And deliver the basket for you,' he added.

Pero raised his eyebrows and then eyed Aldara with suspicion.

She glanced down at her dress. 'Why not? I'm dressed for a stable outing. Perhaps I could assist with cleaning the tack while I am there.'

Tyron eyed the plain dress. 'You actually look good as a maid.'

She laughed, despite having no idea if the comment was a joke or a genuine attempt at a compliment. Pero took the basket from her, and she thanked him before he walked off down the corridor. She was imagining Fedora's composed expression collapsing with the arrival of Tyron's squire carrying the women's laundry.

The rest of the castle was coming alive by the time they stepped outside. Maids stood talking, bed linen piled at their feet, ready to be hung. Servants clutching pails of soapy water were waiting for those above them to wake. They scattered like uncovered mice at the sight of Tyron, but he did not seem to notice. She snuck glances at him as she watched the sun rise in front of them. Whenever the breeze stilled, she closed her eyes for a moment, enjoying the warmth.

'In Asigow the people worship the sun,' she said. 'It makes complete sense.'

Tyron kept his eyes ahead. 'I'm sure the bishop would suffer heart failure at hearing you say such a thing.'

Aldara tensed up next to him. She could now add blasphemy

to her list of failures. 'Apologies, my lord. I meant no offence to your God.'

'My God?'

'Our God. The only true God.'

He studied her for a moment. 'It makes sense the Asigow people worship the sun because they do not see it very often. Even when the snow stops, the clouds remain.'

'They must have a lot of trouble growing food.'

They were walking side by side, and Aldara noticed he had a distinct scent, a combination of clean cotton and pine needles.

'Thinking like a farmer,' he said.

Her eyes went to her feet. She needed to stop discussing her previous life. 'Old habits.'

He turned back to the sun. 'There is no shame in a farming life. We all need food.'

She glanced up at him. 'I have no shame, my lord. I had a wonderful life.' She bit her lip to silence her mouth.

'Had?'

Apparently it had not occurred to him that she might have preferred that life, a harder life.

'I suppose you miss it. Fedora is no replacement for a mother,' he said.

She laughed. 'You have not met my mother. Fedora is delightful in comparison.' He was watching her. When he did not reply, she added, 'I am grateful for the opportunities I have been given here.'

He looked at the ground and smiled. 'What an entirely appropriate response. I have had conversations with Fedora in the past, and you sound just like her.'

His expression confirmed her suspicion that he was teasing her. 'Then you would also know Fedora does not approve of sarcasm. What would you prefer to hear?'

'Something honest.'

'Honesty is not always appropriate for a Companion.'

He was staring at her again. 'Honesty should always be appropriate. What do lies achieve? Only distrust.'

Aldara laughed again. 'Think about your own daily existence. How much of it is honest? You must have obligations also.'

'Ah, so I am an obligation?'

She glanced at him to see if he was teasing her again. He appeared to be enjoying himself. 'Perhaps we should discuss Galen history before I get myself into trouble.'

'You can converse with me honestly. There is no need to construct answers that will please me. I would prefer not to second-guess everything you say.'

She was sceptical, but she nodded. Tyron was not done with the conversation.

'Many of the Companions come from poor living conditions, and this is a privileged life they want desperately.'

'I believe that is true for many.'

'But not for you?' His tone suggested he did not believe her.

'You are assuming happiness is dependent on wealth, and I can tell you from experience it is not. Some of my fondest memories were born during times of hunger.'

Tyron stopped walking. They had arrived at the stables, but he was not looking at the horses. 'An honest response, how refreshing.'

Aldara kept her expression neutral. 'I am glad I was able to construct something that pleased you.'

They stood still for a moment. A groom approached them before anything further could be said.

'Can I saddle a horse for you, my lord?'

Tyron's eyes remained on her. 'Fetch my horse. We need to inspect his condition.'

The groom hurried off and returned moments later, leading the gelding. Aldara stepped out from Tyron's gaze and held a hand out to the horse. He sniffed at it before nudging her for a pat.

'I see who is in charge here,' she said, rubbing his face. The gelding did not object as her hands ran down to his shoulder. There was less heat, and he did not react to the pressure she applied. 'He seems to have improved.' She ran her hands all the way to the hoof and lifted it. 'Though you might want the opinion of an actual marshal,' she added, before letting go. 'And his shoe is loose.'

Tyron did not call for the marshal. He did, however, instruct the groom to get the gelding reshoed. Once the horse had been led away, the two of them began a slow walk back up the path. Their time together was coming to an end, and he had no further reason to keep her with him. As they reached the steps of the castle, Pero came running up to them. He stood in front of them, breathless.

'My lord,' he panted. 'The king has urgent news and wishes to see you immediately.'

Tyron nodded. 'Of course.' He glanced at Aldara.

She smiled up at him. 'I pray it is good news, my lord,' she said, curtsying.

He was already walking away. 'Good day,' he whispered.

She watched him until he was out of sight. Then it was time for her to return to her quarters and face Fedora's scrutiny. As she walked, she lifted her hands to her face so she could once again breathe in the lingering scent of horse. She stopped and looked at her hands. Something else lingered on her skin. It was the scent of clean cotton and pine needles.

CHAPTER 10

When Tyron entered the throne room, his father was leaning on the back of a chair behind a large, empty table. His face was creased and tight. Pandarus was pacing behind him.

'What is it?' Tyron asked, walking over to them.

King Zenas stared at the empty table in front of him, a sixty-year-old family dispute pressing down on his shoulders. Two Archdale brothers, one the rightful heir of the Corneo throne, and the other worthier of ruling. The people had been divided and eventually so had the land. The newly established kingdom of Syrasan was meant to end the ongoing civil war in Corneo. But the solution proved to be temporary. At some point it stopped raining in the East, and the crops in Corneo failed. Syrasan had enough to feed the people and a little left to trade with Galen across the Arossi sea channel. King Nilos of Corneo watched his people starve for some time before sending an army of men to take back some of the fertile land. Sixty years later they were still fighting. Periods of peace aligned with periods of rain. No one fought when there was enough food.

'My informants tell me King Nilos has laid claim to a section of land in the South.'

His tone was flat. Pandarus continued to pace behind him.

'What could he possibly want land in the South for? Our people have trouble keeping sheep alive down there.' He could not fathom another fight so soon. Historically both sides required time to rejuvenate their armies. Syrasan relied on volunteer footmen, and morale was still low. Families were still grieving their losses. 'Are you sending men?'

Zenas stood up and rubbed his greying beard with both his hands. His eyes crinkled as he thought. 'Our aim is always a peaceful outcome. Even if we do not always get it. The Syrasan people will begin to think we do not value their lives if we fight.'

Pandarus spoke up before Tyron had a chance to respond. 'A swift, firm response will send a clear message. Any display of weakness will just encourage them over the border.'

Easy for him to say, Tyron thought. The man had never fought a battle in his life. 'We must put pride aside and think of what is best for the kingdom, not just our family. We will soon be dealing with our own food shortages if we send all of our workers to their death. Then what? Do we expect the women and children to provide for the kingdom? Perhaps we can send them off to fight next.'

Pandarus waved his hand, dismissing the comment. Zenas rubbed his forehead and then pulled the chair back from the table. The silver buttons on his tunic strained as he lowered himself into it and let out an exhausted sigh.

'Tyron is right. We must try to diffuse. Find out what has taken their interest in the South. They may be rebels for all we know.' He studied his hands, which were pressed flat against the table in front of him. 'Leave the men in the South be for now. Send a messenger requesting an audience with King Nilos. Both of you will go. Stamitos will remain here.'

Pandarus stopped walking. 'Is that so you have one living son after we are both killed crossing the border?' He crossed his arms in front of him.

Zenas turned to face him. 'Yes. This kingdom will still need an heir if anything should happen.'

Pandarus did not appreciate the honesty. 'Send Tyron with some men! I am next in line to be king.'

Zenas shot up out of his seat with surprising force. 'I should be sending only you. It is *your* duty to manage relations with our neighbours! That is why you do not fight. Your inability to keep hold of a sword means I am forced to send Tyron also, to protect *you*. You should be thanking me.' He signalled for them to leave him.

Pandarus turned his clenched face to Tyron. It was an expression Tyron had seen many times, as though Pandarus's inadequate fighting skills were somehow his fault. Tyron gave a short bow to his father.

'We will leave today. Just five men so as not to appear threatening. But let's make it five of our best.'

Zenas nodded. 'As you wish.'

Pandarus left without saying a word. Tyron predicted the bad mood would accompany them on the journey. He would include Leksi in his five men to perform the role of mediator and protector of his sanity. The other four men Pandarus could choose to allow him to feel in control.

Tyron sent Pero off with preparation instructions. Once his affairs were in order, he made his way to the hall to fill up on roasted duck, soup, and bread. There were no food guarantees while travelling. When he could eat no more, he stepped out into the corridor half expecting to see Aldara standing across from him, a basket of laundry on her hip. He stood looking down the empty corridor. Moments later he found himself standing outside of the Companions' quarters. He could hear the hum of conversation from the women inside. The air smelled of perfumed oil and burning wood. He had just decided to leave when Fedora walked out and noticed him.

'My lord,' she said, genuinely surprised. 'I am so sorry, I had no idea you were here. What can I do for you?' She took a few steps towards him.

The problem was Tyron did not have an answer. 'Nothing. That is, I wanted to let you know I will be away for a week or two. Or rather, Pandarus and I will be away.'

They both knew there was no need for him to advise her of such things in person. Those messages were usually sent via a squire or messenger.

'I appreciate you taking the time to inform me, my lord.' She paused. 'Would you like any assistance with preparations for your journey?'

He was already walking away. 'No. Thank you.'

He almost walked straight into Aldara, who had just arrived behind him. She was holding a book against her chest, and her cheeks were flushed from the sun. Aldara glanced at Fedora, who discreetly reminded her to curtsy.

'Good afternoon, my lord,' she said, curtsying.

He nodded at her. Fedora excused herself in hope it would ease his discomfort. The two of them were left alone.

'I was just telling Fedora that I will be away for a while. Possibly a few weeks,' he said.

'Oh. So it was not good news then?'

He did not respond to that point. 'I am afraid my horse's rest period will be cut short.'

'It appears yours also. Any business that takes you from your home so soon must be of some importance.'

He nodded again. 'I should be going.' He gave her a wide birth before starting down the corridor.

'My lord,' she called after him. He stopped and turned around. 'Injured or not, he will return you home. He always does.'

'Yes, he does.' He nodded again before disappearing.

When the seven men rode out that afternoon, Tyron glanced once at the north wing where the Companions' quarters were located. He was annoyed at himself for being distracted. All he could think about was what he intended to do with her. He would need to find a use for her or someone else would. Pandarus would hand her around to his guests, and she would do what she was told, without question, and with all the grace that had been instilled in her. Perhaps he would not return and the decision would be out of his hands. No, that was not better. In that scenario he would be dead. He blinked away the thoughts of her and tried to focus on the task at hand. First, he had to stop a war.

CHAPTER 11

The women grew bored with the princes away. Idalia was the only Companion requested as King Zenas had no use for the others with his sons absent. They filled their days as best they could, but there were only so many lessons they could have, songs they could sing, and books they could read. And read again. The evenings were long and silent.

'Why is the king receiving no guests?' asked Violeta, one evening. She snapped her book shut and stood up. 'I feel as if we are in mourning.'

Rhea was always happy to spend an evening reading. 'You do remember that Leksi is with the princes? What other guests could you possibly hope to receive?' She did not even bother to look up from her book as she spoke.

Violeta glared at her. 'Anyone at this point. I may as well remain in my nightgown all day if the only faces I see are yours.'

'Leksi always returns with a fresh appetite for Syrasan women. A longer journey can only work in your favour,' said Panthea. She had long ago given up on her book and was watching the flames of the fire.

The sound of Astra's book slamming shut made them all

jump. 'Listen to yourselves. If Pandarus could hear this conversation, you would all be sold off to the first household to make an offer.'

'Pandarus stopped listening to me the moment you arrived,' Rhea said, without looking at her. 'We do not remain here for him.'

Astra stood to leave. 'Be grateful you remain at all. I need to get out of here. Your brooding is draining me of my youth.'

Aldara avoided the women when they were bored and self-destructive. She could not sit around and watch the kingdom's most gifted women claw at the walls confining them. She read in the dressing room, seated on the floor with her back against the wall. When the books became too familiar, she volunteered for more chores. She even learned to sew. The alternative was unbearable. She did not share Hali's indulgent love of leisure time. Hali could spend an entire afternoon soaking in a tub or trying on dresses.

Fedora reminded the women that the time was an opportunity for self-improvement. 'This is your chance to recapture the interest of princes. Offer up something new upon their return and they will not look elsewhere for it.'

Astra laughed. 'Prince Pandarus is always looking elsewhere. We will never be enough.'

Fedora folded her arms in front of her. 'Or perhaps he will find love and sell you all off. You are possessions that need to remain useful. Need I remind you what happens when you are no longer of use?'

Nobody responded. Astra did not laugh again. If the aim of the speech was to motivate the women, then it served its purpose. With books, instruments, and ink in hand, there was newfound focus for the rest of the afternoon.

Two more weeks passed, and the princes did not return. There was talk among the servants of them being in Corneo for negotiations. Some said they had likely been imprisoned. Aldara tried not to listen to the talk. She had seen him ride out with a handful of men and told herself if the threat had been dire he would have left with an army.

One month later, clouds settled in the sky. They did not lift, and they did not move. The air was sharp and clawed at Aldara's throat whenever she went outside. The maids stopped hanging laundry outdoors as nothing dried in the damp air. Servants dedicated entire days to chopping wood. Aldara watched the pile grow as the smell of imminent snow closed in on them.

Still there were no princes.

The rain fell first. Lots of it. It pooled in the castle grounds, drowning the grassed lawns and turning the paths to mud. In the mornings, a layer of frost would cover every surface, a warning of what was to come. There was no longer any sunshine through the windows. Whenever Aldara looked out of them, she saw only grey. And empty roads.

King Zenas held a small feast for the sole purpose of distracting Queen Eldoris and Stamitos. All the Companions were requested to socialise with the guests who were invited to simply fill the room. Even with the large crowd, the mood was strained. Eldoris attended only for a short while, and her smile did not reach her eyes. When Idalia performed, Eldoris excused herself and did not return. Princess Cora sat alone and drank more wine than most of the men. She was unimpressed by the guest list since most of the guests were acquaintances of her father—much older, married, and of no interest to her. Aldara held dull conversations with awkward guests. She danced when she was invited to and laughed when she was expected to. She thought the other Companions appeared more relaxed with Pandarus absent. Hali spent the entire evening seated with Lord Yuri, whom she described as the politest man she had ever encountered. His gentle nature and light sense of humour put all who spoke with him at complete ease.

'Why have we not had the pleasure of seeing you perform this evening?' he asked Hali.

She laughed, and Aldara was surprised to hear it was genuine.

'Hali and I remain seated for good reason,' Aldara said. 'We leave the entertaining to those with skill.'

Lord Yuri placed his cutlery neatly on his plate and pushed it away from him. 'Well, the art of good conversation should not be underestimated.'

Hali smiled at him, a smile that Aldara had seen only on rare, private occasions. She suddenly felt like she was intruding on their conversation.

'Any news on the princes?' he asked.

Hali shook her head. 'We are not privy to updates, my lord.'

Lord Yuri picked up his cup and looked into it. 'I have no doubt they will both return in good health. It is a long journey, and bad weather can see travellers stranded in small villages for some time until conditions improve.'

Aldara could have hugged him.

'But let us hope they make it here before the snow sets in,' he added.

A week later the temperature fell, and so did the snow. The women sat silently by the windows, watching the grounds turn white. The overnight falls were heavy, and each morning the servants would wrap themselves in cloaks and trudge through the fresh covering, shovels in hand. They laboured to keep paths clear and accessible. Whenever Aldara took laundry down to the maids, she noticed the doorways had to be continually doused with boiling water to keep them clear of ice. It reminded her of the farmhouse, which was hazardous in the cold season. She could not recall the amount of times she and Kadmus had slipped in the doorway. Her more experienced father always managed to stop himself from going over, and of course, her mother was incapable of falling.

One afternoon, Aldara asked Fedora if she should assist the

laundry maids in the mornings since she had the time. Fedora agreed to it for the period the princes were absent.

'It is freezing down there. Do not come back to me ill,' Fedora warned.

Aldara boiled water for them and used a shovel to keep the path clear so they could access firewood without injuring themselves. Her hands had softened over the months she had been at Archdale, and they blistered on the first day. But she found that the physical work improved her ability to fall asleep at night, though she still woke early, with each day looming ahead of her. So she got up and shovelled snow.

One week into her gruelling morning ritual Fedora noticed the state of her hands during their morning meal. 'For heaven's sake,' she said, grabbing hold of her wrists. 'Do you listen to anything I say? Your hands are to touch only meals, books, and the inside of gloves until they are completely healed. Do you understand?'

Aldara found some red leather gloves in the dressing room and went back to work. The other women thought she had lost her mind and barely engaged with her. But not Hali. She viewed Aldara as a form of entertainment. One day when they were keeping each other company, Hali had asked her what she hoped to find underneath all that snow. The sun, she thought.

One morning, Aldara was standing with a shovel at the laundry door, working up the courage to step through it, when she heard a woman crying. Tia, one of the maids, had her face buried in the linen she was meant to be pressing.

'We may need to rehang that,' Aldara said. 'What's the matter?'

Tia brushed away her tears and began folding. 'It's my husband,' she said before another sob escaped her. She put the linen down and covered her mouth with her hand to stop the noise. 'He is ill. There is a sound when he coughs, the same sound I heard from my father right before he died.'

Aldara picked up the linen and began to help her. 'What has the physician said?'

Tia laughed. 'That he needs rest. He is out there shovelling snow. The man should be in bed, but we cannot survive on a maid's wage.' She wiped her nose with the back of her hand. 'We have two of our own children to feed, along with my sister and her three. Her husband died at the border. She takes care of our children while we work. That is how we all get to eat.'

Aldara placed a hand on Tia's arm and thought for a moment. 'There are plenty of indoor chores that need tending to. Perhaps he can move indoors to work so he is out of the cold.'

Tia looked at her. 'The same three men shovel those paths every day. They don't come in until the paths are clear.'

'Perhaps I can replace him,' Aldara said.

Tia stared at her for a moment. 'You will not be permitted.'

'We won't tell anyone. No one out there in this weather will be asking questions.'

Aldara could hardly see the men through the snowfall. The thick cover on the ground hugged her knees and filled her boots. She waded through it, dragging her shovel behind her, glancing back to ensure Fedora was not watching her from a window. Where was the path these men were supposedly clearing? She paused and glanced about while the snow bit her face. She had let her hair out for extra warmth, but it was not helping. When she reached the men, her eyes moved up the path and back again. 'This seems a bit pointless,' she said into the icy wind. No one could hear her; their ears were tucked under thick hats. They looked up only when one of the men began to violently cough, pausing to watch before continuing. Aldara walked over to him and tapped his shoulder.

'Your wife needs to see you,' she said. 'I am here to relieve you.'

The man's red, swollen eyes moved over her. 'Who sent you?'

'You are needed inside,' she said again. She thought she would leave the explanation to Tia.

He hesitated before trudging off towards the castle, head slumped, chest wheezing. Aldara ignored the glances from the other men and dug her shovel into the snow, tossing the load a good distance behind her. The wind erased her efforts. She had only been shovelling a few minutes when the men stopped and laid down their shovels. She watched them, wondering if they were finished. It was not until they bowed that she figured out someone was approaching. When she spotted men on horseback, their faces shielded by scarves, she curtsied as best she could. Hooves padded the snow in front of her, the horses grunting with their efforts. One of them stopped, and she looked up, recognising the exhausted gelding. The shovel in her hand dropped to the ground. A frost-covered Prince Tyron stared down at her. He lowered his scarf, revealing chapped lips and a concerned expression.

'What on earth are you doing out here?' His voice was hoarse.

'Helping,' she said. 'How was your journey, my lord?' Her eyes moved down his body, checking for visible injuries.

'Longer than expected.' He gave a weak smile. 'Go inside. It's cold.'

She nodded towards his horse. 'He has returned you safely once again.'

Tyron glanced down at the frosted mane. 'Yes.'

Pandarus was a few yards ahead and swung his horse back around. 'When you are done catching up with the servants can we please get out of this weather? If I arrive without you, father may not let me in.'

Aldara did not look at Pandarus. She kept her face buried deep in the hood of her cloak. Tyron nodded at his brother and clicked his tongue to move the gelding forward. His eyes returned to her though, taking in the sight of her matted hair and blue lips. Aldara curtsied and stared at the shovel by her feet. Her heart was pumping extra blood through her body, providing extra warmth. She had made a promise and had no choice but to resume working. When she glanced over at the stables, she saw a frowning Pero striding towards her, his body angled against the wind and his hands ungloved. She stopped shovelling when he stopped in front of her, wiping snow off his ear.

'You are to return to your quarters,' he said.

He spoke loudly and the servants looked over at them. Her eyes went to the stables. The princes had already disappeared.

'I have permission to be here, helping.'

He shook his head. 'No, you don't. His lordship wants you inside now.'

She glanced at the men who were watching her and then stepped closer to Pero. 'One of the servants is very ill. If I leave, he will be forced to return out here.'

His expression softened a little. 'You have to go inside.'

She nodded and followed him. He took the shovel from her as they walked. Once they were inside the laundry room, she stripped off her wet cloak and gloves and handed them to Tia, who glanced nervously at Pero.

'I hope you're not in trouble on my account,' she said.

Aldara touched her arm. 'No one is in trouble.'

Tia's husband was slumped by the stove, still in his coat. When he coughed they all looked at him.

'Keep him here,' Pero said to Tia. 'I will speak with his lordship.'

Pero escorted Aldara all the way to the Companions' quarters. He said nothing when he left her. She watched him scurry away and then walked into the main room. It was empty, a rare treat. She spent a few moments shivering in front of the fireplace, brushing her hair with her fingers and drying the skirt of her dress. Once she was presentable, she went in search of Fedora. Fedora's private bedchamber was a curtained-off section of the bedroom. On her way there, she found a robed Hali seated on her bed with a broad smile on her face.

'So you have heard the news then?' Aldara said, stopping next to her.

'Yes! All the women are preparing for the inevitable feast. You should get ready also.'

Astra and Panthea walked in, collected their robes, and left without a glance in their direction.

'Has it actually been announced?' Aldara called to their backs.

'No. But it will be,' Astra said. She did not seem pleased. 'And it will be a long and messy evening.'

When they were out of the room, Aldara looked at Hali, who shrugged at her. She grabbed her own robe and followed after them. As she stood shivering by the occupied tubs, she found herself waiting for Fedora to appear, waiting to be told to assist the others and then get an early night. By the time the others were finished, the water was not hot enough to defrost her. She stood by the warm stove, willing the water to boil. When she finally made it to the dressing room, Fedora was nowhere to be seen. She laid out dresses, did hair, painted faces. Waited. Helped the women dress and select jewels. Waited. Fedora arrived just as Aldara had run out of things to do. She nodded approvingly at the women, all except Aldara, who was still in her robe with her hair drying to one side.

'There will be a feast to celebrate the safe return of Syrasan's princes and the amicable outcome of their journey into Corneo. This is a celebration of peace,' Fedora said.

The announcement was a formality. The women were ready to depart.

Fedora's eyes swept over Aldara. 'Get dressed. You will be attending also.'

Aldara exhaled.

Fedora stepped closer to her. 'The prince will be seeking

warmth after his cold journey.' She spoke quietly. 'Choose your dress accordingly.'

'Yes, my lady.'

Fedora left them, and Aldara looked over at Hali, whose face mirrored her own relief. It was time for her to be truly seen. If it was warmth he needed, then she would become the sun.

CHAPTER 12

When Tyron left his father's chambers, fatigue weighed down his legs and arms. He struggled to walk the distance to his quarters. The outcome of the long journey was best described as a delay of a war that would one day take place. Negotiations had been slow and hindered by Pandarus, who was unwilling to compromise on anything. They had eventually agreed to trade a small amount of grain in exchange for skins and furs they did not need. Pandarus had called it charity. Tyron had told him he could call it whatever he liked. Pandarus had insisted no food leave Syrasan during the cold season. Tyron reminded him their food grew on land that was King Nilos's by birthright, and if they did not agree, they would be forced to fight or starve.

'We shall all starve if we continue to give away our food,' Pandarus said.

'We can increase our supply from Galen if need be.'

Pandarus shook his head. 'People can barely afford to buy it at the current price. Who is going to pay for it to be transported?'

'I suppose we will.'

'And that is why I am in charge of the gold.'

The marriage of Zenas to Eldoris had been for the sole purpose of securing an alternative food supply. Everything grew in Galen. The entire kingdom seemed to flourish beneath blue skies and gentle showers. They also happened to have an army twice the size of the Zoelin army, though no one knew what their soldiers did, as they had never fought a war in the time Tyron had been alive. They could afford to maintain their values when their bellies were full and their young were thriving. Meanwhile, Corneo and Syrasan were prepared to kill one another for a bit of grain.

While the negotiations had slowed their return, it was the flooding in Corneo that had prevented them from leaving. They had found lodging in a village close to the border, a village scarred by the death of many Corneon men a few months earlier. The people there had reluctantly provided beds and soup for the men at five times the going rate. The soup was salted water containing only horse meat and potato. There were no herbs in it, no bread served with it. They took it without complaint. Even Pandarus remained silent on the matter. The women served them without speaking, watching them with suspicion from a safe distance. Tyron's men took no chances, sleeping with their swords and taking turns keeping watch.

The heavy rains turned the roads into dangerous mud pits. When the water level dropped, progress was slow. The rain was followed by heavy snowfall, and they were forced to stop once again just inside the Syrasan border. By the time it eased, Pandarus had fallen ill after spending the night with a woman in the village. The stomach ailment was so severe they were forced to remain there for four days before he was strong enough to ride again. Soon after, two other men became ill. Tyron decided to quarantine the group in a village two hours south of Minbury. He didn't want to take a contagious illness into Archdale and put others at risk. It turned out to be a sound decision as Tyron and Leksi fell ill a few days later. By the time they mounted their horses and rode out of the village, they had been gone for months.

Tyron moved his thawing limbs down the corridor towards a hot bath. Pandarus's suggestion of a feast had come as no surprise. What came as a surprise was Tyron's willingness to attend. When Pandarus had suggested all the Companions attend, he had found himself nodding in agreement. The reason was simple—he wanted to see her again.

He woke much later than he had planned. Cold food sat on a tray by his bed. He sat up and grabbed the bread, swallowing it down with a few mouthfuls of water. After a wash, he got Pero to trim his hair and beard to a more acceptable length. He dressed in the clothes laid out for him, marvelling at Pero's ability to carry out chores around his sleeping body. He was still buttoning his tunic as he left for the feast. It occurred to him he was rushing. Never had he rushed to a feast in his life. His pace slowed only when he reached the noise.

∽

QUEEN ELDORIS MISSED nothing at social gatherings. She saw every drunken display and every conversation in every dark corner. She knew the Companions by name, who they belonged to, their talents, and their tactics, though she made a point of never saying their names aloud. She knew Pandarus continued to bed most of them, and Stamitos could not wait to. She was aware of every moment her husband spent with Idalia, and was painfully aware of the fact their relationship was not only sexual, but something more. He had found friendship and had grown to trust her in a way one trusts a spouse. She had told herself Idalia would eventually be replaced like the others before her. She was wrong.

Tonight she watched Pandarus drink too much, too early in the evening. She resisted the urge to say something as she knew it would not change the outcome. He cared only for the opinion and approval of his father. At least Tyron and Stamitos allowed her to be their mother. Cora cared for no one's approval. Elders glanced to Eldoris's right, where Cora was seated next to her. One of the few things they had in common was she too watched the room with great interest. Particularly Leksi, whom she had watched since she was ten years old.

'Tyron has finally made an appearance,' Cora said, signalling to the door.

Eldoris's gaze swept over the unruly crowd and spotted him immediately. She watched as the noise threatened to push him back through the open door. She held her breath, willing him forward. The guests were long done with eating, and they were either dancing or filling their cups. Tyron looked at her, and she offered a small smile, hoping to encourage him in some way. It was the first time she had laid eyes on him since his return, and she wanted to hear his voice. He made his way towards her. She stood and waited for him to navigate the people between them. But soon his feet stopped moving. Something had caught his attention.

She followed his line of vision to where a young girl stood a few feet from where Astra was playing the harp. Her hands rested lazily across her arms as she watched the performance. She was a collection of gold, from her immaculate hair right down to her jewelled shoes. She was lit up like the sun. Eldoris could almost feel the heat from her.

'Who is that?' she asked Cora, already knowing the answer.

Cora followed her gaze. 'Pandarus's *gift* to Tyron,' she said, sounding bored. 'Fresh off the farm. How have you not seen her before?'

The queen shook her head. 'I have. But not like this.'

She looked back at Tyron, who still had not moved. By the expression on his face, she was no longer an unwanted gift.

He did not make it over to her. From the moment he saw

Aldara standing alone, radiating light, he saw nothing else. She had not noticed him enter the hall, so he watched her for as long as he could get away with doing so. He watched her exposed back, which was crisscrossed with embroidered silk, and the backs of her arms when she applauded at the end of the song. He watched the fabric move against her hips. When Aldara turned and saw him, her painted lips move into a smile.

∼

ALDARA WAS ABOUT to take a seat when she saw Tyron standing alone, watching her. His stillness contrasted the crowd crashing about him. She smiled at him because it was her role to do so, and because she could not help it. Once he realised he had been seen, he nodded in her direction. She began walking over to him, allowing her arms to fall by her side and moving at a pace that had been dictated to her since her arrival. When she reached him she curtsied. 'Good evening, my lord. Would you like to sit? You must be exhausted.'

He seemed relieved.

'I was afraid you were going to ask me to dance.'

'I will spare you the embarrassment. I am afraid I am not very good.'

He glanced around for some seats. 'I see Fedora has been teaching you modesty.'

Aldara gestured towards an empty table. 'Do you really believe modesty can be taught? I thought we agreed to be honest.'

'If you are good at your role, I will never know.'

He offered her his hand while she took her seat. Aldara managed to appear casual as she took hold of it, but inside she felt something very different. Once he was seated, it took her a moment to work up the courage to look at him again. She was more nervous than she had imagined she would be. Her mouth was drying up, so she reached for the jug of water in front of her.

Before her hand could take hold of it, Tyron caught her by the wrist and turned her hand palm up. She stilled and stopped breathing as he studied the calluses on them.

'Who instructed you to shovel snow?' he asked, releasing her hand.

Forgetting the water, she placed her hands in her lap. 'No one instructed me to. I was trying to help.'

'The sick servant.'

'The very sick servant.'

He kept his eyes on her. 'He was sent home to rest.'

She blinked. 'Thank you.'

'He was always free to return home. We do not force sick servants to labour.'

'Of course. I was simply trying to prevent him losing his wage.'

He continued to watch her. 'Can I see your other hand?'

'Why?' she asked, not moving. He seemed taken aback, so she immediately held the other hand out for his inspection.

'You are not here for hard labour. Fedora should never have allowed it.'

She was having difficulty reading his mood. He seemed angry at her. 'I prefer to feel useful.' She looked into her lap.

Tyron's eyes did not leave her. 'It appears I am more tired than I realised.'

Aldara reminded herself to breathe. 'You did well to show up at all. I am sure the last thing you feel like is difficult company.'

He nodded. 'You are right. That is why I am seated with you and avoiding my family.'

His body language suggested he was relaxing. 'Have you eaten?' she asked, eyes on the food in front of them. The duck was sitting in a pool of spilt wine. 'I don't think that is a sauce.'

'As appetising as it looks, I think I'll pass. But you go ahead,' he said, resting a hand on the table.

Aldara had a strange urge to reach out and touch it, but she kept both hands in her lap. His gaze seemed to be fixed on her. She was about to ask what he was looking at when a brass cup slammed onto the table in front of her, its contents splashing onto the linen dressed table and the surrounding food. Pandarus stood on the other side of the table, his face flushed from dancing and drink. He was holding Hali tightly by the wrist as though she might flee from him. She was also drunk, but Aldara could tell by the panic in her expression he was hurting her.

'You know, you two are the most boring people here tonight,' Pandarus said, staring down at her. 'Does she not dance either, brother?' His eyes shifted to Tyron.

Tyron stood up, and Pandarus staggered back a few unsteady steps. Hali gave a small cry of pain as he pulled her along with him.

'What are you doing?' Tyron asked.

Pandarus looked at Aldara, who remained in her seat, eyes on Hali.

'Trying to decide if we got our money's worth,' he replied. He stepped forward and leaned across the table in her direction. 'Is your only talent how tightly you can keep your legs closed?'

Tyron's hands clenched into fists, but before he had an opportunity to use them, Leksi appeared next to him.

'There are people waiting to speak with you,' he said, placing a hand on each of Tyron's shoulders. A clever tactic in case he should need a decent grip.

Tyron and Pandarus stared at one another. The guests seemed to have gone quiet for a moment, their attention on them.

'Go!' Pandarus spat, waving him away. 'People are waiting to speak with you. I am surprised they have not formed a line.'

Aldara slowly stood up. 'I wonder if perhaps I could borrow Hali from you, my lord? We were invited to dance earlier, and it seems the guests might need some encouragement.'

Pandarus was holding Hali at arm's length, and Aldara could see all the veins in her hand protruding. He looked around, and when he realised all eyes were on them, he released his grip on her.

'Tell me we are not quarrelling over women,' Leksi said. 'There are plenty to go around.'

Pandarus took a drunken step back from the group. Guests returned to their conversations.

'Go, dance,' Pandarus said to Hali. 'I need a drink.' He walked over to where Astra was seated and barked an order at her. She reluctantly stood and followed him.

'I suppose we better dance,' Aldara said.

Leksi nodded. 'Good idea. And we better find someone for you to talk to so I don't appear a liar,' he said to Tyron, leading him away from the table.

Tyron's eyes remained on Aldara.

'I will leave you to your social duties, my lord,' she called after him.

By the time she had finished curtsying he was out of sight. The girls looked at one another. Hali's eyes almost welling over.

'Let's go,' she said, hiding her red wrist behind her back.

Aldara danced with five guests, forgetting their names almost immediately. As she spun and turned around these strangers, Tyron would occasionally flash into view, intense eyes always watching. By the fifth dance she felt dizzy and breathless. The song was long, and her feet struggled to keep up with the music. When it was over she thanked her partner and excused herself. She slipped through the messy crowd, searching for the door on the other side of them. She kept her eyes straight ahead, hoping no one would notice her exit, or remember the quarrel between the princes with the mute Companions standing next to them. Her powerlessness in that situation was a reminder of who she had become. Someone who could not speak up at injustice or demand a man let go of a woman. Not any woman—her friend. As she neared the door, she made the mistake of looking back at the royal table where she locked eyes with Queen Eldoris, the last person she saw before slipping through the small gap in the door. The corridor was dark and cool. Two guards watched her as she gulped at the air. At some point she had stopped breathing. She moved away from the men, her pace quickening as the air returned to her lungs. She had intended to get some air for a moment and return to the banquet, but the closer she came to the Companions' quarters, the faster her feet moved. Within minutes she could see the glow from the main room fireplace ahead of her. She was practically running then. She was almost there when someone grabbed her hand from behind and spun her around to face the other direction. Instinctively, she pulled her hand free.

Tyron stood in front of her, breathless from his pursuit of her. 'Why are you running from me?'

Aldara placed a hand on her heaving chest to steady her heart. 'I am not running from you, my lord.' Her voice was quiet. 'Forgive me.'

He held out his hand to her. 'Come with me,' he said.

She glanced at the open hand, twice the size of her own. When she reached out and placed her hand in his, it immediately closed around hers. He turned, leading her back down the corridor. She had no choice but to follow. She did not ask questions—it was not her place. They neared the great hall, and she felt relieved when they continued past it. They arrived at the main entrance of the castle, and he told her to wait there while he went to get a few things. She waited, shivering, beneath the curious gazes of the guards. The cold air was seeping through the door and taking all the warmth from her exposed skin. Tyron returned carrying thick cloaks lined with fur, gloves, and boots. She did not know whether to feel excited or terrified.

'Where are we going?'

'Somewhere where we can breathe,' he said, helping her into the cloak.

The warmth from it was immediate. A childlike excitement rose within her as the doors opened in front of them. They stepped through them into the frosty darkness. Tyron took her hand again, and they broke into a run. The snowfall had stopped, but there was a thick covering on the ground. Whenever she stumbled he simply pulled her upright without needing to slow his pace. They did not stop until they were inside the softly lit stables. It was still and quiet. Tyron managed to find a surprised and sleepy groom, who ran off to saddle two horses for them. He offered to fetch them an escort, which Tyron refused. He turned to help Aldara into the saddle, but she had already mounted and was tucking her cloak around her legs for extra warmth. Her hair had started to come loose after their run. She looked at him, her face beaming.

'Where are we going?'

'So many questions.'

'One question, repeated.'

He smiled to himself. 'There is no agenda. I thought we could just ride for a while.'

They rode to the portcullis, and as it lifted in front of them, Aldara remembered her brother's face, blocked on the other side. It was her first time outside of the walls since her arrival. Tyron led them off the main road and into the tall pines. They padded through the snow, which was knee deep on the horses at times. The moonlight was blocked by clouds, so they had to trust the vision of the horses over their own.

'You are very trusting letting me lead you through a dark forest,' Tyron said, breaking the silence.

Aldara grinned. 'I would wager you know every inch of this forest, my lord. You would have played here with your brothers when you were young, before transitioning to hunting?'

'I barely remember. Sometimes it feels as though I skipped childhood.' They came upon a path that widened. 'That was lucky,' he said, turning onto it.

Aldara rode up next to him. She could see the faint glow of his teeth through his smile. The smell of the woods reminded her of home. Memories flooded her as she inhaled.

'About earlier…' he began.

'There is nothing for you to explain,' she said, shaking her head. 'Please do not feel you have to say another word about it.'

Tyron was silent for a moment. 'You were a gift from him I did not want.'

She laughed. 'Definitely do not say another word about it.'

It had been a long time since he had heard her laugh. He felt as though he had just stepped into warm water. His horse moved closer to hers.

'I was going to say my feelings had changed, but I will skip that part now.'

Aldara smiled. 'Fedora sees me as a complete disappointment despite her best efforts to bring me up to the standard of the other Companions. There is not much you could say that would surprise me.'

'Is this more of your modesty?'

She laughed again. 'I invite you to come by the Companions' quarters and see my paintings sometime. You will see I am simply stating the facts.'

He really could not look away from her when she laughed. 'You can't paint or dance. What *can* you do? Shall we have you sing at the next gathering?'

She glanced across at his playful eyes, sparkling away in the dark. 'It would be an effective way to get rid of unwanted guests.'

The horses remained side by side, their strides in unison. Tyron loosened the reins so his horse could relax its head. He looked across at her, and she deliberately pulled her horse to the left, causing them to collide. He barely moved in his saddle.

'Ah,' he said, a smirk on his face. 'I used to play this game with my brothers when we were children.'

'I guess you didn't erase all of your childhood memories,' she said, smiling. 'I used to play this game with my brother also, but it was not that long ago.'

'And did he ever succeed in knocking you from the saddle?'

'Only once he grew bored. He would give up and shove me by hand. The last time we played I was on the ground with the wind completely knocked out of me. I could not move for the longest time.'

'I bet he felt rather bad then.'

She shook her head. 'No. He took my horse and went home. He thought he was hilarious. Father not so much.'

Tyron was a little taken aback. 'If I had done that to my sister she would have poisoned me in my sleep.'

'Kadmus is not a graceful loser,' she said, remembering how furious she had been.

She went silent again. After a few minutes Tyron pulled his horse to the right, but Aldara was ahead of the game and stopped her horse before he could make contact. Again he smiled.

'What village are you from?'

She closed the gap between them. 'Roysten, my lord.'

He thought for a moment. 'Ah, sheep?'

'Yes, and a few other animals for our own use. And barley when the weather is kind,' she added.

'Sounds prosperous.'

She glanced across at him. 'Not prosperous enough to prevent my mother from selling me. But there is a chance we were secretly rich and my mother simply invented an excuse to be rid of me.'

Tyron did not laugh, so she said nothing more on the subject. They listened to the haunting sound of a boreal owl.

'Can you read now?' Tyron asked suddenly. 'I imagine Fedora has you writing also.'

Aldara nodded. 'Yes, my lord. I was fortunate enough to have both skills prior to my arrival at Archdale.'

It was the one thing she could thank her mother for. Dahlia

had insisted both children learn from a young age. Isadore had called it a waste of time. Farmers did not need a different skill set. Dahlia had ignored him. She had different plans. Coincidentally, it had since become common for farmers to have written agreements for large sales at the market. Aldara had eventually realised her father's objections stemmed from the fact he had never been taught and was too proud to admit it.

Aldara began to shiver, and Tyron noticed.

'Let's go back,' he said, turning his horse.

She reluctantly turned her horse also.

'Pandarus's new Companion,' he began. 'Are you two close?'

'Hali and I left our families on the same day. We arrived together. We have learned everything together, made mistakes together. Yes, I would say we are close.'

He had never imagined friendships between the women before. 'I have always assumed the women had a more competitive existence.'

'There is a little of that. Survival instincts are stronger than most friendships.' She paused for a moment. 'Hali left behind more siblings than I could count that day. I was fortunate enough to meet her before we became something else. She wanted to come to Archdale as Pandarus's Companion, but she still needs family.'

'So you have become her sister?'

'I suppose I have in a sense.'

He looked at her. 'And what has Pandarus become? We agreed to honesty,' he reminded her.

She was silent for a moment. 'Hali understands her place in his life. She is aware of her own disposability. All the Companions know they are replaceable.'

His eyes remained on her. 'I suppose they understand that emotions are pointless in their positions. The tradition has survived because of its simplistic nature.'

She could see he was trying to gauge her position on the

subject. 'It's just a shame tradition disregards the welfare of these women once they are used up.' Her reply was too quick, not thought through.

He observed her for a moment. 'I am of the understanding the women move on to respectful positions and are taken care of.'

'They are *sold* on,' she pointed out.

'Yes, they are educated and therefore of value. An asset that is theirs to keep for life.'

She shook her head. 'I am curious as to what sort of life you imagine them having, with only their knowledge for company?'

Tyron was enjoying the fact she had forgotten herself. Her well-rehearsed manners were melting under the heat of the conversation. 'One day Pandarus will be king and the women will have much bigger worries.'

She looked away then. 'And what kind of king do you imagine him to be?'

'Probably the kind of king *you* imagine him to be. Quite like my father, except that he will not fight or show any compassion towards the poor.'

She smiled. 'Given a large portion of the kingdom is poor, he will find ruling almost unbearable.' She could see him smiling also. 'And what of the Prince of Mercy? What sort of king would you be?'

He glanced across at her, confused. 'Prince of Mercy?'

'Yes. That is what they call you all around the kingdom. You did not know?'

He shook his head. 'No. It seems you are educating me on many things tonight.'

That comment worried her. 'I hope this evening is not some sort of test, because I have most certainly failed.'

He looked away. 'I won't tell Fedora if you don't.'

'I am more concerned with you sharing the details of our conversation with Pandarus. He will have me hanged in the courtyard.' She kept her eyes ahead.

'It's a risk I am prepared to take in my effort to remain honest.' They had arrived at the stables, and he wondered if she would have laughed if they had still been among the pines.

They dismounted. Aldara insisted on unsaddling her own horse while the confused groom stood awkwardly nearby. She then spent a few moments saying goodbye to the mare before the horse was finally led away. Tyron watched her the entire time.

'Perhaps you need a pet,' he suggested.

'I already have Hali,' she replied. Tyron laughed. *Laughed.* She could see the entire brilliance of his teeth.

They stepped out into the light snowfall, and she took the offer of his gloved hand. She was determined to make it back up the path without falling.

'No harm will come to you or your friend at his hand,' Tyron said suddenly. 'His self-interest is a problem, but I don't believe him to be a dangerous man.'

'Of course not, my lord.'

The Companion within her had returned. She was no longer free among the trees to say as she pleased. Once inside the castle he stepped away from her, walking in silence all the way to her quarters. They stood in the candlelit corridor, weighed down by fatigue and damp cloaks. Aldara's nose was red from the cold, and her hair had long ago come loose. A few pine needles poked from it. He thought she was beautiful in that moment and was forced to look away from her. His feet did not move though.

Fedora came out through the door and was surprised to find them standing there. Her eyes moved between them.

'My lord,' she said, curtsying. 'Would you care to warm yourself by the fire?'

Tyron shook his head and glanced at Aldara. 'Thank you,' he said, stepping away from her. 'I hope you don't catch cold.'

Aldara curtsied also. 'Thank you, my lord.'

He turned to leave but then stopped. 'Actually, Fedora, there is one thing you can help me with.'

She stepped forward. 'Of course. What is it, my lord?'

'I have heard a great deal about Aldara's new-found artistic abilities. Could you please have one of her paintings delivered to my quarters?'

Aldara did not know whether to laugh or beg him to take back his request. She glanced at Fedora, who was masking the concern on her face rather well.

'Of course. I will have something sent immediately. Was there something specific the two of you discussed?'

'Have Aldara select something,' he said, glancing at her. His eyes were smiling.

Aldara curtsied. 'I hope it does not disappoint, my lord.'

He nodded and left them. Aldara resisted the urge to watch him walk away.

'Where on earth have you been?' Fedora asked, once they were inside. 'You left here looking like a Companion and return to me looking like a beggar. And you smell of horse.'

'I don't think Prince Tyron noticed or cared,' she replied, stifling a yawn.

Fedora took hold of her shoulders and turned her to face the door. 'Go bathe, and thank God Prince Tyron does not have the choice of Companions that Prince Pandarus does.'

Aldara was thankful for that. As she retreated to the warm water to thaw her bones, she realised her logical mindset was eroding. When selecting a dress to capture his attention, she had forgotten her armour. And Companions could not afford to be vulnerable.

CHAPTER 13

When Tyron arrived at his chambers, Pero informed him that Princess Cora was waiting inside. He hesitated at the door and thought about not going in at all, but sooner or later she would hunt him down. It was best to get it over with before the wine wore off.

'Sister,' he said. 'To what do I owe the honour of this private visit at this ungodly hour?'

When she did not respond immediately, he stood still and studied her. She was seated in the chair by the window, staring at the floor in front of her. The paint on her lips had long ago worn off, replaced with the stain of red wine. The paint around her eyes was smudged, making her appear sleep deprived. He knew by her state she had crossed into dangerous drunk.

'Where have you been?' she asked, not looking up.

Her speech was sloppy. One sleeve of her dress hung down her arm, and she did not notice or care. He was far too exhausted for one of her drunken interrogations.

'Does it matter?'

She looked at him then. 'Your whore,' she began. 'Please tell me she is for your amusement only and your good judgement has not been impaired as a result of too much time spent stranded with Pandarus.'

Too much free time was not a good thing for a woman like Cora. She needed to be kept busy or else she became destructive. 'Really, Cora, all this spite is ageing you.'

She sat up and poured herself some water from the nearby jug. It was a miracle it did not spill from her unsteady hands. She lifted the cup to her mouth and then changed her mind and sat it back down. 'Royal men having sex with women of inferior birth will never make sense to me. Teaching them to read does not change what they are.'

'An interesting speech from you.'

'What do you mean?'

'You have loved a knight for as long as I can remember.'

She picked up the cup again and took a small sip from it. 'Leksi should not flatter himself with such thoughts.'

Her charade was wasted on him. 'I'm sure he gives it no thought at all. It is just the observation of the rest of the kingdom.' Cora's eyes flashed at him then. Although she had never loved anything more than herself, he knew Leksi was the closest she had come. 'What do you actually want?' he asked her.

She sat up straight, moving as though it were painful. 'I will not have our family made fools of by these women. A peasant farmer in a pretty dress should not be coming between two princes of Syrasan. You both embarrassed yourselves at the feast.'

He remembered the gold dress. The golden hair. That laugh. 'What is between Pandarus and I is years of bad blood fuelled by his need to beat me at all things. If you must scold someone, speak with him about his collection of women.'

She stood and walked unsteadily towards the door. 'Pandarus remembers they are just expensive whores. He beds them and moves on.' She stopped at the door and leant against its frame. 'He is indulging his overactive libido while he waits for the crown. I saw you with her tonight. I saw it all.'

'I am sorry there were not more exciting things to keep you entertained.'

Her face softened for a moment. 'Do not embarrass yourself.'

She pushed gently off the support beam and left him. Pero immediately replaced her in the doorway. He was holding a small oil painting in his hands.

'Forgive me, my lord, but this was just delivered for you. What would you like me to do with it?'

Tyron stared at it. 'Bring it here,' he instructed.

Pero walked over and held the painting up so Tyron could see it in the poor lighting. 'I believe it is the view of the stables from the castle, but I cannot say for sure. It is not entirely…clear.'

'It is terrible,' Tyron said, studying the amateur colour mixing and rushed application.

Pero lowered it. 'Shall I have it sent back?'

'No. Have it hung on my wall.'

The confused squire leant it against the wall before leaving him. Tyron collapsed onto the bed and stared at the painting. He did not undress, and he did not pull back the linen. The lit fire was making him sleepy, but Cora's words lay with him. She was protecting her own interests of course, but she was right about one thing, he had lost himself to her. Like Pandarus, he had the ability to spend the night with a woman and move on from it the next day. What kept her from his bed was the knowledge he might not move on easily from this one. He struggled to leave a conversation with her. What would happen if he let her into his chambers, let her undress, and let his hands do as they pleased? He would have to regain some perspective and control. And the only way to do that was with distance between them.

∼

When Aldara returned from her bath, the first thing she noticed was Hali's face. There was a red and purple bruise under her left eye. She was about to ask what had happened when she realised she already knew. A fire lit in her stomach as she sat down on the bed next to Hali and gently turned her head to study the mark on her face.

'He does not get to treat you like that, prince or not.'

'Of course he does.' Hali's face was puffy from tears and lack of sleep. 'On the upside, I won't have to see him again until it has completely healed. Fedora's orders.'

'So Fedora has seen this?'

She nodded, lay down, and pulled the blanket up to her chin. 'He has changed.' A few tears spilled across her nose.

Aldara spoke quietly so as not to disturb those who were sleeping. 'He has not changed at all. He is the same person he has always been. It is just becoming clear to you now.'

Aldara's father had never laid a hand on her mother, and she had loved him all the more for it. Drunken beatings were not uncommon where she came from. She had grown up seeing bruises like these on women all around Roysten. They were the actions of desperate and uneducated men. No one seemed to expect any better from them. But she wondered what the queen would think of her son buying women for his bed only to beat them when he needed to vent frustration. She lay down next to Hali and stared at the roof. What would the Prince of Mercy say in defence of his ill-tempered brother who was meant to pose no threat? Perhaps he did not know him that well after all.

'What did Fedora say?' she asked.

But Hali was already asleep. Perhaps dreaming of home—a place where the smell of bread and the banter of family spilt out onto the road. No amount of dresses and indulgent food could substitute that. They could not afford to forget what was real and be swept up by the charade they had been sold into. And that was what was happening. Aldara was no different from Hali, forgetting herself as she was stripped of her good sense. Princes did not care for the women they bought. They did not marry daughters of farmers and raise half-peasant children together. They used them for as long as it suited them and then disposed of them.

In that moment Aldara was forced to re-evaluate what she was doing. She needed to find a way to survive that did not rely on the whims of men.

CHAPTER 14

Aldara knew how to work hard, so that is what she did. Prince Tyron did not request her company, and she did not let herself wonder why. She was grateful. She told herself she was grateful. She told herself stories about how much easier it was and how the distance gave her more control. These are the things she told herself—so it would not hurt.

Fedora did not speak of him, and Aldara took it as an act of kindness. She mended dresses, washed linen, scrubbed the floors and wooden tubs. She helped everybody else. She did no more paintings. In exchange for her hard work, she was rewarded with silence on the subject.

Once Hali's face had healed, she began to follow Aldara around the castle, observing her as she did chores, pretending to learn but actually just fulfilling her need for constant company.

'I always wondered what mischief you got up to all day while the women play,' she said deviously. 'I have to admit, I am disappointed to discover no mischief at all.'

'You could help you know,' Aldara said, carefully loading firewood into her spare arm. They were standing outside by the wood pile, searching for dry pieces.

'I was hoping to discover something scandalous. An affair with a handsome servant perhaps.'

The snow had stopped falling, but the air was cold and the ground was turning to ice. Hali held her dress up to keep it dry while Aldara's hem sat in the muddy snow that covered her boots.

'Why? So you could see me beheaded?'

Hali regathered the hem of her dress and looked at Aldara horrified. 'No! So you could have some fun.'

'Can you imagine what would happen to a Companion found sharing a bed with a servant?' She kept adding logs even though she was already struggling with the weight. 'Fun is for the rich. Anyway, who says I am not having fun? This is fun.' At that moment the wood tilted in her arms and the entire pile tipped onto the wet ground. They both stared at the logs lying at her feet.

'That does seem like fun,' came a voice behind her.

Both women looked up to see Prince Tyron in royal dress. Pero stood next to him. Hali immediately dropped into a curtsy while Aldara stood still. She had planned to put on her façade and exhibit all that had been hammered into her every single day since her arrival. Now he stood in front of her with his smiling green eyes and her mask was crumbling, leaving her exposed. His eyes remained on her, and she was surprised to feel a burn of anger in her stomach as she looked back at him. His complete disregard of her since that evening had wounded her more than she cared to admit. She forced herself into a barely acceptable curtsy.

'What are you doing out here? Why do you insist on taking work from the servants?' he asked her.

Aldara bent down and began to pick up the wood. 'I was raised with pigs, my lord. I enjoy the mud.' She did not meet his eyes when she spoke, which showed complete disrespect.

He noted her tone as he watched her re-stack the wet wood on one arm. 'That wood won't burn now,' he said, crossing his arms in front of himself.

'No, it will not. But I cannot leave it on the ground for the servants to fall over.' She stood up then and looked straight into his eyes. His expression gave nothing away, and she feared hers gave far too much.

Pero stepped forward. 'You are forgetting your manners in front of the Prince of Syrasan.'

Tyron held up a hand to silence him, watching Aldara swallow her feelings and try to take control of them. Her expression softened slightly. She knelt down and finished picking up the last of the wood before stepping aside.

'I apologise for delaying you, my lord.'

They looked at each other for a moment. He had informed Fedora she was not to socialise without his consent. He had made her an outcast of sorts.

'If you are bored, read a book. You are not to move firewood. Is that clear?'

The humour was gone from his voice. It was an effort for Aldara to keep her tongue still while her mind processed an appropriate answer.

'Perfectly clear, my lord.' She curtsied, determined to do it without dropping the wood again.

He was about to continue past her when a guard came out of the laundry door dragging one of the maids behind him. The four of them watched as the woman was hauled towards them, pleading with the guard the entire time. As they got closer Aldara recognised the maid. It was Tia. Aldara moved towards them, but Tyron held a hand out to stop her.

'Say nothing,' he said to her.

He walked towards the guard. 'What is going on here?' he asked.

The guard stopped walking and nodded at Tyron. 'My lord, I have been instructed to carry out the punishment for petty theft.'

Tyron glanced at the woman. 'What did she steal?'

'Food from the kitchen, my lord. My orders come from Prince Pandarus.'

Despite a glance of warning from Hali, Aldara let go of the wood and strode up to where they were standing. 'I can vouch for this woman,' she said. 'She is no thief.'

The guard's eyes moved over her. 'She has already admitted to the theft,' he said, not happy with her interference.

Aldara shook her head and looked at Tia.

'You know,' she cried to Aldara. 'You know how it was. He couldn't work.'

Aldara's eyes returned to the guard. 'What is the punishment for petty theft?'

'A hand,' Tyron said quietly, unable to meet her eyes.

Hali came forward then and took Aldara by the arm. 'We need to go,' she whispered.

Aldara pulled her hand free and stared at Tyron. 'You cannot let him do this. A desperate act does not make her a thief. She was feeding her children.'

'Let's go!' Hali said.

Seeing Tyron standing there so passively only made Aldara more upset. She turned to the guard. 'Let go of her. If you take her hand she will never work again.'

'Aldara,' Tyron said, taking a step towards her.

'No!' Aldara said, stepping back from him. 'I cannot pretend along on this.'

Tyron blinked and turned away from her. 'Pero, get the physician. Hali, take her inside.'

'Please!' Aldara pleaded, tears spilling over.

Hali took her hand and began dragging her, with surprising strength, towards the laundry door. She shoved Aldara through the door, closed it and leant on it. 'Have you lost your mind?' she asked, wide-eyed.

She had. She had completely lost it. And the sound of an axe coming down finished her.

CHAPTER 15

Over the next month, Aldara moved like a mole through the castle. She avoided the great hall and the adjoining corridors, instead using the outdoor paths and servants' rooms where possible. The thought of running into Tyron drove her outside into the cold winds. The plan worked well for a short period. She did not see one member of the royal family for weeks. But when the cold winds subsided, and the ice began to melt, an announcement came from Pandarus that he would be hosting a flag race in Pelaweth. All the Companions were to attend at his request. Flag racing events were typically held in the warmer months, but boredom was chaffing Pandarus. He had purchased a new horse that had been trained for tournaments and he refused to wait any longer.

The races drew spectators and competitors from manors and villages all across Syrasan. It was an exhibition of the kingdom's most skilled riders, as well as a chance for commoners to show off their best horses in hope of a sale. Everyone in attendance wore masks to keep identities concealed, a tradition that had begun forty years ago when King Zenas's father decided to compete. He had instructed all of the riders to wear masks to keep his identity concealed and ensure an unbiased outcome. It was not long until spectators began to wear masks in keeping with the spirit of the event. Constructing masks was almost a competition in itself. Even the poor managed to create elaborate masks using old clothing and whatever they could scavenge from nearby forests.

Aldara had never attended an event, but Kadmus had. He had described to her in detail the stretch of clean field, marked off with pegs and rope dyed red. Spears with coloured flags stood like soldiers across the grounds. It was a race against time. Each flag had to be retrieved in a specific order, one at a time, and returned to the barrel that stood by the timekeeper. While the princes did occasionally compete, it was mostly noblemen with insatiable egos.

Aldara had once discovered Kadmus practicing when he thought nobody was around. He was using large sticks in place of flags. She had watched through the trees as his large, heavy horse struggled with the tight turns. When she had asked him if he was planning to compete, he had laughed at her. 'Against princes and knights? What do you think?'

'Loda could do it. And she could probably win,' she had replied.

'And who would ride her? Women do not compete. It is a sport for men, a sport of speed and agility. Your skirt would slow you down,' he teased.

'Women would have an advantage with less weight,' she said, ignoring his insult.

Strength was irrelevant, so she failed to understand why any good rider could not compete. She had even offered to race him.

'Absolutely not,' he had laughed again. 'I couldn't take the embarrassment of losing to you.' He had wrapped his arm around her neck then and squeezed her like a child.

The Companions were excited about the event for different reasons. For some it was a trip outside the castle walls; for others it was a chance to glimpse their families from a distance. A few were looking forward to masked encounters with guests. Figuring out identities was part of the fun. Hali was looking forward to the dresses, which were always extravagant and almost costume like. Aldara knew there was a good chance Kadmus would attend in the hopes of seeing her. It was her only motivation outside of obligation.

On the day of the event the women travelled in two concealed wagons not too dissimilar from the royal ones. The wagons were trimmed with vibrant red fabric and silver fringe. The horses were matched by size and colour, and the Syrasan symbol was stencilled onto each rump. Their heads were secured with leather straps to maintain perfectly arched necks. Aldara knew they required some freedom of their heads to manage the weight of the wagons, and for that reason she did not enjoy the journey. When they arrived in Pelaweth, the horses were slowed to a walk to better navigate the busy roads. Many spectators were packed into carts pulled by one tired horse. Families walked beside the road, carrying small children and encouraging the older ones to keep up. Their wagon was directed past the main entrance where people were queuing to a private entrance framed by large fires blazing from drums. Guards stopped the wagon and peered inside to view its occupants. Aldara wondered what they were assessing since they were all masked. Upon seeing the women, the guards waved them through. The wagon stopped in front of the undercover berfrois, which was also heavily guarded to keep the commoners from disturbing the noble guests. The common people wandered as close as they could to better admire the attire of the rich as they arrived.

When the Companions stepped down from the wagon, the women in the crowd made noises of appreciation while the men stopped their conversations altogether. They all watched the elegant parade of beauty walk to where the richest men of Syrasan were waiting for them. For this tournament, the women had taken their inspiration from species of birds. Aldara was a goldfinch. Her dress was layers of gold and black silk. It had raised shoulders with gemstones. She wore a black mask across her eyes and her hair was sleek and tucked low with dark feathers spraying from it. Black pearls wound her neck and wrist.

Hali was a snow goose. It was an idea the other women had laughed at until they saw her. She was a vision in white lace, with a cluster of soft feathers at the base of her back that moved with her hips as she walked. Fedora had permitted her to wear the diamonds usually reserved for Idalia or Astra. As it was Hali's first social event since her recovery, she needed to impress the guests. That would in turn impress Pandarus.

Idalia was the peacock. Aldara had spent almost the entire morning on her hair. Emeralds and fine silk had been woven through it, with the fabric extending across her forehead and joining with her mask. Not to be outdone, Astra had transformed herself into a flamingo. She was draped in soft pink silk and matching rare pearls Pandarus had sourced for her as a gift. The dress climbed her neck but was shredded below the waist to ensure her long legs flashed through the fabric whenever she moved. The Noble Companions reluctantly made do with the remaining resources provided to them by Fedora, and after some research, added a pheasant, eagle and kingfisher to the mix of birds.

The women walked up the steps of the berfrois, bathing in the stares of the noble guests who had arrived before them. The air was still cold, and they all pretended it was not. Any mention of cloaks by Aldara had been shut down. Their feathers were far too fragile and their efforts far too great to be covered up.

The wives in attendance remained close to their husbands. There were few social occasions they were invited to join, and flag races gave them an opportunity to try to take back possession of their straying men. The Companions were invisible to them. Their pride stopped them from glancing at the birds weaving between them, stealing all the attention. The masks may have covered their individual identities, but they did not disguise what they were. Thankfully, Fedora had taught them all early on how to rise above feelings of shame while remaining grounded. They learned to accept their outcast status among the married women, but it did not prevent them from socialising with the willing husbands who found ways to free themselves of their wives.

'How on earth are we meant to socialise when all the men are heavily guarded by their wives?' Hali asked, careful to keep her face neutral.

'They are not *all* guarded,' Aldara replied without looking at her. She felt tiny against the icy backs of the noble women.

Aldara and Hali saw Lord Clio, a young inheritor of a successful manor near Veanor, standing alone by the refreshments table. They went over to him and got to work. He was painfully shy and struggled to maintain any form of eye contact during their conversation. Aldara made a point of speaking softly and leading the conversation in a way that minimised his discomfort. She found the task much less daunting tucked behind the safety of a mask.

A few minutes into their conversation, King Zenas arrived on horseback flanked by four guards, each flying the Syrasan flag. His crown, elaborate tunic, and familiar physique made him still recognisable, despite a polished wooden mask that covered most of his face. He stepped with great effort up into the berfrois, and people stopped their conversations. His tone was warm and welcoming as he greeted his guests. He acknowledged all of the Companions with a respectful nod before spending a few private moments with Idalia, who escorted him to the adjoining royal berfrois. There he took a seat to await the arrival of the rest of his family.

When the royal women stepped out from their wagon, Aldara noticed Eldoris was dressed conservatively and had chosen not to wear a mask. Cora, on the other hand, was dressed more elaborately than all of the Companions combined. She was draped in heavy jewellery, and her deep blue embroidered dress had a long tail, a feature usually reserved for weddings. Her mask wrapped one side of her head and was painted blue, with tiny gemstones scattered about the eye. Aldara thought she looked like moving water as she slipped past the Companions without so much as a glance in their direction. Aldara rose from her curtsy to find Hali in a panic next to her.

'He's here,' Hali whispered.

Aldara followed her gaze to where the three princes had arrived on horseback. The crowd cheered and whistled, always hopeful that a member of the royal family would compete with enough encouragement. The three princes spent a few moments greeting the serfs who waited at the foot of the berfrois in hope of an audience. Aldara was aware of her change in heart rate at seeing Tyron. She noticed he remained behind to listen to some of the complaints of the thin men who stood with their masks respectfully in their hands. He nodded attentively as they spoke and responded with patience. When he stepped up onto the berfrois, he paused, eyes roaming. She should have looked away, but instead she met his eyes through the holes of his black mask. She waited for the anger to hit her. For weeks she had replayed their last meeting in her mind. But as she stood watching him, she realised he was also stuck in a role he did not want. He was as trapped as she was. He could have had her flogged for the way she spoke to him that day.

Tyron was forced to look away from her when a lord brought his wife to him for introductions. Aldara turned back to Lord Clio.

'I apologise, my lord. You were telling me about the success you have had with wool.'

He smiled politely and glanced down at his feet. 'I do not wish to bore you.'

'Not at all,' she said, glancing at Hali. Her eyes had not shifted from Pandarus since his arrival. 'I am curious how the quality could vary so much from one year to the next.'

His gaze returned to her again, his confidence growing. However, the conversation was shut down once again by the sudden presence of Tyron and Pandarus next to them. Prince Stamitos had not made it past Violeta. She had his undivided attention. Aldara and Hali curtsied.

'How was the journey to Pelaweth, my lords?' Hali asked, her most brilliant smile on display.

'Dull,' replied Pandarus.

Aldara glanced at Tyron, who was watching her. 'I believe you both know Lord Clio?' she asked.

Pandarus nodded. It was clear he would not make the conversation easy for anyone. Tyron spoke up for both of them.

'Yes, how is the manor shaping up for the coming season?'

While the men spoke, Pandarus ran his eyes over Hali, who was pretending to listen to Lord Clio's response. 'And where have you been hiding?' he whispered to her through his silver mask.

Aldara could not stop herself. 'She has been waiting for the bruising on her face to fade, my lord,' she whispered to him, careful not to disturb the flow of conversation between Tyron and Lord Clio.

Pandarus turned to her. 'Well, it looks beautiful now,' he said, keeping his tone light.

'It does indeed, my lord,' Aldara said.

Lord Yuri joined their group and bowed before the princes. 'Good day, my lords.' His eyes moved to Hali. 'Prince Stamitos informs me that all of the ladies are different types of birds,' he said, sounding pleased. 'I guessed you to be a swan, not a goose.' He began to laugh.

Hali smiled politely at him. She seemed to be wilting under the presence of Pandarus.

'Only Hali could take an ordinary bird like a goose and make it so extraordinary,' Aldara said to the group.

'Goodness, you are awfully harsh on the humble goose,' Pandarus said to her.

'Did any of your sons make it along?' Aldara asked Lord Yuri, ignoring Pandarus. 'I was looking forward to meeting them.'

Lord Yuri was the father of four sons. Two of them living. One had died in battle four years earlier and the other as a newborn during a difficult childbirth that had also taken the life of his wife. The two living sons were both knights of the king. It was the job of a Companion to know the histories of the noblemen, but they were only ever to discuss the aspects of their lives that were directly conveyed.

'Yes!' he said. 'One is competing today.'

'Wonderful. I will cheer for him. Though I may need a hint as to which rider he is.' She was about to say something else when she noticed Kadmus seated upon Loda across the field. She reached out and grabbed hold of Hali's arm to steady herself for a moment.

Tyron narrowed his eyes on her. 'Are you all right?'

It was the first time he had spoken directly to her. She watched as her brother disappeared into the gathering crowd and then looked up at him.

'Yes,' she said, forcing a smile. 'Yes, my lord.' She removed her hand from Hali's arm.

A trumpet sounded, announcing the tournament would soon commence.

'Hali, get me a drink. Then we should go take our seats,' Pandarus said to Tyron.

Aldara's eyes went to him, appalled by his manners. 'I'll help you,' she said to Hali.

'How many Companions does it take to get one drink?'

She stared at him. 'I was being courteous.' She knew he got her point because his eyes flashed at her.

'There are servants in our berfrois,' Tyron said to Pandarus. 'Let's get drinks brought to our seat.'

He glanced once at Aldara before moving his brother along. The women curtsied and watched the princes walk through to the royal berfrois.

Hali turned to Aldara. 'What's wrong? Why did you grab me?' she whispered.

'I saw Kadmus, and it threw me for a moment.'

A look of pity came over Hali. 'Let's find seats before the trumpet sounds again.'

They took the two remaining seats at the front of the berfrois. The spectators had gone silent as they waited for the race to begin. Hali took Aldara's hand and squeezed it. 'Don't worry, you will see him again. My father will be here selling bread. Though he may not recognise me.'

Aldara turned to her. 'Perhaps we can ask Lord Yuri to accompany us later to sample bread. I'm sure he wouldn't mind,' she whispered. 'You could speak with your father.'

Hali shook her head. 'I can't risk any further trouble. And your comment before didn't help the matter.'

'The man is a pig.'

Hali looked around to ensure no one had heard before turning back to Aldara. 'If you want to completely ruin your chances with Prince Tyron, go ahead, but please leave me off your path of destruction. I'm not as strong as you. I would not survive if something were to happen.'

Aldara swallowed. 'You are right, and I'm sorry. I should not have said it.'

The final trumpet sounded. There was a small eruption of excitement from the spectators, which built up the suspense. Aldara's gaze shifted to the field where a mounted horse now stood. It pawed at the ground and pulled its head against the reins. It was fitted with one of the lightest saddles she had ever seen, but the rider was a heavy man. She guessed his boots alone weighed as much as her. The timekeeper's horn sounded, and the horse took off, using the full power of his hind legs. Within a few strides they were moving at a gallop, and when the rider retrieved the first flag, the crowd thundered with applause. Aldara pressed her hands together in her lap, and from that moment on, she could not look away from the race.

The skill of the riders made her heart quicken. The horses knew what to do, negotiating tight turns at almost horizontal angles. Each time a flag was retrieved the crowd would stir and glance at the timekeeper, whose arm was poised, ready to fly up whenever a faster time was recorded. By the time the second rider had finished Aldara understood the challenges of the sport. By the third, she had memorised the course. When the fourth rider exited the field, she had some thoughts on how their times might be improved.

The trumpet sounded to signal a break, and she exhaled and sat back in her chair. 'That was incredible.'

'Let's find the wine,' Hali said, seeming disinterested.

When they arrived at the refreshments table, they came upon two guests having an animated conversation about the last rider.

'He wasted time on the last two turns. He would have been in the lead if he had maintained his technique,' one said.

'If he had taken those turns any sooner, he would not have cleared them,' the other replied.

'I would recognise your quarrelling anywhere,' said Hali, interrupting them. 'Your masks cannot hide your never-ending difference of opinion,' she laughed. 'Aldara, allow me to introduce Lord Thanos and Lord Xerxes.'

The two men bowed before them.

'My dear Hali, is it possible you get more beautiful each time we see you?' asked Lord Xerxes.

'Not only possible, but very probable,' she replied.

'Don't worry, we can speak of something more suitable for ladies,' he assured her.

'No, please, continue,' Aldara insisted. 'However, I am afraid I will have to agree with Lord Thanos on this matter. The rider could have saved time on the last two turns. Though I am not sure all blame falls on the rider. His horse was tiring.' The men exchanged a look of surprise. 'Perhaps a little more work on the horse's fitness would have been beneficial,' she added.

She saw him then. A few yards away Kadmus stood with Loda among the trees, watching her. When he was sure she had seen him, he raised his hand in a wave. Without thinking, she raised a hand and waved back. She stood frozen with her hand in the air, perplexing the men next to her.

'Aldara,' Hali said, trying to pull her focus back before she was noticed.

But it was too late. Pandarus stepped into Aldara's vision, snatching her attention. A tiny gasp escaped her. When she looked at him, she knew from the smug fix of his mouth he had seen the exchange.

'Forgive me, my lord,' she said in her warmest tone. 'My mind was elsewhere.' Both of the women curtsied. 'How are you enjoying the tournament so far?' she asked, drowning before him.

They all stood waiting for him to reply, but instead of responding, he turned to Kadmus and raised his hand also. Aldara felt her body tighten as her brother returned a reluctant wave. What had she done? She watched as Kadmus turned and led Loda away from them, willing them to go faster.

'Friend of yours?' Pandarus asked, turning to face her.

Hali tried to take the attention off her. 'My lords, can I refill your cups? It helps mask the cold,' she said, gesturing towards the drinks on the next table.

Aldara watched as they stepped away towards the table and fought her instinct to follow them. Her eyes moved to the royal berfrois, where she could see Tyron chatting with a guest who had been invited inside. He glanced over also, and she watched his expression change. His feet were moving towards her before he had even concluded his conversation.

Pandarus was still waiting for an answer. 'An old farmhand of yours perhaps?' he prompted.

Aldara realised he was hoping for a scandal. A fling with a farmhand would suit his needs. She smiled. 'That was my brother, Kadmus, my lord.'

'Really?' he asked, sounding disappointed. He thought for a moment. 'Does he compete? We are always searching for new talent. He certainly appears to have the horse for it.'

He would take her apart any way he could. 'I am afraid the horse holds all the talent. Kadmus is a spectator in every sense.' Her eyes flicked past him in search for Tyron.

'In that case, I must see this horse of his. I am in need of a new mount.'

She pressed her tongue against the roof of her mouth, thinking. Thankfully, Tyron arrived and placed a hand on Pandarus's shoulder.

'Apparently Leksi is entering,' he said, eyes only on Pandarus. 'He has a new horse. Come join me for a laugh at his expense.'

Pandarus did not take his eyes off Aldara. She did not dare look at Tyron.

'No,' he replied. 'Aldara's brother is here. Did you know she has a brother?'

Tyron glanced at her. He knew of her brother. 'She is not an orphan. I assumed she had family. What of it?'

Pandarus took on a lighter tone. 'Well, he has a horse here I am going to take a look at.'

Aldara shook her head, but Tyron spoke before she could say anything further.

'A farm horse? What on earth for?'

It was no good. Aldara could see he was enjoying himself far too much and there was no way out of it now. To make matters worse, her brother was visible across the field, standing with some men from her village. Pandarus called his squire over and instructed him to fetch Kadmus.

'Would the two of you care to join me?' Pandarus asked, walking ahead of them.

The three of them stepped down onto the wet grass and watched the conversation from a distance. They all saw Kadmus' reluctance and confusion at the request, but soon the mare was trotting towards them, her tail lifted slightly and muscles toned from farm work. Her condition was immaculate. Aldara imagined Kadmus taking extra care with her that morning knowing she would be at the tournament. When they were close enough, Aldara heard a small whinny of recognition from Loda. That also did not go unnoticed by Pandarus.

Kadmus lowered his head. 'My lords,' he said before looking to Aldara. 'Sister,' he added quietly.

'Good day, Kadmus,' she said. Her voice was barely audible, but she remained composed, because she had to. 'Prince Pandarus was interested in viewing Loda. It seems there is a shortage of working horses at Archdale,' she added in a light tone.

'I am quite sure she is useless on your farm,' Pandarus replied as he walked around her. 'I see her as a hunter.'

Kadmus looked at Aldara, confused. He was trying to read her wishes.

Aldara tried again. 'She is far too spirited for hunting, my lord. You would be greatly disappointed with her.'

There was no way she could bear Pandarus on her horse, but Pandarus did not care about her wishes. He had had enough of the polite banter. Enough of her.

'How much for the mare?' he asked Kadmus.

'Brother, you do not need another hunting horse,' Tyron said.

Kadmus spoke up then. 'I apologise, my lord, but the mare is not for sale. She is needed on the farm.'

Aldara blinked with relief.

'Everything has a price,' Pandarus insisted. 'Right, Aldara?'

'Not everything, my lord,' she said, looking away for a moment.

'Tell you what,' said Pandarus. 'I will race you for her.'

Kadmus studied his sister, noting her panicked expression. 'In the flag race, my lord? I have not raced before, nor has the mare.'

Pandarus placed a hand on Loda, who stirred beneath his touch. 'If you win, you keep her, *and* I will give you the mare's worth in silver. If I win, I will *buy* the mare from you at a fair price. Either way, you get paid.'

Tyron interrupted. 'Perhaps we should make it a fairer race. I will ride on behalf of Kadmus. There will be no honour in beating an inexperienced farmhand on his workhorse,' he added.

Pandarus thought the suggestion over for a moment. 'You would race on behalf of a stranger you have just met? Very noble, brother, even for you.'

Kadmus was about to decline the offer, but a gentle shake of the head from Aldara quietened him. Pandarus sent word to the timekeeper, and the challenge was announced to the spectators. Two princes had never competed against one another in the history of the tournament. The excitement moved over the crowd like a wave.

'Have the mare paraded while we prepare,' Pandarus said to Kadmus.

He glanced at Aldara one last time before leaving them. Tyron went to follow after him, and Aldara placed her hand on his arm. He stopped and looked at her.

'Your horse will not win against his,' she said.

Her touch was light, yet her hand anchored him. 'I'm quite aware of that,' he replied. 'I will borrow Leksi's.'

She retracted her hand. 'Thank you,' she said, exhaling. 'I am so sorry.'

'Don't thank me yet.'

He walked away without a backward glance. Loda was unsaddled, cleaned up, and led out onto the field by a groom. The applause unsettled her, and her handler was struggling to keep hold of her. This increased the excitement of the crowd, if that was possible. Aldara re-entered the berfrois and held on to a table, trying to keep herself steady. Hali rushed up next to her, asking questions she could not process. All she could do was watch her overwhelmed mare, panicking in the hands of a stranger.

'If Pandarus wins, Loda will become meat for his hunting dogs,' Aldara said. 'He has no other use for her. It's all about winning.'

'The tournament?' Hali asked, confused.

'Not just the tournament.' Her eyes remained on Loda.

'For God's sake, let him have the horse,' Hali pleaded, finally understanding. 'Let him have this small win now. Then perhaps he will move on.'

But it was not a small win. It was another part of her he would own.

When the trumpet sounded, Hali forced Aldara into a nearby seat. An unmasked Pandarus appeared near the timekeeper on a magnificent chestnut gelding. Hali shook her head, confused.

'Why has he taken his mask off? I thought the point was to conceal your identity.'

Aldara could barely look at him. 'Because it's now a race between two princes, and he wants everyone to know who they are watching.'

The horn sounded, and the gelding leapt forward without delay. Pandarus manoeuvred the horse around each flag like a snake moving through dense forest. It was almost effortless. Aldara was not surprised when he finished the race with the best time of the day. The crowd erupted into applause, and she was forced to slap her hands together in an awkward rhythm as she tried to clap for him. Hali was a little more believable, but only a little.

Tyron rode up to the timekeeper on Leksi's brown mare. He was masked, but he fooled no one. The horn sounded, and Tyron swept forward with incredible ease, handling the unfamiliar horse with no difficulty. At the third flag, the timekeeper raised his arm, confirming Tyron was ahead of the best time. He gained a little more with each flag, and Aldara sat forward in her chair, her hope growing with each flag returned to the barrel. But when he approached the last flag, the mare's back legs slipped out from beneath her. There was a collective intake of breath from the spectators as they watched the mare go down onto her hind legs. Tyron was an experienced enough rider to prevent her from going over onto her side. In a few motions they were upright again and finishing the turn. The gallop to the finish was fast, but it was not enough to make up the time lost because of the stumble.

Aldara felt her stomach twist as she watched the still timekeeper. His arm did not move. Pandarus had won. Only just, but it did not matter by how much. Loda was his, and her brother would return to the farm with only the silver pieces in his pocket. Apparently there was nothing Pandarus could not have. She watched him return to the timekeeper among deafening applause. He even moved closer to the berfrois so he could witness her misery. Aldara stood and applauded. She had no idea how she was doing it. Hali beamed and cheered while Aldara tried not to be sick.

'Does your brother have any other representative riders who want a go?' he shouted to Aldara. 'Unless you have another challenger, I think I will take the mare back to the castle and see what she is made of.'

Aldara stopped applauding. She stilled for a moment as her mind continued to run. She raised her arm to gain his attention, and when he looked at her, she shouted, 'I will challenge you.'

No one heard her except for Pandarus. The smirk fell from his face as he registered what she had said.

'I challenge you for the mare, my lord,' she repeated louder, so that the timekeeper could hear her.

Hali grabbed her arm. 'What are you doing?' she whispered, pulling her back from the edge.

The crowd quietened, trying to listen to the exchange. Aldara pulled her arm free and stepped forward again. 'If you win, she is yours at no cost. If I win, she is mine to do with as I please. No money will be exchanged.'

Pandarus laughed loudly. The spectators joined him. Aldara was too scared to look away from him for fear of what, or who, she might see. Perhaps Kadmus and Tyron were laughing along with them. The confused Companions looked between themselves as if they had missed something. Hali stood frozen next to her. The rest of the royal family watched on quietly.

'You arrived in a wagon,' Pandarus said loudly. 'Do you plan on unhitching one of the horses? Or shall I organise a driver to trot you around the field?' Laughter rolled across the crowd, which only encouraged him. 'This is quite different from the chicken races you held on your farm. You will actually require a horse.'

'I will ride the prize,' Aldara responded calmly. 'You wanted to see what she was made of.' The crowd cheered with approval. 'Then perhaps after I win, we can all stand around listening to more of your jokes, my lord.'

His eyes narrowed on her 'Saddle the mare,' he shouted to a nearby groom.

'No need,' she responded. 'Saddles are just extra weight.' She said it loud enough for the crowd to hear. They cheered her insanity.

As she turned around, Hali grabbed her arm again. 'Have you lost your mind? You will get yourself killed. And even if you survive the race, Pandarus will strangle you in your sleep.'

Aldara was already exiting the berfrois. 'I will be fine,' she said, the adrenaline and terror moving like waves through her.

Hali followed her. 'Bareback, in a dress? What are you even thinking?'

Aldara kept walking. 'That I can't afford the extra weight of the saddle. I have enough disadvantages.'

Tyron and Kadmus were waiting with Loda. Aldara kept her eyes on the mare. 'You should see your face,' she said to Kadmus. She was not brave enough to look at Tyron's.

Hali rushed up to Prince Tyron. 'Please, my lord, tell her she cannot do it.'

Tyron did not need prompting from anyone. He stepped in front of her. 'It's too dangerous, and you cannot win.' He spoke as if that were the end of the conversation.

She looked at him then. 'My lord, unless you are forbidding me, in which case I will be forced to obey you, then I would like to try.'

Kadmus spoke up. 'My lord, she may not be able to win, but she will have no trouble finishing.' All eyes went to him. 'She rarely used a saddle on the farm. It will not be a disadvantage.'

Tyron turned back to her. 'Do you understand what you are doing?'

'Yes. I have not stopped watching since my arrival here.'

He shook his head. 'I'm not talking about the tournament. I'm talking about the dangerous enemy you are making.'

'The one you said would pose no threat?' He continued to look at her. 'It's only an issue if I win, and you have declared it impossible.'

He stepped aside so she could pass and then made a step with his hands to help her mount. She did not need the help, but she stepped onto his hands, anyway. As she mounted, her dress slid up, gathering about her thighs. Tyron tried not to stare at the milky, bare legs wrapped around the mare while Aldara took off all of her jewellery and anything that could distract, slow, or injure her during the race. She even took off her shoes, handing everything to Hali, who was looking at her as though she were riding to her death.

'Are you sure about this?' Tyron asked for the last time.

'I have nothing else to lose at this point.'

He shook his head. 'I disagree, but here we are. Take a wider turn at the seventh flag. There is a lot of clay in the soil and the mare will slip if you take it too closely. And I don't need to warn you about the final flag.'

'No. Thank you.'

He gave the mare a quick pat before turning around and walking off towards the berfrois.

'Don't die,' Hali said, pretending to be furious. She fought back tears as she followed Tyron.

Aldara glanced at Kadmus, who said nothing. Loda stepped sideways as excitement built in the crowd. Kadmus kept hold of her, walking them up to the timekeeper. He squeezed Aldara's bare foot before leaving her. She was trembling as she mapped out her surroundings and tried to look only at the flags in front of her. She did not want to see the disapproving faces watching her from the berfrois or the laughing faces in the crowd.

Tyron knew his brother saw through his neutral expression, so he made a point of seating himself as far away from him as possible. It was not far enough from Cora though. She took a last-minute seat right next to him without saying a word. The anxious tap of his foot drew her attention. He immediately stilled it, keeping his eyes ahead. The sound of the trumpet caused him to stand involuntarily, drawing the attention of his entire family.

The sound of the horn scared both Aldara and Loda and delayed their take off. Aldara weaved one hand through Loda's mane and loosened the reins so the mare had freedom of her head. She rode with her legs, the way her father had taught her. 'Bridles are just accessories for good riders on well-trained horses,' he had told her. They had broken her together using traditional methods, but they soon realised bridles were handy for stopping her.

Once they were moving, Aldara worked at regaining the time lost from the delayed start. They moved around the first flag, collecting it in one sweeping motion. One thing Aldara had not counted on was the heavy weight of the flag itself. It threw her balance considerably and caused Loda to circle more than was necessary. She knew she did not have time for delays and made a point of shifting her body weight for the next flag. With each flag retrieved she became more efficient.

The crowd grew excited as they noticed her improvement. At the halfway point she glanced at the timekeeper, whose arm remained down by his side. They would need to be faster. Loda's speed was all she had. Cheers of support reached her across the field as she increased speed again. With three flags remaining, she tried not to look at the motionless timekeeper. The field was a soggy mess with muddy holes that swallowed Loda's hooves. The faster they moved, the more mud was sprayed into the air, covering her face and body. She could not afford the distraction of wiping it from her eyes, so she blinked through it. At the final flag, she took a risk and leaned in further to tighten the turn. She had to trust that Loda's sure-footedness would be enough to keep them upright. The mare's body moved close to the ground while her legs stretched out, trying to push off an impossible surface. As she finished the turn, Aldara saw out of the corner of her eye the timekeeper's arm fly up into the air. The roar of the crowd confirmed it. She pulled the flag from the ground as though it weighed nothing, and dug her heels into Loda's sides. The mare's stride lengthened beneath them as she returned to an upright position. The gallop to the finishing point was just a few moments of pounding heart and hooves.

Aldara's body was flush against the mare as she heaved the flag into the barrel. Her head turned to the timekeeper as she tried to slow the mare. It took her half the length of the field to stop her. Loda's neck was foaming with sweat and her breaths came in heaves. Aldara's eyes remained on the timekeeper, disbelieving. The crowd had erupted. She tore the mask from her face and wiped at the mud in her eyes with the back of her hand. She saw then the timekeeper standing with his arm as straight as an arrow in the air. The fastest time recorded for the day. She looked over at the royal berfrois where Pandarus was sitting motionless with his arms crossed in front of him and his jaw set. That is what confirmed she had actually won. She slid her hands down Loda's steaming neck and buried her face in the mare's mane. Kadmus appeared next to her, a gleaming smile on his face.

'You have ruined what appears to be a very expensive dress. You should see yourself right now. Why did no one else finish with a face full of mud?'

Aldara lifted her eyes to him. 'Because they did not win,' she said, smiling. Her leg swung over Loda's rump, but before her feet touched the ground, she felt hands on her waist, catching her weight and easing her to the ground. She knew it was Tyron without turning around.

'Congratulations,' he said. 'You have a new enemy.' When she turned to face him, his hands slid around her waist before dropping to his sides. He reached for the shoes and cloak Pero was holding next to him. 'Hali wanted me to give you these.' He handed the shoes to her one at a time, and when she had finished putting them on, he held the cloak open for her. She turned again, and he slid it over her shoulders. He took her hand, then faced her to the crowd. When he lifted her hand into the air, the roar was deafening. A royal Companion had just won the flag tournament against Syrasan's princes and knights.

When Aldara looked again at the royal berfrois, Pandarus was gone. The king and queen were clapping politely, but their faces were blank. Princess Cora sat still, watching with her hands folded in her lap. Aldara had shown up her brothers in front of

Syrasan's most important people. Tyron was right—there would be fallout from it. She had placed a target on herself.

'Take Loda and leave,' she said to Kadmus. 'Before Prince Pandarus changes his mind.'

She ran a dirty hand down the mare's shoulder. Kadmus nodded, but when he tried to take the mare, Tyron placed a hand on her. He turned and spoke to Pero.

'Organise an escort home for Kadmus. The mare will come to Archdale.'

Pero left to follow out the orders. Aldara could not find her voice. Her gratitude was choking her. She stood with one hand on Loda and the other pointlessly holding her filthy dress off the wet ground. She stared at the mare and blinked. Tyron watched her struggling to hold her emotions together. He had one hand on Loda and the other by his side. It was Kadmus who found some words on Aldara's behalf.

'Thank you, my lord. She is very appreciative. She rides much better than she speaks.'

'Much,' Aldara agreed, turning her face up to him.

Tyron looked away from her shiny eyes. 'No need to thank me. You won her. That was the agreement with Pandarus.'

Kadmus brushed her cheek with his lips and squeezed her shoulder before following after Pero. The crowd had quietened and was beginning to disperse. The noble guests had refilled their cups and were talking among themselves. Food was being served before their long journeys home.

'I can escort you if you would prefer to ride the mare to Archdale,' Tyron offered. 'I suppose the offer of a saddle is offensive to you?'

She laughed. His new favourite sound.

'It is much more fun without one,' she said. She sprang onto the mare's back and held out her hand to him. 'I'll show you.' When he did not move, she retracted her hand. 'Sorry. I forget myself sometimes.'

It was one of the things he liked most about her. He took hold of Loda's mane and hauled himself up behind her. The mare sprang sideways in surprise, and Aldara squealed. All eyes were on them then. Common, noble, royal.

'Go,' he said, attempting to hide behind her. That only made her laugh more. She clicked her tongue, and Loda moved into a canter, weaving through wandering spectators until they were free of them. They did not slow until they had made it out of Pelaweth, away from the people and busy roads.

For a few moments, they were free. But it was just an illusion.

CHAPTER 16

The sound of Loda's walk was the most relaxing noise in the world to Aldara. The combination of rhythmic hooves and Tyron's body heat made her eyes heavy. When Tyron noticed her head drop, he spoke up.

'Please tell me you are awake. I have no stirrups or reins back here.'

Her laughter was laced with fatigue. 'Perhaps we should find some cold water to throw over me.'

'You could definitely do with a wash.'

Another laugh.

They were riding alongside farmland, where new grass was pushing up through the icy surface. Sheep stopped grazing to watch them pass. Aldara spotted a well among them, not far from the road.

'Water,' she said, stopping Loda.

Tyron dismounted and then held a hand out for her. She took it and slid down to the ground.

'You will need to wash that now,' she said, glancing at his hand.

He was inspecting his tunic. 'Thankfully your back was clean.' His eyes returned to her. 'You really are a mess.'

'Fedora is going to drown me in the bath when we get back.' She turned towards the well. 'What are our chances of getting water without being caught?'

He suppressed a smirk. 'I think we'll be okay. Wait here with the mare.'

'Be careful,' she called after him. 'I was literally chased by a farmer with a pitchfork once for crossing his property on horseback. If we are caught stealing their water supply, we may hang in their barn.'

He turned to look at her standing on the edge of the road in front of a giant horse, nervously searching their surroundings. A smile tugged at his mouth. She really did forget he was a prince sometimes. Farmers did not chase him. They bowed before him as he took what he needed from them. 'I'll be sure to keep my wits,' he whispered loudly back in her direction. Only once he had turned away from her again did he allow himself a grin.

The sheep fled as he made his way through the muddy paddock towards the well. As he lowered the pail, his eyes sought Aldara. He found himself doing that a lot lately. It was some distance before he heard a crack as the pail broke through the thin layer of ice on top of the water. When the rope began to creak from the weight of it, he turned the large wooden handle and hauled it back up. As he was untying the pail, he thought he heard shouting. When he looked up, he saw an older man running towards him, waving his fist and shouting profanities. Tyron stood still, waiting for the man to recognise him. He was a few feet away from Tyron when he noticed the royal emblem displayed on his arm. He stopped running, an expression of concentration on his face.

'A knight?' he asked, confused.

'A prince.'

The man dropped to his knees, his eyes on the ground. 'My lord, the water is yours, and whatever else you need.'

Tyron stepped forward and lifted the old man to his feet, the soggy knees of his woollen pants clinging to his legs. 'Thank you. I only need the water.'

The man glanced nervously at the road. 'Is the girl with you also, my lord?'

Tyron followed his gaze and saw a man holding Aldara by the arm. She was shouting at him as she tried to free herself. Tyron took off at a run and reached them in seconds.

'Release her,' he shouted at the young farmer.

The older man arrived a few moments later, breathless. 'Please forgive us, my lord. We did not know.'

The young man panicked when he saw Tyron and released his grip on Aldara. She fell forward, and Tyron caught her and returned her upright. He gently pushed her behind him with one arm.

'I've seen pigs handled with more care than that,' he said to the younger one.

'So sorry, my lord. She didn't look like...she was travelling with you.'

Aldara placed a hand over her mouth to stifle a laugh.

Tyron turned his head and stared at her. 'Something funny?'

She glanced between the men. 'He has a point. I look like a beggar. There is not a man alive that would believe I am travelling with you.'

His eyes swept over her and his shoulders dropped. Her vulnerability terrified him.

The two farmers retrieved the water for them and then left them alone. Tyron insisted Aldara drink first. When she was finished, he had a drink himself and then took his handkerchief from his pocket, wet it, and handed it to her. Aldara crouched by the pail and washed her face, neck and hands. She let out her hair and wiped at the clumps of mud as best she could. Black feathers floated down to the ground around her. When she was done, she wrapped her damp hair into a bun and secured it with the comb again.

'It's a good thing I wore black,' she said, looking down at her dress.

When she had finished with the water, she rinsed the handkerchief and placed the pail in front of Loda to drink from. Tyron stood still and tense, watching her. She stepped up to him to hand him the wet handkerchief, and he surprised himself by catching hold of her wrist. She was waiting for him to say something, do something, but he released her, took a step back, and glanced down the road.

'We should leave before we run into any more of your farming friends.'

Aldara laughed, and his eyes returned to her. He was not a reckless man, but all sense left him in those moments. She stopped laughing when she saw his expression and swallowed.

'What is it?'

He shook his head. 'Nothing. Let me help you up this time.'

∼

She glanced at the empty pail lying by his feet. 'I just need to return the pail to the well.'

He blinked at her. 'What?'

'It won't take me long,' she said, scooping it up.

He caught her by the arm again and the strength of his grip made her entire body pay attention.

'Just to be clear, you are going to return the pail to make life easier for the men who would have done God knows what to you had I not been here?'

She looked at him, confused. 'I am going to be courteous to the farmers who gave us their water.'

And there was that expression again—thoughtful, conflictual, but this time he did not let go of her arm. She did not move. The pail fell from her hand, and she turned her head to watch it roll along the ground. Tyron pulled her close and slid his spare hand up her neck. She stared up at him, and then his mouth was on hers. He let go of her wrist and pressed his hand into her back so she was flush against him. Her entire body softened under his grip.

Aldara could barely breathe beneath the weight of his hands. The heat coming from him made her shudder in the cold. She had no idea if her feet were on the ground. Just her toes. She freed one of her hands that was crushed against his chest and found the side of his face, pulling herself up to him. She did not want him to stop. When a puff of hot breath hit the back of her neck, her eyes snapped open, and she squealed into his open mouth and pulled back from him. He immediately released his grip on her. She turned around and Loda's muzzle found her face.

Tyron stepped back from her, trying to steady his breathing. 'She's jealous.'

He seemed to be at a loss as to what to do with his hands, so he leant on his knees, watching as she stroked the mare's face before placing a quick kiss on the tip of her muzzle.

'There is no chance I will go back for seconds now,' he said.

She laughed and there was that expression on him again. He looked as though he were about to pull her to him again when the sound of approaching horses made him turn around. Some wagons were making their way along the road.

'Soon the royal wagons will pass and we will have to face the judgemental stares of my family,' he said. 'I would prefer to face them one at a time—and later. Let's go,' he said, wrapping her waist with his hands and lifting her up onto the mare.

She sat behind him for the last part of their journey, hands on him, and her forehead occasionally resting on his back. The air was cooling quickly, and Tyron wanted to give her his tunic to wear beneath her cloak. She laughed off the suggestion.

'I'm going to be in enough trouble. If I return to Fedora wearing men's clothing, I won't be permitted to go anywhere ever again.'

When they arrived at the castle, they watched the portcullis rise in front of them. Neither of them wanted to go in, yet both of them had to. Tyron reluctantly moved Loda forward, their pace slow until they reached the stables. A groom rushed out, surprised to find the prince sharing a horse with no saddle. He ran off to get a stool for Aldara. By the time he came back Tyron had lowered her to the ground and was standing next to her.

'How was your saddle-free experience, my lord?'

They were inside Archdale, so the formalities returned.

'I may never sit again. Or produce children.'

She smiled at him, and they both watched the groom take Loda off to a stall. She was too tired to protest being handled by a stranger.

'Will you send for me?' Aldara asked quietly.

He looked back at her. 'That depends. Will we have separate horses next time, with saddles, like normal people?'

He did not want separate horses, and she had not been talking about going riding, but they said nothing more. They walked in silence up the path towards the castle, and then they stood outside of the Companions' quarters, hands by their sides, stretching the time. It did not take long for Fedora to discover them. She came out of the door and stopped walking to take in the sight of Aldara. Not a muscle moved on her face.

'Good afternoon, my lord. How was the tournament?'

'Eventful,' he replied, eyes on Aldara. 'I will let you get cleaned up,' he said to her.

The women curtsied and waited for him to turn the corner of the corridor. Fedora turned to face Aldara.

'Have you been socialising with pigs?' she asked without humour.

Aldara sighed, inwardly. 'No, my lady.'

Fedora's arms were folded and her lips were pressing together. She was showing restraint. 'Then why are you covered in mud?'

Aldara would have explained, but Fedora did not even let her speak.

'Never mind. I have heard enough from the messenger. I cannot bear to hear it again.' She sighed *outwardly*, a forbidden gesture. 'You are endangering your life with these defiant acts. And you are endangering the lives of the other girls as well.' She paused to let her words linger between them. 'The last thing we need is a very powerful prince with a vendetta against the women he bought to worship at his feet.'

'I don't worship at his feet,' she replied.

Fedora uncrossed her arms. 'Yes, that is why we have this problem. What concerns me most is he is also aware of it. Your actions show a lack of understanding of your situation.'

Aldara said nothing.

'Go clean yourself up,' Fedora snapped, showing a rare glimpse of anger. 'You better hope Prince Tyron sends for you tonight, because you need to be in favour with at least one prince right now.'

Those words remained with Aldara as she walked to the bathing room. She replayed them in her mind as she washed. Then she replayed them for many nights after, as Tyron did not send for her.

CHAPTER 17

Tyron stood in front of his mother and tried very hard to look at her. All of that disappointment in her eyes was making it difficult.

'My son,' she began. 'I am worried about you. It is not like you to be distracted from your responsibilities. I want to talk to you about the girl.'

Tyron could have predicted the script exactly. Not much passed his mother's observant eye, especially when it came to her children.

'Your concern is unnecessary.'

He walked over to the table and poured himself some water from the jug. Eldoris tried a more direct approach.

'You have not taken much of an interest in these women before, and suddenly you are riding off on horseback like a rebellious ten-year-old. Actually, I am not entirely sure you would have behaved that way as a ten-year-old.'

He laughed at her. 'It was not an act of rebellion. I went for a ride with a girl.'

She studied his face. 'Not a girl. Your Companion.'

'Does the title matter?'

'I am trying to understand your relationship with her.'

He was trying to understand that himself.

'History is full of great men who have been undone by ordinary women. I am simply cautioning you to be careful and not throw away the respect of your kingdom.'

'She is not ordinary.'

It just came out of him. Fuel to the fire. When he looked at his mother, he saw pity and disappointment. *Pity*. He took another drink so he could stare into his cup.

'If you think it is love, it is not,' she said. 'If you believe there is any kind of future with her, there is not. If you are hoping for a different outcome than the inevitable one, then you only have to look to your father to see what is ahead for you both.' She waited a moment to ensure he was following the conversation. 'Is that what you want for her? In a few years she will be barren and lonely, watching you live your life while her own slips by.' Pity filled her face. 'I do not wish ill upon these women, but there is a reality to their situation that needs to be faced.'

'I suppose you wouldn't believe me if I told you she was different from the others?'

'On the contrary, it can be the only truth. I cannot imagine any other reason you would be so foolish with your heart.' Her tone was not unkind.

Tyron looked at her. He wanted to argue the point, but there was no argument in what she was saying.

'She did not want to come here. She would have remained happily poor.'

'Those women…' She thought about what she wanted to say. 'The Companions' entire lives are dedicated to making men feel and think like that. They are trained to be desirable in whatever form is appropriate for that person. That girl has been custom made just for you, so it is natural you feel this way. If she was Pandarus's Companion she would be different again. Suddenly you would have a woman who shares his love of sports, expensive things, and bedroom antics.'

Tyron could not imagine Aldara as Pandarus's Companion, nor did he want to.

Eldoris stood up, keeping her eyes on her son. She fought the impulse to touch his face, knowing better than to trespass in his personal space.

'I am not saying you should not take a Companion. The tradition stands—for now. Rather choose a Companion you can guard your heart against. I am about to have this same conversation with Stamitos, who has just followed in the footsteps of his father and brothers.'

Tyron shook his head. 'What do you mean?'

'He bought a Companion at the tournament today.' Her tone was mournful.

Tyron tilted his head. 'You think we are the bad influence? Men have been buying women for their beds for centuries. The tradition existed in Corneo long before Syrasan flew its first flag.'

'I am aware of our history,' she reminded him. 'It is just that Stamitos is a kind boy with a big heart. I fear he is trying to buy love and will not be able to differentiate the two.' She touched his shoulder briefly as she passed him. 'The decision on her future is yours to make. You are smart, so make a smart decision that benefits both of you. The time for a true companion, a wife, will be decided by your father when a suitable match is found. This too is the way it has been for centuries.'

'It is also the reason why the tradition of a Companion came about. If you want marriages of convenience, you are expecting your sons to live their lives with closed hearts.'

She stared at him. 'And what of my daughter? This is not a problem only for men.'

Tyron looked away. 'You're right.'

'I am trying to protect you. And your heart most of all. Open your heart to the right person. If this girl does care for you, which she may do, the pain for her will be far worse. She will have nothing after you. No one. No prospects of any sort. If her virtue is intact, there are still other possibilities for her.'

She slipped from the room, leaving Tyron to stare at the empty doorway. Her words remained stagnant around him. She had spoken complete sense, truths that were clouded by Aldara's sunlit presence and golden laughter. End it, a simple resolution for everyone. He could send her somewhere where she would be safe from his world. It hadn't really begun, which should have made it simpler still. *Liar.* It had begun long ago—the moment he had seen her stumbling down the path towards him.

∽

ALDARA WENT TO BATHE. She added boiled water to the tub, climbed in, and slipped beneath the surface so she could free the mud from her hair. The water clouded around her, and she could hardly see through it. What she could see were Tyron's hands tangled in her filthy hair, his fingers holding her head in place so the air she breathed came only from his lungs. She emerged to the surface of the water and found herself face to face with a girl she had never seen before. She gasped and pushed herself to the back of the tub. The girl stepped back.

'I am so sorry,' she said, trying not to smile. 'You were under water for so long I thought you might have drowned.'

She had a round, pretty face and fair hair cut above her shoulders. She was wrapped in a robe, her long legs visible. Aldara looked around for her own robe. It was well out of reach. She sank lower into the dirty water.

'Who are you?'

'My name is Sapphira. I arrived a few hours ago.' An expression of recognition came over her face. 'Oh, you are the girl from the tournament. I watched you race today. I watched you win.' She stepped closer again. 'You are the reason I am here.'

Aldara leant forward. 'What do you mean?'

Before she could reply Fedora walked in, soundless as always.

'Good, the two of you have been introduced.' She stood between them. 'Sapphira will spend time with you over the coming months. She will shadow you on chores and lessons. Prince Stamitos is eager for her to be available socially before the warm season ends.'

Aldara looked at the young girl who now belonged to Stamitos.

'Sapphira made quite an impression on the prince at the tournament today,' Fedora added.

'It must have been some impression,' Aldara said. 'How did the two of you meet?'

Normally Fedora would have shut down such a conversation, but she stood waiting to hear the reply.

'He watched me shoot,' Sapphira said. 'The lads were running a small contest in between the riders. It drew quite a crowd in the end. I had no idea Prince Stamitos was among the spectators when I split my own arrow.'

Fedora was not impressed. 'Archery?'

Sapphira was oblivious to her disapproval. 'Yes, my lady. The best in the kingdom, let me assure you. Better than any man. My father is an artillator in Veanor, one of the finest craftsmen in Syrasan. I was never one for toys as a child. I played with crossbows as soon as I had use of my hands.'

Aldara lowered her head and smiled to the water.

'Let us hope it is not your only skill,' Fedora replied. 'Your boyish tricks may have impressed the young prince, but they will not take you far inside these walls. The lords require ladies, not knights, so your archery will be about as useful as Aldara's horsemanship.' She walked over and checked the water jugs. 'Aldara, find something suitable for Sapphira to wear, and then you can both help the ladies prepare for this evening's feast.'

Aldara stood up in the tub. 'Tonight's feast?'

Fedora was already leaving. 'Yes. You will not be attending.'

'Did Tyron not request I attend?'

That made Fedora stop and turn. Her expression was fierce. 'That is Prince Tyron or His Lordship to you. Do not forget your place here. Your actions today have done you no favours. Perhaps he could not trust you to keep clean for the occasion, or perhaps the embarrassment to his entire family was too much for him.'

She turned and left then. Aldara shook her head and sat back down in the water. It did not make sense to her. But then, she would not be the first naive girl to believe she was different, to imagine something more than fleeting lust. She winced at her own stupidity. How many more times would she find herself fooled by the ridiculous life she had been sold into? Every time she was forced to check herself, she found herself in the same tragic state.

Not that long ago she had found contentment in shovelling snow from the castle paths, out in the cold where her thoughts were frozen and her hands hurt. She had been away from the beautiful women in their beautiful dresses, living their pretend lives that could be snatched away from them at any moment. But then the tired prince had returned on his tired gelding and melted the snow and stripped her of her tools. His weak smile had undone all of her work. Undone her. She had rejoined the beautiful women and put on a beautiful dress and pretended to be one of them. And now she would be forced to pick up the shovel yet again.

Sapphira was still standing by the tub, holding onto her robe. 'You captured the attention of an entire kingdom today,' she said. 'What is the attention of one man compared to that?'

Aldara looked at her. She had a lot of confidence for someone so young.

Sapphira stepped closer and whispered, 'Today you showed everyone that Companions are not just pretty playthings for the princes. You showed women a way to be noticed that has nothing to do with sex. I want people to see what I can do—that's why I'm here.'

Aldara closed her eyes. She did not want to feel responsible in any way for the fate of this girl.

'My father is ageing,' Sapphira went on. 'His hands shake. There will come a time soon when he'll no longer be able to work. When Prince Stamitos made an offer to him, I said yes, before Father had a chance to say no. It was a lot of money. I could not have done it without seeing you race.'

'I am afraid you have been misled,' Aldara said, staring into the filthy water. 'I doubt you will ever pick up a bow or arrow again.'

Sapphira shook her head. 'You're wrong. It was my archery that caught the prince's eye.'

Aldara thought about this. It was probably true. He would have found her exciting. He would have thought they would run wild in the woods together and shoot deer. Youth did that to you, it made you stupid.

'*You* caught the prince's eye,' she said. 'And now you belong to him. There are rules and strict ways of conduct here. I broke them when I rode today. The other women, the real Companions, are not like me. You will be expected to conform, or you will become an outcast and requested by no one.'

When she found the strength to look up, she expected to see a mirrored reflection of her own disappointment. Instead, Sapphira appeared sceptical.

'I am not here to be like them. I am not beautiful like them. I am also not one for conforming. I think you will find Prince Stamitos chose me for different reasons.'

Aldara had just wanted to save her mare, not start an uprising. But it was too late for both of them. They would have to find a way to exist that kept Fedora happy and their sanity intact.

'You say you are from Veanor?'

'Yes.'

That explained her optimism. Veanor was on the coast and was the main port used for Galen trade. It was a wealthy village. People could afford to be optimistic about their futures.

'Do you play the harp?'

Sapphira raised her eyebrows in surprise. 'No.'

'Dance?'

She shook her head. 'No.'

'Paint? Sing?' Aldara continued.

She crossed her arms and nodded. 'Yes, I sing a little.'

Aldara let out a tired breath. 'Then you are already ahead of me. I can do none of those things.'

Sapphira frowned at her. 'Why on earth would you want to paint and sing when you ride as I imagine Epona to ride?'

Aldara stood up, stepped out of the tub and retrieved her robe. 'Who is Epona?'

'Epona is the protector of horses. A goddess actually.'

Aldara laughed. Her first thought was how amused Tyron would be by that story. His eyes would laugh even if he did not. He would wipe at the mud on her face and call her Epona with that smirk of his. A coldness came over her as she realised she could no longer afford those thoughts if she were to survive.

'Come,' she said. 'I'll introduce you to the true goddesses of Archdale.'

CHAPTER 18

She found a way to exist. There was no choice but to pretend it was enough and hope it would eventually become enough. She tried not to notice the days growing warmer, slipping past without a word from him. She tried to forget the sweet suffocation she had felt in his crushing grip. She tried to toughen herself against him in hope that if they met again, she could say, 'Good day, my lord,' and smile with warmth but feel nothing inside. She tried and pretended, but she was still suffocating against him.

One morning, Fedora announced to the women there was to be a banquet in honour of their Galen guests. The men had arrived the previous day, sent to review all food trade agreements prior to the cold season. Zenas needed to know there would be enough grain to feed his people, and for that reason he wanted all the Companions to attend the banquet and keep the men in good spirits. The women were props to aid negotiations in any way they could. No one said as much, but everyone understood their role.

'The Noble Companions are awfully quiet,' Hali said. They were in the dressing room, and Aldara was fixing her hair.

'For good reason,' Aldara replied.

She was already dressed in a sleeveless, orange silk dress with a belt of pearls. Her own hair was loosely tucked to one side and wrapped with black silk.

Hali was watching her in the mirror.

'Are you afraid?'

Aldara looked at her. 'Of what?'

'Being sent to their chambers.'

She had been trying not to think about that possibility, but now that it had been said aloud she could not hide from it.

'There's no point being afraid is there? I have no control over it.'

Hali appeared sympathetic. 'The only reason I bring it up at all is because there are four guests and three Noble Companions.'

Aldara had already done the math. Her eyes did not return to the mirror. She was trying to keep it together. There was a small, naive part of her that insisted Tyron would not allow it. But there was also a bigger part of her that knew his kingdom came first and he would follow the wishes of his father. Her mind flashed back to the savage removal of Tia's hand. The wood chopping block was stained with her blood.

'You must be looking forward to socialising without Pandarus hovering over you for the evening,' she said, changing the subject. Pandarus was in Zoelin for business, and Hali seemed to have more bounce than usual.

'That's an understatement,' she whispered.

Fedora slipped into the room at that moment, glancing about, checking the women. 'All right, ladies, remember everything we went through today. Make sure our guests feel welcome. Off you go.'

Aldara kept her eyes down as she passed Fedora, but she felt eyes on her back.

The gathering was extravagant but civilised compared to previous celebrations Aldara had attended. Guests were seated at tables and talking at polite volumes. A lute played at the far side of a room, a song Aldara did not recognise. No one was dancing.

She did a quick surveillance of the guests. She knew most of them. There was no sign of Lord Yuri, and one look at Hali's face confirmed her suspicion. 'Perhaps he is running late,' she offered.

Hali pretended not to understand. 'Who?'

Aldara smiled, her gaze moving about the room. She had already prepared herself for the fact Tyron would be in attendance, but when she saw him on the far side of the room, watching her, she guessed he did not know *she* would be. She curtsied from a distance and then turned away from him. That was etiquette ticked off—now she could go about avoiding him.

'They don't seem so bad,' Hali said, eyeing the Galen guests. 'I think I was imagining men with far too much access to food.'

Aldara followed her line of vision back to where Tyron was seated just beneath the dais, with all four Galen guests. There would be no avoiding him now. Hali was right though, the men were rather handsome, and much younger than she had been imagining. That relaxed her slightly.

'Let's find the wine, and then we can introduce ourselves,' Hali said.

Aldara rarely drank much at social gatherings, but that night she was feeling an overwhelming desire to do so. 'Good plan,' she said, glancing at Tyron, who was showing no sign of moving. As if the evening was not awkward enough from a distance, now she would have to include him in the conversation and smile at him all night.

They found some refreshments on an abandoned table. Aldara poured herself a cup of wine and emptied it in a few gulps. She picked up the jar and poured another.

Hali looked at her. 'What is happening here?'

Aldara took a large gulp from her cup and set it down. 'I'm just trying to survive the evening.'

'Should I be worried about you?'

'Of course not,' she replied, picking up the cup and taking another mouthful. 'Let's go.'

The guests broke into applause as Astra replaced the lute player across the room. Hali glanced at Aldara as they made their way over to the guests and rolled her eyes. When they arrived at the table, Tyron shifted in his chair. Aldara took another drink and then set the cup down on the table.

'My lord,' she said, curtsying alongside Hali. The women then turned to the Galen guests who were watching them curiously.

Tyron stood up. 'Allow me to introduce two of Archdale's most beautiful residents,' he said to the men. 'This is Hali and Aldara.'

All of the men were fluent in the Syrasan language, which was lucky for Aldara, who was not yet fluent in Galen. The men stood up and bowed.

'Ladies,' Tyron continued. 'May I present Alcaeus, Caelius, Philo, and Lysander.'

The women curtsied again.

'How was your journey across the Arossi?' Aldara asked. 'I understand its waters are calm at this time of year.'

'I am afraid we were not that lucky,' replied Philo. 'I was the only passenger who was not ill for most of it.'

Aldara guessed Philo to be around the age of twenty. He was fair and tall, common traits of pure Galen bloodlines. 'I'm sorry to hear that,' she said. 'I imagine you are still finding your land legs.'

Rhea and Panthea stepped into the conversation, pulling the attention of the men.

'I think it's time for some dancing,' Rhea said, a purr in her tone.

'If only we had willing partners,' Panthea added, pretending to look about.

'I believe that is our cue,' Alcaeus said, turning to Lysander.

'You do not have to ask me twice,' Lysander replied.

Rhea and Panthea led the two men into the middle of the room. Astra began a slow, traditional Galen song she had been practicing on the harp for over two weeks.

'I don't suppose I can tempt you to dance,' Hali said to Philo.

But his eyes were on Aldara. 'I think I will get myself another drink, but Caelius is champing at the bit, aren't you, old man?'

They all laughed, even Tyron. The visit was too important not to laugh.

'I will have to see if I can remember this one,' he said, bowing to Hali.

'I am happy to refresh your memory,' she said, curtsying.

Caelius led Hali out to join the others, leaving Philo, Tyron, and Aldara standing as spectators. Aldara picked up her cup and finished what was left. Both of the men noticed.

'Can I get you another?' Philo offered.

Tyron seemed concerned. 'Perhaps some water?'

She looked at him as she placed her cup back down on the table. 'I would love some more wine,' she said, turning to Philo. 'It is a banquet after all.'

He picked the jar off the table and filled her cup. 'This is actually Galen wine,' he said, pride in his tone as though he had bottled it himself.

Aldara took the cup from his hand. 'Yes, I can taste the quality,' she lied. 'Produced in the South I believe, where growing conditions are ideal.'

Fedora always ensured they had a few relevant and impressive facts on hand.

'The lady knows her wine,' Philo said to Tyron, smiling appreciatively.

'She's full of surprises,' Tyron said, smiling back.

Aldara took another drink. Just a little more and she could pretend the situation was not happening at all. Up went her cup, then on with the conversation. 'What part of Galen are you from Philo?'

They did not use titles such as *lord* in Galen as they did not want to segregate people.

'I'm from Klovotor, on the coast. I have a substantial amount of land there. However, I am rarely there to make use of it.'

'Perhaps you can try your hand at wine,' Tyron said.

Philo laughed, and Aldara emptied her cup.

'Would you like to dance Philo of Klovotor?' Aldara asked. The women had also been practicing Galen dances. She felt confident she could get through most of them without injuring herself.

'An excellent suggestion. I believe we are now properly fuelled.'

'I shall leave the two of you to enjoy the evening,' Tyron said.

He bowed with such grace that Aldara believed him to be sincere. That is until he turned to leave and his dark eyes burned in her direction. She remained tall and unblinking against them. The wine had given her courage. It had also given slight dizziness.

They joined the others who were lined up facing each other in the middle of the hall. Astra had finished playing, swiftly replaced by three musicians with wind instruments. Aldara stood opposite Philo, heart pounding from the wine.

'I should warn you I am not a strong dancer,' she said.

'I have been told I am rather good. If you will allow me, I will lead you.'

∼

TYRON DRIFTED BETWEEN CONVERSATIONS, discovering he could not focus on any of them. Aldara was swirling about in his peripheral vision, apparently enjoying herself. At one point he heard her laugh and looked over to find her smiling and flushed as she weaved between the other dancers. She was a little out of time with the others, but Philo did not seem to mind. He was besotted. His eyes remained on her through every partner change. Tyron gave up trying to talk and went to sit down. Cora sniffed out his vulnerability from across the room, and within moments, she was seated next to him, ready to narrate his thoughts.

'You're surprisingly sober,' he said, attacking first.

'My, my. She has got to you.'

Tyron said nothing.

'Look at her, out there, playing the game so well. And you're playing right along.'

'You always assume people share your twisted mind. Not everyone plays games, sister.'

Before she could reply, Leksi came and sat in the empty chair on the other side of Tyron. Cora pretended not to notice.

'I thought you would be out there,' Leksi said to Tyron, smirk on his face. He leant back in his chair to watch the dancing for a moment. 'Well, well. Philo has taken a shine to your Companion.' He leaned forward, eyes on Cora. 'Tell me, Cora, is that against the rules?'

Cora gave him a lazy glance. 'Do not ask me about men's rules. I just follow them.'

'That's not true,' he replied, winking at her.

The dance had stopped, and they were all staggering about, out of breath and clapping one another. Tyron watched as Philo led Aldara to a table and poured her another cup of wine. She drank it fast, thirsty from her efforts. They were back out dancing before Tyron had collected his thoughts. That was his fault. He had meant to send her away and had delayed the decision for far too long. The truth was, she belonged to no one at that moment, and everyone seemed aware of that fact. Cora could not resist the opportunity to push him a little farther.

'Is it just me or is his hand slipping inside her dress every time they come together?' she asked, keeping her voice neutral.

Tyron was out of his chair and walking towards them before

Leksi had a chance to point out she was wearing a closed dress, making the suggestion impossible. It did not matter anyway—Tyron could not have watched it for a moment longer.

'Forgive the interruption,' he shouted to Philo, trying to compete with the music. 'Do you mind if I steal Aldara from you?'

Philo studied his face for a moment and then nodded. 'By all means.' He turned to Aldara. 'You have worn me out. You will have to excuse me.'

Aldara curtsied. Once Philo was out of earshot she looked at Tyron. 'What did you say to him?' There was accusation in her voice.

Tyron took hold of her hand and led her through the maze of dancers and out of the hall. He was walking fast, forcing her to run to keep up. Once they were away from the noise and the stares of the guards, she pulled her hand free and stood still. He spun around on her, losing patience.

'Where are we going?' she asked.

He took a step towards her. 'Where are we going, my lord?'

Her eyebrows shot up. 'Really, that's how you want this conversation to go? All right. Where are we going, *my lord*?'

He took hold of her arm again. 'I am taking you back to your quarters to sleep off the wine.'

She pulled herself free again, this time using more force. 'I really hope you are joking.'

'Am I laughing?'

'You never laugh, so how am I to tell?'

He lowered his arms to his side and looked at her. 'You should not have even been here tonight.'

She folded her arms in front of her in a manner that would have had Fedora reeling. 'And where should I have been? Scrubbing floors with the maids? Tucked up in bed losing my mind to boredom?'

'I don't know. Not in here.'

She stared at him, feeling the heat of anger in her stomach once again. 'I can make my own way back to my quarters. And then I will spend the evening explaining to Fedora why I was asked to leave the banquet so she can point out, once again, all of the reasons I am a failure.'

She looked away and tried to walk past him. Tyron reached out and grabbed her arm.

'I will explain to her…'

She reeled on him then, eyes burning. 'Explain what? What will you explain? Tell me. You have explained nothing from the moment we were introduced.'

He could not find the words he needed. Or perhaps he did not know where to start. Either way, she was not done.

'If you don't want me, then hand me over to your guests or sell me! Those are my options, and the decision is yours to make!'

He let go of her arm, and she stood there panting, trying not to cry. Because he could not say the things he wanted to, he said something else.

'Lower your voice. You will be taken away and whipped if you are caught speaking to me like that.'

She took an unsteady step away from him. When he said nothing more, she curtsied and said, 'Good night, my lord.'

All the venom was gone from her tone. She stood upright, turned, and walked away down the corridor, leaving him standing alone, hands open and words still missing.

She did not see Philo again.

CHAPTER 19

Twenty-seven days. Aldara could not help but count them. Twenty-seven days without one word from him. She listened for news, but none of the maids knew anything more than she did. He had not left Archdale to fight a secret war or returned to Galen with his guests nor any of the other excuses she had dreamed up. His horse remained in the stables, and he was safely inside the castle walls—just never anywhere near her. She had to stop listening for mention of his name. So twenty-seven days after the incident, she found a way to distract herself.

'You want what?' Fedora asked, clearly displeased.

Aldara was undeterred. 'Some archery supplies,' she said again. 'Sapphira believes that archery is the only talent Prince Stamitos wants from her.'

Hali was pretending to read by the fireplace. She wanted nothing to do with it.

'Absolutely not,' replied Fedora calmly.

Aldara remained calm also. If there was any chance of getting her way, it would need to be Fedora's way ultimately.

'There are plenty of girls that can sing. There are no others in the kingdom that can shoot a longbow over four hundred yards.

His lordship chose her for that reason—the reason she stood out from all others that day. She just wants the equipment and the chance to maintain her skills in case the need arises.'

Fedora walked away. 'The need to shoot someone?'

Aldara walked alongside her, remaining calm. 'The need to entertain the prince or his guests in a form of his choosing. Or perhaps the need to accompany his lordship on a hunt.'

Fedora picked up the pace. 'Companions do not hunt. And she will not be entertaining guests with her…archery.'

She had one more try. 'This is the first girl that really captured his attention—the girl with the longbow. Are you sure you want to offer up something different?'

Fedora stopped walking. It was a long enough pause to be a good sign. 'Very well. I will send a squire to fetch her equipment from her father. I don't want to cause scandal by sourcing it within the castle walls. Any practise is to be done outside of her singing and other lessons. Am I understood?'

'Yes, my lady.'

It was a small win, but a much-needed one. It would give them both more access to the outdoors. Sun, fresh air, a chance to breathe properly.

The following day, a messenger arrived with the equipment from Sapphira's father. Inside the leather quiver, hidden among the arrows, was a letter that Sapphira read in private. Afterwards, she washed her face and returned to Aldara, who said nothing of her red eyes.

Fedora allowed them to spend the afternoon at the butts where archery training took place. She felt armed Companions roaming the castle grounds alone might be cause for alarm, so she sent a guard to accompany them. The guard carried the equipment and trailed behind them as they stepped out into the sunshine that had finally broken through the clouds. There was just enough warmth to remind them the warm season had begun. The girls stopped walking to bathe in the light for a moment. The guard, impatient and resentful of his duty, hurried them on. They did not walk, they strolled. Aldara breathed deeply, occasionally spinning around so the sun reached her entire body.

Sapphira laughed at her and then reached over and unclipped her hair. 'You may as well completely relax,' she said, using her fingers to detangle the waves, so they fell about her shoulders.

'Don't lose that clip, or Fedora may not let me back in.' Aldara lifted her arms, bathing her cold hands in the warmth.

They continued alongside the castle, weaving through hung linen and maids elbow deep in soapy water. Sapphira could not help but join in on Aldara's insanity. She spun faster and faster until she was so dizzy she had to grab hold of a wet tunic to keep herself upright. The maid scolded her, and Aldara laughed, surprising herself. It was a sound she had not heard in weeks.

'We should go,' Sapphira said. 'I think Fedora is having us watched.'

Aldara went silent and followed Sapphira's line of sight up to a figure standing in the window above them. A dark shadow against the brilliance of the sun. Familiar enough to wipe away her smile and slow her heart beat. She used a hand to shield the sun, trying to get better vision, but the window was now empty. Her hand fell to her side, and she looked at Sapphira. 'Yes, we should go.'

They walked away from the castle and stepped onto the new grass that was taking over the mud. They walked amid lines of flowering populus, finding themselves in a quiet place where the noise was just a distant hum behind them.

'In there,' the guard said, pointing to a gap in the trees.

The girls walked through the opening onto a large, grassy lawn. They stopped, looking around at the target mounds positioned at varying distances. Behind the mounds, protective fencing ensured no stray arrows took out unaware passers-by. Each mound had five coloured rings.

'I assume the aim is to hit the yellow circle in the centre?' Aldara said.

'You're a natural.'

Sapphira collected her things from the guard, handling the equipment with ease and familiarity. She strapped her quiver to her hip, so the arrows hung beside her. When she raised the bow, her loose cotton dress slid up her arm, revealing toned muscle beneath it. Aldara stood behind her, a quiet observer.

'Nock, mark, draw, loose!' Sapphira shouted.

She released the arrow, and it pierced the heart of the yellow centre. She shifted her footing and aimed at the next target. Aldara noticed the guard next to them shift his weight.

'Nock, mark, draw, loose!' she shouted again, hitting another bulls-eye. She found a rhythm and released another six arrows consecutively.

'You don't have to call it when there are no other shooters,' the guard said.

Sapphira rolled her eyes. Aldara guessed the shouting made him uneasy.

'All of that effort and it turns out you do not need any practise after all,' Aldara said. 'I should also mention I wish to remain your friend now that I have seen what you can do with that thing.'

Sapphira tucked her hair behind her ears and offered the bow to the guard. 'Fancy a little competition?'

'*I* most certainly would,' a voice came through the trees.

Prince Stamitos appeared through the opening, smiling on top of his chestnut gelding. Leksi followed behind him, loose rein and appearing relaxed. Aldara glanced past them, but no one else followed. The women dropped into a curtsy.

'Good day, my lords,' they said in unison.

'Indeed,' Stamitos replied. 'So this is where Fedora has been hiding you. Can't pretend I am not pleased.'

Leksi's eyes rested on Aldara, and he nodded politely.

'Actually, I have been lost among a sea of dresses and suffocating on songs,' Sapphira said.

Stamitos looked between the targets. 'I'm not one for songs.' He smiled down at her. 'Pandarus has organised a large hunting party in a few days' time. I am hoping Fedora will let you join us.'

'I will not hold my breath.'

Aldara laughed. 'Sapphira has figured out the hierarchy of the power around here,' she said to Stamitos.

'Yes, I have heard even the bravest of princes do not go up against Fedora.' He glanced at the bow in Sapphira's hand. 'Have those arrows ever been used on a moving target?'

Sapphira went completely still. She appeared to be listening for something. Aldara was about to speak to fill the silence, when suddenly, Sapphira lifted her bow towards the sky and released an arrow at a vertical angle. A few moments later, a large, black crow, fell to the ground in front of them, making the horses stir and Aldara squeal. Sapphira stepped forward and yanked the arrow from the dead bird. Aldara cupped her hands over her nose and mouth in horror. Stamitos and Leksi were smiling, and the guard just stared in disbelief at the lifeless bird.

'I'm afraid I could not possibly join the hunt,' Sapphira said. 'Women are forbidden from taking part, and it would not be fair to your guests.'

Stamitos laughed, eyes lighting up at her. 'Perhaps you can give them a few pointers beforehand then.'

'We should go before Fedora's spies discover the two of you breaking the rules,' Leksi said, interrupting their flirtation.

Stamitos kept his eyes on Sapphira for a moment. 'Ladies,' he said, bowing his head.

Leksi nodded in their direction, then the men turned their horses and trotted off towards the stables. Both of the girls curtsied and did not rise until the horses were some distance away.

'Well, Fedora will be pleased to hear you have no nerves in the presence of royalty,' Aldara said, eyes going to the bird.

'Why would I be nervous? When I am armed, they should be nervous.' She put down the longbow and retrieved her small crossbow, holding it out to Aldara. 'Come, I'll teach you.'

Aldara hesitated before taking it from her. Kadmus owned a simple crossbow he used for hunting. She had played with it a few times, and had been terrible. She had never put too much effort into learning because if she was not able to use it, then she was not expected to hunt with it.

The afternoon slipped by, and Aldara proved to be an enthusiastic student when her target was a lifeless, painted mound. When she finally put the bow down, her hands were raw and the ring finger on her right hand had a large blister.

'We'll have to get a glove made for you,' Sapphira said.

Aldara laughed. 'Fedora would love that request.'

They reluctantly began their walk back to their quarters with a bored guard shuffling behind them. They passed the empty clotheslines and abandoned washing bats. Aldara glanced again at her hands, enjoying the familiar burn of work. It reminded her of a different life. One with purpose. Her life before him.

∽

LEKSI FOUND Tyron in the stables, loading his horse with supplies. The sun was setting behind him, and soon there would be nothing but shadows.

'Where could you possibly be going at this time of day? And without me?'

Tyron glanced at him. 'I am meeting with Lord Clio at his manor in Veanor.'

'Veanor?' No response. 'Shouldn't Pandarus be taking such meetings?' Leksi glanced at Pero, who had already mounted and was waiting with two guards nearby. 'Why are you running off to Veanor? Is there a sheep crisis I'm not aware of?'

Tyron mounted. 'There is no sheep crisis,' he said, looking at him. 'He has a new supplier from Galen staying with him who I want to meet. I'm bored, and happy to go in place of Pandarus.'

He pushed his horse forward, but Leksi did not move aside, stopping the gelding with his hand instead.

'You are bored with this peaceful time? There is no pleasing you.'

Tyron glanced about. 'It appears that is true.'

Leksi was not buying the story. 'I saw your Companion today at the butts.'

And there it was, a sharp return of Tyron's attention and a flicker in his eyes confirming Leksi's suspicions.

'Ah, I see. This trip has little to do with your Galen supplier.'

Tyron did not want to discuss her. He had seen her earlier from the window, bathed in sunlight, spinning like a carefree child.

'You're as bad as my mother. You miss nothing.'

'To me you try to lie?' Leksi let go of the horse. 'Go on then, take your trip. Run away. Torture yourself some more.' He turned and walked away.

Tyron did not move. 'Leksi.'

Leksi stopped and turned around, taking in his tortured expression.

'What was she doing at the butts?'

Leksi smiled, satisfied. 'She was with Stamitos's new acquisition. They were shooting birds from the sky. It seems you and Stamitos share the same unconventional taste in women.' He paused. 'When you finally work up the courage to invite her to your bed, be sure to sleep with one eye open.'

Tyron watched him leave. He knew Aldara would find any excuse to be outdoors. He wanted to ask more questions, but Leksi was too far away, and he had already revealed enough.

His horse was waiting for instructions while the younger horses shuffled nearby, impatient to get moving. He preferred an older horse for exactly that reason. They were never in a rush.

They understood there was nothing at the end of their journey worth rushing for. All that was ahead of them was fatigue, thirst, hunger, battle, or death.

He left Archdale, his pace slow, dreading the return when he would send her away. But he had let it drag on for long enough, and it was hurting them both. No more excuses. No more indulgent glimpses. He would do it as soon as he got back.

CHAPTER 20

On the morning of the hunt, the cold air took the women by surprise. They reluctantly covered their gowns with thick cloaks. Aldara laid them out on a chair and then stood by the door, watching them disappear, one at a time.

'Can you finish my hair?' Hali asked, giving up.

Aldara's hands were sore from archery practice, making her wince occasionally. Hali threw looks of disapproval at her in the mirror.

'How are you meant to paint your masterpieces if you can barely hold a brush?' Hali asked. Her hair was too thick for many of the new hair pieces that had arrived.

'I'm doing the kingdom a favour and refraining from that particular talent. Your hair has gotten longer. It is fighting with me.'

Hali tried to help her. 'We shouldn't bother. Pandarus will be too drunk to notice. It will be a tangled mess in his hands by evening.'

Aldara had forgotten he had returned from Zoelin. She was about to say so when Fedora appeared behind them.

'I assume you are talking about *Prince* Pandarus,' she said. 'You will do well to remember he is the firstborn son of our king and heir to the throne. That position deserves a title. Don't you agree, Hali?'

Nobody openly disagreed with anything Fedora said.

'Of course, my lady,' Hali replied before walking over to retrieve her cloak.

'Why are you not ready?' Fedora asked, looking at Aldara.

It took Aldara a moment to realise the question was directed at her. 'Because I am not attending, my lady.'

'Of course you are. The princes have requested the company of *all* Companions, which I relayed to you all earlier.'

Aldara's gaze went to the chair where one cloak remained like a corpse. Perhaps she had known after all.

'Forgive me, but *all* does not usually include *me*. My understanding is that Prince Tyron is not at Archdale and will not be attending.' It was also her understanding he wanted nothing further to do with her.

'Prince Tyron will not be attending. However, you will be, as per my clear instructions. The king has important guests from Zoelin in attendance, so get yourself ready.' She glanced down at Aldara's hands. 'And for goodness' sakes, put some gloves on your hands. There will be no more playing with bows.'

After Fedora left, Hali made her way back over to Aldara. They looked at each other; the exchange said they would speak of it later. They dressed in a rush. Hali painted Aldara's face, choosing a vibrant red for her lips. They did a simple plait of her hair and threaded some purple silk through it to match her dress. When Aldara saw her reflection, the only thing she felt was relief at the conservative nature of the gown. The less attention she drew, the better.

Aldara took the final cloak off the chair and put it on. The two girls made their way over to where Sapphira stood, fiddling with a bracelet on her arm. She was being introduced for the first time.

'He will laugh when he sees me,' she complained. 'That is if he recognises me at all. There is so much fabric at my hips I fear my quiver won't make the distance around me.'

Aldara smiled at her. 'As explained to you, several times, Fedora would prefer you spend time with the prince without a weapon in your hands. Let him see who you are without a bow.'

Sapphira wiped at her painted face, and Aldara reached out and stilled her hands.

'I am nothing without a bow. I may as well show up with a leg missing.'

At that moment Astra passed them, a serious expression on her face. 'Do not embarrass us again. Any of you. Let the men be men and try to behave like women.'

As she walked, the tail of her blue velvet dress shushed the ground beneath her. Her fiery hair was smoothed back and tucked. Her nude lips shone. She seemed to be missing a crown.

'I can't make any promises,' Sapphira called after her.

Astra returned a warning glare before exiting.

The hunting party had already gathered by the time the women arrived. Men stood in expensive tunics, trimmed with silver and gold thread, and tall black boots that repelled the dust they stirred. The king's presence made the occasion more formal than usual. He moved about the guests with Idalia by his side, her long hair out and brushed over one shoulder. She spoke the correct words and laughed at an appropriate volume. Her social skills rivalled that of the queen's, and she often liaised with the most important guests. Many of them did not hear a word she spoke—they just watched her. Without question she was the most desired woman in the kingdom. And that was why she belonged to the king.

Stamitos stood before Sapphira with the largest grin Aldara

had ever seen on a man. Aldara averted her eyes to let them have the moment to themselves. He invited Sapphira for a walk through the stables. Aldara wished she could join them and see Loda. It was not appropriate for her to wander off alone. She looked over to where Hali stood with Lord Yuri, gazing at one another and then smiling down at their feet. It seemed the day would be filled by these small moments. Aldara remembered a similar moment, a long time ago.

The dark faces of the Zoelin sat above the cloud of pale skin. Black ink markings licked their necks and spread down one shoulder, an arm, a hand. Zoelin people used permanent ink on their bodies to indicate their level of importance within a village or to their king. The more important the man, the more extensive the ink. First marks were always to the hand, and they grew from there. The marking on the guests told Aldara they were of great importance. She glanced at their thick, exposed arms, which appeared not to feel the cold. The men around them wore tunics to shield the morning air and to display their own level of importance via embroidered symbols that represented the manors they came from.

The sound of applause pulled Aldara's attention. Pandarus was arriving on horseback, unusual for a pre-hunt gathering, but he clearly wanted to show off his new horse. That was his display of importance. She found a smile to disguise her clenched jaw. It was the first time she had seen him since the tournament, and she noticed a slight shake in her hands as she joined in the applause. The attention of the guests breathed life into him. He dismounted and gave a small bow before beginning a charade of greetings to those around him.

It did not take him long to spot Aldara through the small crowd. He stopped talking and gave an exaggerated bow in her direction. She felt her face flush, which is exactly what he would have wanted. She lowered into a curtsy and kept her eyes on the ground as she composed herself. The moment she was upright he moved towards her, eyes fixed as he manoeuvred the crowd. She forced her feet to remain still, fighting her childish instinct to flee.

'So pleased you could join us,' he said, stepping into her personal space.

She did not move away. 'My lord. I was pleased to have received the invitation.'

'I suppose you are wondering why you were invited?'

That was exactly what she was wondering. 'It is not my place to question. I am just honoured to be here.'

She could see his mind working, and she sensed he was building up to something.

'I wanted to introduce our Zoelin guests to our latest tournament winner.' He turned towards the men, gained their attention, and signalled for them to join him. 'You have become something of a spectacle,' he said, turning back to her. 'The first female competitor to enter, and the first to win. Faster than the princes of Syrasan.'

There was mockery in his tone, and his insincerity was not lost on Aldara. She glanced at the ground for a moment, a gesture that destroyed any illusion of confidence. She knew his pride had taken a hammering, but she could not have predicted how long its recovery would be.

When the two men came to a stop next to Aldara, she was forced to adjust her posture to hide her immediate discomfort. They towered over her, a head taller than Pandarus, who already made her feel small. Their eyes roamed her body before coming to rest on her lips. She reminded herself that the Zoelin people had different social etiquette. Had Fedora mentioned leering?

'This is Aldara,' Pandarus said, already enjoying himself. 'Winner of our most recent flag tournament. I am disappointed you could not join us and witness the making of Syrasan history for yourselves.'

The men smiled, but Aldara found their expressions patronising.

'I am not sure I believe him,' one said with a heavy Zoelin accent. 'I am Pollux.' He took hold of Aldara's gloved hand and studied it. The other man just observed her. His hair was shaved behind the ear to allow for the growing ink that was taking over his skull. 'You will have to forgive my friend. He does not speak the Syrasan language,' Pollux explained.

Aldara curtsied and resisted the urge to pull her hand away. 'Pleased to meet you both.'

She spoke in the native Zoelin language to include his companion. Fedora had spent the last two weeks reminding them how important relations between the two kingdoms were. She did not have the luxury of demanding space. She stood with her best impression of warmth. However, the scent of stale drink on Pollux's breath almost knocked her down.

'You have travelled far to join the hunt, my grandors. I hope the boars appreciate your efforts.'

'Your mentor has taught you well,' Pollux replied, referring to her correct use of title. 'There are alternate ways to pass time if the pigs are not willing,' he added, stroking her glove with a finger. 'Why would you cover your hands? In our kingdom a woman's hand speaks for her. How am I to know you when you keep yourself hidden?'

'You can simply ask me, and I will answer you.' Now both of his hands were holding hers. He was bent slightly, and she could see the fur trimming of his vest also lined it, the source of his warmth. She glanced at Pandarus, who was drinking up her discomfort. 'I am afraid my hands will give you the wrong impression of me,' she said, pulling away. 'I have been learning archery of late, and my hands are yet to toughen.'

Pollux laughed at her. 'Are they training you to fight?'

Aldara made a noise that was meant to resemble a laugh. It

was not convincing. Pollux did not seem to notice. Pandarus, on the other hand, missed nothing.

'Perhaps you should use your hands for more suitable activities from now on,' Pollux said, raising a suggestive eyebrow at her.

'Like playing instruments? I am afraid I am not musical,' she replied, pretending not to understand. She turned to Pandarus. 'Shall I introduce our guests to Astra?' she asked, before looking back at the men. 'She is very gifted with the harp.'

It was unkind to lay Astra out as bait, but Aldara knew Pandarus would protect her. He would not let them lay one finger on her. There were some possessions he did not share. She searched for Astra and found her already preparing to play. 'You are in luck. It seems her performance is about to begin,' she said, gesturing towards Astra. 'I will leave you to enjoy the music.' She gave a small curtsy and excused herself before any of the men could object. Her exit was inappropriate, and as she left with three sets of eyes burning into her back, she knew Pandarus was not done with her yet.

Aldara joined a safer social circle made up of Hali, Lord Yuri, and a freshly shaven Lord Thanos. They were discussing his hunting dog, who was sitting obediently by his feet without need for restraint. Hali, who cared little for animals, was feigning interest in the topic.

'And you trained him yourself?' she asked, appearing impressed.

Lord Thanos' shoulders lifted. 'Yes. It seems I have a way with dogs. They respond well to my methods.'

Lord Yuri nodded his head. 'You have a gift.'

'Perhaps you can teach the royal dogs some manners,' said Aldara, joining in.

They all looked over at the excited hounds that were barking and pulling against their restraints.

'It seems there is a large market for well-trained dogs. People need them for all sorts of reasons, from herd protection to sport,' Lord Yuri said.

Hali was watching him as he spoke. 'What a clever business idea.' There was pride in her tone, and the wonder in her eyes was not feigned.

And that is how the conversation continued, with the women listening attentively and speaking when appropriate. They laughed when the men made jokes, but never too loud. They encouraged conversation and made sure everyone was at ease. They did everything they had been taught to do. And when the men left to collect their horses, they moved to another social group, slipping seamlessly into the conversation with a clever comment and a facade of confidence, and the process was repeated.

Aldara was the perfect companion to every guest, right up until the moment they mounted their horses and galloped off. Only when the sound of hooves became a distant rumble did she go silent and let out her stifled yawn. The shivering women collected their cloaks from the servants and wrapped them around their blue skin and impractical dresses. As they came together to begin their walk back up to the castle, they all noticed Sapphira's shoes were covered in dirt.

'You will need to learn to lift your feet higher at outdoor events,' Astra commented, staring at Sapphira's feet in disgust.

Sapphira's did not care about the shoes. She said nothing as Astra slipped past her and walked ahead. Aldara walked over to her.

'Astra is right. It will be the first thing Fedora notices when you return.'

'They are just shoes,' Sapphira replied.

Aldara knew life was easier with Fedora on your side. 'I know. But why make things harder for yourself?'

The women returned to the warm baths that awaited them. Lavender, palmarosa, geranium, and cedarwood had been added to the steamy water to protect the girls from illness after exposure to the cold. While Aldara was waiting for a tub to become available, she noticed Idalia sitting by the stove, clutching a pot as though she may be sick into it. Aldara walked over and pulled a stool up next to her. She brushed the hair back from Idalia's wet face and let her hand rest on her forehead for a moment.

'You're burning up. Does Fedora know you are ill again?'

Idalia lowered the pot and fanned her flushed face with her hand. 'No. Say nothing—please,' she whispered. 'There is no need to worry her.'

Before Aldara could respond, Fedora walked into the bathing room and stood observing the women for a moment. One look at Idalia gave the secret away. In a few steps Fedora was standing next to her.

'Are you unwell?'

Idalia smiled. 'It is the heat in here,' she replied. 'The sudden change in temperature has made me faint.'

Fedora studied her, her expression doubtful. 'The king has requested you this evening.'

Idalia stood up, smiling. 'Wonderful. Let's not disappoint him.'

'I need not remind you what would happen if you knowingly passed on an illness to our king?'

'Absolutely nothing,' Astra said as she passed them. 'They have shared more germs than meals over the years. He forgives all when it comes to our Idalia.'

Fedora turned away from them and faced the other women. 'All of you have been requested for this evening's banquet,' she said loudly.

Aldara's body stiffened. 'Am I to attend also?'

Fedora was silent just long enough to make her regret her question. 'Yes, Aldara. You are a part of everyone. You can assume you are included when I use that term.'

Sarcasm was not tolerated—except by those who made the rules.

'Yes, my lady,' she replied.

'We still have the day to brush up on your Zoelin, so do not linger about in the baths for too long.'

Fedora was addressing everyone but looking at Hali. She turned to Aldara then, noting the worry on her face. She was not obligated to explain her instructions, but she did.

'It is for social purposes only. Ensure our Zoelin guests enjoy themselves. Teach them a Syrasan dance, make them laugh, fill their cups, and then return here to your bed.'

Astra, who was still standing with them, spoke up. 'She understands her role; she is simply pining.'

'Leave her be,' Idalia said, taking Astra by the hand and leading her away.

Fedora's expression softened a little. 'You are still Prince Tyron's Companion until I am instructed otherwise.'

That did not ease Aldara.

That evening, the women began all over again. Painted faces, new dresses, new hair. Aldara worked mechanically and efficiently, beginning with a pale-faced Idalia. She applied colour to her clammy cheeks and washed out lips, saying nothing more about it. Hali and Sapphira moved around the room fetching silk and swapping paints. The room was unusually quiet. Even Astra seemed tense, shaking her head at every dress Aldara suggested. Eventually she stood up and sifted through them with a savage thrust of her hand. Aldara watched her, remembering a time not long ago when she had owned one good dress. It was for church, weddings, and all social occasions not related to chores—like the day she was sold. That dress had been burned, its ashes most probably used to make the lye that cleaned the valuable dresses hanging before them. As she glanced around her excessive rainbow prison, she could not help but think of some of the families in her village who could have used the money from just one dress to feed their family for an entire month. Families just like her family.

Astra finally pulled a pale blue silk dress from its holder and held it at arm's length. 'This will have to do,' she said, giving up. 'Find me jewels in contrasting tones. I do not want to completely bore the prince.'

Aldara helped her into the dress first. 'You could wear a chambermaid's uniform and still draw attention. What are you worried about?'

Astra locked eyes with her for a moment, and Aldara saw it. It was panic.

'I worry about what we all worry about,' Astra replied, looking away.

When all the Companions were dressed and ready, Aldara put on the dark green velvet dress Hali had selected for her. She was grateful for the thick fabric as the sun had failed to warm the air that day and the small fire did little to shift the cold that seeped through the walls. Sapphira attempted to help her with her hair, and then Hali discreetly came and fixed it. Hali aged Aldara by using large amounts of dark paint on her eyes.

'Let the rest of the kingdom enjoy you if he will not,' Hali whispered, rubbing shimmering oil onto Aldara's arms and exposed collar bone.

Aldara sat like dead weight in front of her.

The women had to wait. They passed the time reading by the fireplace. More staring at the words than reading. They looked up each time a messenger arrived with words for Fedora's ears only, errands ran by her spies carrying out her secret business. It was almost dusk when someone sent for them. The women touched up the colour on their lips and followed their escort to the banquet room where they awaited the arrival of the hunting party, noble guests, and royal family.

'What's with the blue wall hangings?' Sapphira asked, looking about the room.

'I feel as though I am under water,' Hali added. 'Did I mention I get seasick?' She was calming herself with slow breathing. Her hands opened and closed, her fingers stretching each time. A taught technique used to calm one's nerves.

'Blue is Zoelin's royal colour,' Aldara whispered. 'It is all for them.'

Sapphira did not lower her voice. 'Seems a bit over the top if you ask me. This is Syrasan, is it not? We should be proudly displaying red.'

'No one cares what we think,' Aldara replied. 'We just smile neutrally.'

'There seems to be a lot of that,' Sapphira said, keeping her eyes on the door.

The hunting party arrived first, spilling into the room, drowning the polite hum of conversation with their loud voices and drunken laughter. Aldara and Hali exchanged a knowing glance before turning their smiling faces towards the guests.

'Perfect,' Aldara said, barely moving her mouth. 'They had an opportunity to drink, but not bathe.'

Hali did not have time to respond. Pandarus entered the room, flanked by Pollux and his silent friend. His gaze swept the room, landing on Hali. She curtsied slowly, her breasts bulging at the top of her dress as she bent.

'Show some class,' Astra said to her as she glided towards him.

Hali maintained her position until Pandarus turned his attention from her to Astra. 'I have to play my strengths,' she said as she returned upright.

'I wish I could say you are wrong,' Aldara whispered.

'Am I the only one who thinks that man is a pig?' Sapphira whispered. No one replied. 'I am going over to sniff Stamitos and make sure that odour is not coming from him,' she said, before walking away.

The men grinned appreciatively at the women dotted about the room. It was amazing what copious amounts of wine did for their confidence. The servants brought out silver trays filled with pigeon, chicken, and hard-boiled eggs covered with saffron. They laid the trays on the buffet around the colourful centrepieces, which were also blue. Lord Yuri was the only man to wash his hands upon entering the room. Afterwards, he stood in Pollux's giant shadow and looked about the room. His eyes stopped on Hali, and his face softened into a smile. Hali's body relaxed at the sight of him. She raised a hand in greeting. Aldara glanced at Pandarus, hoping he would not witness the moment between them. She need not have worried because Queen Eldoris and Princess Cora came through the doors, snatching the attention of the entire room. Men bowed before them, women lowered themselves all the way to the ground. Even Pandarus was forced to put his own importance aside for a few fleeting moments. The other men were happy to watch Cora saunter past, draped in an open-back lavender silk dress. The royal women nodded at the noble guests as they passed by them. As usual, Cora refused to acknowledge the Companions. She kept her eyes ahead. Eldoris gave a small nod in their direction, but she did not let her eyes rest on them for long. Idalia curtsied low as Eldoris passed her, holding the position for some time. As she had explained once, it was her small way of showing respect to the woman she disrespected every day.

'Lord Yuri appears well,' Hali said, once the royal women had taken their seats.

Aldara smirked at the floor. 'Very well.'

'You should go and socialise with the Zoelin guests. They have not taken their eyes off you since they arrived.'

Hali's expression gave nothing away of their conversation. Aldara glanced in the direction of the men who were indeed looking straight at her.

'They are literally twice my height. The conversation is awkward, and my Zoelin is weak.'

Hali turned to her. 'What's wrong? Were they rude to you earlier?'

Aldara shook her head. 'No. The opposite actually. They were…attempting to be charming, I suppose.'

Hali laughed. 'Ah. They were flirting. No wonder you're confused. You are used to Prince Tyron's indifferent glances.'

His name hung in the air for a moment. Aldara tried not to inhale it. She accidently made eye contact with Pollux and he immediately walked towards her. When he stepped up beside her, his body odour made Aldara want to cover her mouth. Hali curtsied and excused herself. Aldara wanted to take hold of her arm and stop her, but she was required to behave like a grown woman.

'You have gotten more beautiful since this morning. How is that possible?' he asked.

Aldara was having difficulty holding her smile. 'One always looks better in a room lit by lamps.'

And so it began.

The evening was slow. At least for Aldara, whose invitation had been for the sole purpose of entertaining the Zoelin guests. She saw that it was part of Pandarus's punishment. She had never seen him so pleased with himself whenever he glanced at her. The more Pollux drank, the more he touched her. The more he touched her, the harder it became for her to laugh and smile. Soon the two men were so intoxicated she had to direct them to their seats. All of her efforts at conversation were lost on them. They were so drunk they exchanged vulgar comments in Zoelin, forgetting she could understand every word.

'I am afraid I am boring you,' she said, thinking through her exit. 'Perhaps I should organise a change in company.'

Pollux stilled for a moment and looked at her. 'There is no need for your words. I am satisfied viewing you. Though once again I find myself wishing you were not so covered up.'

'That is the wine talking,' Aldara replied, careful to keep her tone light.

Pandarus, who had a knack for appearing at inconvenient

times, staggered up next to her, intoxicated and dishevelled. 'No. It definitely sounded like our guest talking.'

Inwardly Aldara jumped at the sound of his voice. Her outer self was perfectly still. She stood up and curtsied before the looming prince. Pollux placed a large, damp hand on her face as she rose. It spanned her cheek and neck. She remained still beneath it, a calm expression on her face. He leant forward, stopping inches from her face without need to stand.

'I am told Pandarus is more generous with his hunting horses than with his women,' he said to her. 'I hope that is not true.'

Aldara swallowed, feeling the hand move against her throat. 'I am afraid you will have to ask one of his Companions about that.' She forced herself to maintain eye contact. Pandarus appeared to be sobering up in her presence, and that made her nervous.

'I have no claim on this one,' Pandarus said, his voice low.

Aldara stared up at him. Pollux's hand fell away as she turned. She knew what was coming next before he spoke the words.

'Aldara, please escort our guests back to their quarters. They are not familiar with the castle, and they are in no state to find their own way.'

She kept staring at him. She did not want to plead, but that is what her expression said to him. Please. Don't. Pandarus just turned away from her, but not before seeing the slight tremble in her hands as they joined together in front of her. She swallowed again and glanced at Pollux. He appeared to grasp the situation well for one so drunk. She tried to take back control of the situation.

'Of course, my lord. Though you shall all have to excuse me for a moment while I speak with Fedora. As you know, she likes to be kept well-informed of the whereabouts of the women.'

She tried to bring volume to her voice—she really tried. Pandarus was having none of it.

'Let me take care of Fedora. Do not keep our guests waiting.'

And just like that, Aldara was a gift for someone else.

The two men followed Aldara to the door. She was unsure how her legs were even moving. She was aware of Hali watching her from the safety of Lord Yuri's side, but she did not raise her eyes to the others, not even when Sapphira took a few steps in her direction before stopping herself. She did not dare look at Idalia, who stood among gentlemen, protected by the bed she shared. Their pity would break her. As she walked down the long corridor that suddenly did not seem long enough, she tried to tell herself she was helping maintain a union between two kingdoms. She reminded herself it was the purpose for which she had been bought. However, as she stood outside of Pollux's chambers, she had to admit to herself she was not stopping a war. And she had been bought for another.

'Well, my lords, I bid you goodnight.'

It was her final attempt to leave them. She had to try.

Pollux took hold of her wrist and pulled her closer. 'Let us make it a better night,' he hissed into her hair. He pulled her through the door, and his voiceless friend followed them, closing it behind them.

Aldara tried to still her mind as they pulled down her dress. She tried to numb her body when she felt their hands clutch at her small breasts. When she was unhelpful, Pollux lost patience. He pushed her face-down onto the bed. She panicked and tried to get up, so he held her shoulders with one hand and did as he pleased. A searing pain shot through her core as he pushed himself inside her. She began to cry, but he seemed oblivious to her discomfort. When he was done, he held her by the hair while his companion took his turn with her. She was shaking, but she was also hopeful it might be over. They each took another turn. Ashamed of her tears, she buried her face in the linen. They saw then, but they did not care.

As the shock wore off, Aldara became aware of the physical pain. Her instincts drove her to resist them. That angered Pollux. He flipped her onto her back and took a fist to her face. She went still again, forced to watch him this time. She was terrified the night would not end, that the sun might not rise. Her face was wet with tears, no not tears, blood from her nose. She used a free hand to try to stop it, but it poured freely. They were angry at the mess and the inconvenience to their moods, so they covered her face with a pillow and continued.

A little before dawn the sobering men fell asleep in a twisted pile of bloodied linen. Pollux's wet head was pressed against Aldara's back as she lay shivering at the edge of the bed, hoping they would not wake. When she was sure they were in a deep sleep, she slipped from the bed and collected her dress. She stepped into it and pulled it up with trembling hands. She did not bother with the buttons, instead securing it with a clenched hand. She stepped over the undergarments and fled the room.

As she stumbled down the corridor, her eyes remained on the ground in front of her. She may have even been running. If she passed anyone, she was unaware. At one stage she thought she could hear whimpering nearby. It was not until she felt Fedora's hands on her shoulders that she realised the sound was coming from her. She looked up into Fedora's blazing eyes. It was too much, so she looked down again. Fedora secured an arm around her shoulders and led her to the bathing room. She waved away the maid and went to fill the tub herself. Aldara sank down onto the floor as soon as there was no one holding her up. Fedora fetched a stool and placed her on it while she added jug after jug of steaming water to the tub.

'Hali came to me,' Fedora said. 'I went to see Prince Pandarus myself, but he would not see me.'

She lifted Aldara to a stand and tried to pry open the hand holding her dress together. Aldara shook her head and tightened her grip. 'No,' she said, her eyes welling up.

Fedora took hold of her shoulders and turned her so she was facing her. 'You are safe. We need to clean you up.'

Aldara closed her eyes and let go of the dress. She let Fedora guide her out of it and help her into the water. Fedora sat down on the stool next to the tub and watched her tremble. The water was tinted red.

'There are strict rules of conduct. I am sorry those rules did not protect you.'

Aldara tried not to listen. She focused her eyes on the clumps of hair floating in front of her. She could almost feel the large hands pulling at the back of her head. Her eyes moved to the purple rings around her wrists that were wrapping her knees. Beyond that she did not look—could not look.

'This should never have happened,' Fedora whispered into the steamy air. She also did not want to see. 'A virtuous Companion is valuable. They are not given to guests as play things. His actions make no sense.'

'It does not matter now,' Aldara said, jumping at the sound of her own voice. 'It is done. My value was decided by Pandarus long before last night.'

The other Companions began to return from their own engagements. They spoke in hushed tones around her. Aldara remained in the tub, protected by its warmth. She did not look up. Somewhere nearby Hali was crying. Not somewhere, next to her. She was bent over the tub crying into Aldara's wet hair.

'I should have just gone after you,' she sobbed.

Aldara said nothing. She did not move.

~

WHEN TYRON ARRIVED at the stables, he could feel the sombre mood of the castle. He was grateful to have missed the hunt, the feast, and the glances from his well-meaning family. They had ridden overnight, enjoying the quiet and absence of people. He could be anybody under the cover of darkness. He almost forgot about the men riding next to him. There was no one to greet him along the way, no reason to stop, no reason to parade their flags.

As he walked up the path towards the castle with a tired Pero trailing behind him, he tried not to let her back in. He thought about food, a wash. Sleep. It was helpful to focus on the simple things. But that is not what awaited him. Instead, he found Leksi standing at his chamber door, with an expression that could only mean bad news. They walked inside without need for pleasantries.

'I was in a great mood until I saw your depressed face,' Tyron said.

He sat in the chair by the window and poured some water. Leksi's expression did not change. Tyron put the cup down and waited. They had known each other their whole lives and had done the bad news dance many times.

'What is it?' Tyron asked.

'I heard something this morning I think you might prefer to hear from me. It involves your Companion.'

Tyron went to stand up, but Leksi raised a hand to keep him seated. He sat, listening carefully as Leksi spoke. The report took only moments to absorb.

The opening of his chamber door sounded like thunder through the entire wing of the castle. The attending guard drew his sword in confusion as Tyron ascended like a moving storm down the corridor, his pace quickening until he reached the Companions' quarters. There was no opportunity for him to be announced. He tore through each room looking for her. The tired women stood, surprised and unsure what to do. Fedora eventually caught him by the arm, and he spun around at her.

'Where is she?' he yelled.

Fedora spoke slowly to encourage calm. 'She is in the bathing room. Perhaps we should talk in private for a moment.'

He brought a finger to her face. 'You are meant to take care of these girls. That is your purpose here. What were you thinking handing her over to them?'

She said nothing. His anger was misdirected, and they both knew it. His hand dropped to his side.

'Take me to her,' he said, growing quiet.

Fedora hesitated. 'I assure you I am caring for her, my lord. She needs time to recover from a very difficult evening.'

'Take me to her,' he repeated, in the same tone.

Fedora nodded and walked ahead of him to the bathing room. She instructed Hali to leave. He lingered by the door, waiting for the room to be cleared. He was not at all comforted by the sight of Hali's tear-stained face as she rushed past him without a greeting. The room was lit by only a few candles. The air was damp, and the steam made it difficult for him to see. His eyes moved from tub to tub until he saw her. She seemed so small. Like a drowned pup. Her eyes were open, but focused on the water in front of her as she sat shivering. He could already see bruising appearing on her face as he walked over and crouched down next to the tub.

'Aldara,' he whispered.

His chest tightened. Her vulnerability at that moment was constricting it. She turned her head and looked at him. There was a moment of panic in her eyes, and a few tears fell down her swollen cheeks, turning black from the paint. He took the wet towel hanging over the edge of the tub and moved to wipe her face. She shied away from his hand, so he withdrew it. Fedora brought him a bowl of warm water.

'I will be back to check on her shortly,' she whispered.

Tyron stared at Aldara, his eyes moving to the crusted blood around her nose. He looked at the filthy water she sat in and then away. She tucked her knees under her chin and stared back at the water.

'I am so sorry,' she said suddenly. She would have cried harder, but her face hurt too much.

He shook his head to block the words. There was no way he would listen to her apologise. He dipped the towel into the warm water and then reached for her face again. She did not pull away this time.

'I am sorry,' he said. 'I left you defenceless. I left.'

He carefully wiped at her face until it was free of blood and paint. Fedora returned with a robe, holding it open while Tyron gently lifted her from the water. He averted his eyes as Aldara covered what she could of her body with her hands. They wrapped her up, and then Fedora fetched a second robe to put over the top of it in hope it would stop her shivering. He did not know what to do next. He took a few steps back from her. Fedora noticed his unease.

'Aldara needs rest, my lord. I will ensure she is taken care of and update you on her recovery.'

He stepped forward again and lifted Aldara into his arms. Her head collapsed against his chest. Fedora led him to the bedroom and gestured towards her bed. He laid her down on it, and when he could no longer bear the eyes of the other women on him, he left. There was nothing else he could do and was unsure if anything would help. As he walked away, he realised he needed somewhere to walk to, a purpose for the long day ahead. His pace quickened as he moved towards Pandarus's quarters. On arrival he found only Pandarus's squire, who was very nervous at the sight of him.

'Where is he?'

The squire held his hand like a shield in front of him. 'With the king in his chambers, my lord.'

'Hiding you mean.'

Tyron marched back down the corridor and burst into the king's chambers unannounced. He drew his sword and within a few paces he was standing in front of Pandarus with it flush against his neck. The surprise was frozen on Pandarus's face. He did not move a muscle.

'Have you lost your mind?' roared King Zenas. 'Put that sword away before I have the guards lock you up.'

Tyron's sword remained where it was. Pandarus relaxed his face a little; however, small beads of sweat were forming on his forehead. Tyron spoke first.

'Have you told our father about the gift you gave to our Zoelin guests last night?'

Zenas looked at Pandarus confused. 'What gift? What in heaven's name is he talking about?'

Pandarus swallowed against the sword.

'Well?' repeated the king.

Tyron spoke for him. 'He handed over my Companion to those men to be raped and beaten. She is barely recognisable.'

Zenas fell quiet, disappointment on his face. 'Put away your sword,' he said, sitting down. 'So this is about a woman.' He shook his head. 'These women are meant to provide you with company, let you blow off steam, not start family wars.' His tone was flat.

Tyron withdrew his sword but kept his eyes on his brother. Pandarus relaxed, but he did not look away.

'Are you suggesting I played a part in this? I requested the girl entertain our guests. She was not instructed to have sexual relations with them.'

'By the appearance of her she was not given much choice.'

'You have shown little interest in the girl, so I am surprised by your sudden concern. If it helps at all, I heard she was a great disappointment.'

'Enough,' said Zenas. 'The women are under Fedora's instruction when it comes to guests. Why were the Noble Companions not called upon to entertain?'

Pandarus shrugged. 'I thought offering something more virtuous was a smarter approach. We are trying to build relations between our kingdoms after all.'

Tyron stared at his father in disbelief. 'Are you hearing this? It sounds as though we are running a brothel.'

King Zenas closed his eyes and shook his head again. 'Can we continue with more important matters please?'

Tyron turned back to Pandarus. 'If any more harm comes to her at your hand, I will cut your throat.'

'Enough,' his father shouted.

Tyron put his sword away, bowed to the king, and left the room.

CHAPTER 21

During the warm season, the women could take their lessons outdoors. They would sit on blankets in the shade of the large cherry trees, books open on their laps, speaking of other things. Sometimes they would have their meals brought out to them and spend the afternoon eating apples and berries while exchanging stories about particular lords who took their fancy and those they tried to avoid. These conversations always took place in hushed voices out of earshot of Fedora's excellent hearing.

When Aldara's face had healed enough that it could be concealed with paint, she was permitted to leave her quarters for lessons only. She sat under the trees among the women and tried to block out their voices. Fedora left her alone for the most part as she paced around them, directing her questions at whoever was paying the least attention. Occasionally her eyes would drift over to Aldara. The events of that night had disempowered her since she had been unable to do anything to stop it. While Aldara had almost made a full physical recovery, inwardly she suffered. Nights were the hardest, lying in the dark replaying scenes in her mind, sweating beneath the blankets she refused to remove. She needed the weight of them.

One positive to come out of that night was that Aldara was not only allowed to once again accompany Sapphira to the butts, but she was also permitted to learn how to shoot. When Fedora noticed her reddened hands, she organised for a glove to be made. Aldara's eyes welled up when she handed it over, but no words were exchanged.

Each day Aldara threw herself into archery as though her personal safety depended on it. Her progress both surprised and impressed Sapphira.

'I hate what happened to you, but I like this new version of you,' Sapphira said one day.

Aldara looked at her, puzzled. 'What do you mean?'

'Feisty. I suspect you carry a blade under your dress also.'

Aldara looked down the arrow and released it. 'I don't, but that is an excellent suggestion,' she said, smiling. Time had brought more and more of such moments.

Occasionally Prince Stamitos and his guests would join them for a friendly competition. It was a way for Aldara to socialise again. The men who attended were young, good-humoured, and kind. Aldara felt comforted by their sobriety. And the fact that she was holding a loaded bow.

Stamitos reminded her of Kadmus. His mischievous nature and sense of humour brought her the closest she had come to laughter in many weeks. She enjoyed watching Sapphira with him; their playful banter entertained the entire group. She had witnessed a similar sense of humour in Tyron, though she suspected only those closest to him experienced it. She had not seen him since that morning, but she knew Fedora reported to him daily. Pero came for updates each morning, and Aldara would listen from the other side of the wall as he asked all the questions Tyron would have asked himself if he had visited her. 'Is she sleeping and eating? Does she need anything?'

Yes, for the shame to stop.

Fedora would answer as positively as she could. 'She rests often. Food is brought to her regularly. She has rejoined lessons.' What Fedora would not say was that rest did not lead to sleep. Food was left mostly untouched. And Aldara's mind was elsewhere during lessons. Pero would then take all of Fedora's answers back to Tyron. For him to do what with, she had no idea.

One warm afternoon at the butts, Aldara was lying on her back in the grass, covering the sun with her hand and then opening her fingers to let it spill through. She was in a good mood, as she had slept the entire night, waking to sunlight and chatter instead of darkness she could not breathe through. Sapphira and Stamitos were laughing together nearby. The Companion Fedora had created was put aside during real moments like those. They were loud and unrefined, both forgetting that he was a prince. But they were happy. It was hard to imagine four children from one king could be so different.

'Are you actually going to take your turn?' Sapphira asked, waving the longbow above her.

Aldara lowered her hand and looked at her friend, whose face was flushed from laughter. She stood, brushing the grass from her lime-green cotton dress. She took the bow from her and wandered over to be in line with the target. An energy surged through her as she took aim, driving the arrow. It hit just above the bulls-eye. She lowered the bow, disappointed.

'Ah, you've been getting more tips from Sapphira I see,' said a smirking Stamitos. 'An easy win for the lads today then.'

Aldara reloaded her bow. 'Yes, it must be very satisfying for trained soldiers to beat a couple of self-taught girls,' she teased.

Stamitos laughed. 'Do not lose focus now.'

She took aim, this time hitting above her other arrow.

'Is it possible I am getting worse?' she asked Sapphira.

'You need to lift your elbow a little. It's dropping before your release,' came a voice behind her. She recognised it immediately. When she turned to look at him, he appeared as he always did—handsome. And tired. He sat on his tall horse studying the target. She turned back to it also, reloaded her bow, lifted her elbow a little, and released. It missed again, and Stamitos and his guests laughed at her.

She turned back to Tyron and gave a small curtsy. 'I am afraid I will not be of much use if the castle is attacked, my lord.'

They looked at each other for a moment.

∽

THAT BRUTAL MORNING was still there between them, but Tyron was enjoying the sight of her healed and lit up in the sunshine. She wore a short-sleeved dress, and her arms were free of jewels. Her hair was out, and her feet were bare. Her shoes sat in the grass some distance away.

'That's not true,' he replied. 'Just aim for your attacker's leg and you will pierce him straight through his heart.'

She laughed, and his entire body warmed at the sound. The bow swung in her hand as she walked towards him. His horse immediately lowered his head to her. She stroked his face and whispered into his soft muzzle.

'You have never told me his name,' she said, looking up at him.

The others had grown bored of their conversation and returned to their archery.

'We only give names to pets.'

She looked up at him, sceptical. 'I suspect you are playing down the relationship.'

It would not be the first time.

'His name is Otus.'

Aldara smiled, satisfied. 'Hello, Otus,' she whispered. 'What does it mean?'

'Keen of hearing,' he said, continuing to watch her. He could waste hours watching her. 'Want to ride him?'

She looked up, face lit like a child. 'Let me just lose the bow.'

'Keep it,' he replied. 'I'll teach you how to use it.'

He held out his hand to her, and she took hold of it and pulled herself up behind him.

'Ah,' she said. 'I have discovered your secret to winning battles. You have a very unfair height advantage.'

They rode to the stables where Tyron had Loda saddled and sent a messenger instructing Pero to bring his bow and quiver. He filled water skins for them both and then took Aldara into the woods to teach her how to shoot while riding. He wished she was back behind his saddle, and then felt guilty for the intimate thought.

They walked under the cover of large trees, him pointing to various targets, her taking aim. She missed most of them, and they spent much of the afternoon trying to retrieve the arrows.

'Perhaps I'll be better if I am riding faster,' she suggested, remounting.

'No, you won't.'

She pointed to a tree and kicked Loda into a slow canter. Releasing the reins, she lifted her bow, pulled back and released the arrow. She missed the tree by a great distance. Tyron said nothing as he suppressed a grin. She turned to him and was about to defend her miss, when a startled bird took flight from a nearby blackberry bush, causing Loda to leap sideways. Holding the bow threw Aldara's balance, and she slipped from the saddle and landed with a thud on the damp ground. Loda did her the favour of only trotting a short distance away before turning to watch her.

Tyron dismounted and ran to her. 'Are you hurt?' he asked when he reached her, eyes searching her body for visible injury.

She exhaled, remaining on her back. 'No. Just humiliated.'

He pulled her up by the arm into a sitting position and sat down next to her. Her hair was full of leaves, and he watched as she began the tedious task of removing them.

'Do you ever stay clean?'

'Only for short periods.'

He wanted to kiss her at that moment. He remembered well how it had felt to be pressed against her—the heat of her mouth. But then he remembered her sitting in a tub of blood-tinged water. Her swollen wrists, imprinted with large fingers. He looked away, and she noticed.

'I have dragged that night around with me every day since it happened. It is exhausting. At some point I would like to put it down. I cannot do it if I am reminded of it whenever I look at someone. I want to see the desire, not the pity.'

He looked at her again. 'I'm sorry. I feel responsible. It's guilt you see when you look at me.'

She shook her head. 'Their actions are theirs alone. Their lack of manners…'

'Lack of manners? You are being very kind.'

Aldara took a moment to think through what she wanted to say. 'I have spent a lot of time feeling angry and afraid. It's not sustainable. You warned me I was making a dangerous enemy in Pandarus, that there would be a cost.'

Tyron leant back on his hands and looked at her. 'His actions surprised me. I wonder if he knew what he was doing when he handed you over.'

She suspected Pandarus knew exactly what he was doing, but the conversation was pointless now. She brought a dirty hand to Tyron's face, and he leant into it a little.

'I am a Companion, and we both know what that entails.'

He pulled back from her hand. 'I was going to send you home when I returned. I had decided long ago it was the best thing to do.'

She rested her head on her knees. 'Why did you wait?'

'I believe you know why,' he said, falling silent for a moment. 'I know it's been difficult and confusing for you here. I wish I had acted before those men took so much from you. What future do you see for yourself if you were to return to your family?'

Aldara folded her legs and placed her hands in her lap. 'We both know there is no going back there now. The entire village knows where I am and what it means to be here.' She paused for a moment. 'I would like to stay here as your Companion. Of course, I would like to know what you want.'

He stared at her as he thought. 'How am I to know if you speak the truth? I will not settle for Fedora's version of you. Do you really want to be here?'

She reached up and touched his face again. 'I did not want to come here. I did not want to be your Companion. That was my truth, right up until the moment I met you. Something changed that day. I know where this leads and I know where it cannot. Leaving here today will not erase what has happened. Or you.'

The tenderness in her voice made him swallow. She tipped her head forward and rested it against his shoulder. A few leaves drifted from the sky and fell into his lap. All of his apprehension was melting away in the afternoon sun that filtered through the trees.

Loda, becoming bored, walked off in search for grass. They reluctantly stood and retrieved their horses before making their way back to Archdale.

When they arrived at the stables, Aldara unsaddled Loda while the groom looked on in discomfort, and they walked her back to her stall together. They stood leaning against the timber door, watching her drink and checking her food container for grain.

'Send for me tonight,' Aldara said, without taking her eyes off Loda.

He nodded.

She turned to him to make sure he understood. 'Send for me,' she repeated.

He nodded again. 'I will send for you.'

And he did.

CHAPTER 22

When Aldara woke in the morning, she was aware of his warm body behind her. She did not move because she did not want him to move. Perhaps she would never move. His sleepy breaths in her hair made her smile. Not quite a snore. She studied the arm that wrapped her, noticing each small scar. She counted a few freckles on his hand and then remembered that hand on her just hours earlier. And she remembered both of his hands with clarity.

She had been nervous on the walk to his quarters. The only experience she had was as an unwilling partner. They had told her she was a disappointment. They had told her lots of things. She had been a mess of nerves when he opened his door to her, studying her in an attempt to read her thoughts. When Pero had left them, she had thought she might be sick. He had touched her hair so gently she thought perhaps he had not touched her at all. He had leant in then, mouth to her, complimenting her on her *clean state*. She had laughed then—could not control it. He had kissed her neck while her head was tipped back, and then whispered words of reassurance into her mouth. She had been the one to finally slide her dress down her shoulders. If she had left it to him, it might never have happened. The rest had been easy, surprising, intense. She had not wanted it to end. But it did—several times. A familiar flush crept over her skin as she remembered.

'Tell me you have slept,' Tyron said, causing her to jump. 'Sorry, I didn't mean to scare you.'

His arm drew her closer if that was possible. She turned to face him and his hands pressed against her back. She savoured the warmth of them.

'Should I go?' she asked.

'No,' he said, kissing her head.

'The other Companions usually return before the morning meal.'

'The other Companions are not mine. Stay.'

The morning turned into afternoon, and no one emerged from his quarters. When the sun began to sink, Aldara said, 'Fedora will be wondering where I am.'

They were lying face to face, their eyes closed as they fought sleep.

'No she won't,' he replied, his hand resting on her hip. 'If that woman wants to know something, she finds out.'

'She'll be cross with me for disappearing.'

'She will be thrilled when her spies report where you are.'

They slept, and when they woke, it was dark and Pero was knocking on the door. He looked embarrassed when he entered, apologising profusely. Queen Eldoris was looking for Tyron. He sent Pero off with a vague excuse for his absence and told him to return with some food. They ate in bed, wrapped in linen.

'Perhaps it is important,' Aldara said.

He was rolling a grape across her stomach. 'More important than this?' he asked, releasing the grape a final time and opening his mouth to catch it.

Before it reached him, she snatched it up, threw it high into the air and caught it in her own mouth.

'It's the flag tournament all over again. Must you always win?' he asked, trying to sound serious.

She laughed, and he wanted her again. She was not sure where he found the energy. Perhaps he siphoned it from her.

Afterwards, they fell asleep, limbs entwined. They slept properly this time, not stirring until the sun glowed in the sky. She woke first and pried herself free from him. By the time he was awake, she had finished dressing.

'Don't go,' he said sleepily.

'You are mad,' she said. 'You have an entire kingdom waiting for you.'

He propped himself up on one elbow and watched as she fixed her hair. She glanced at the sheet that covered him to his hip, tempted to return to bed. She turned away instead.

'I'll send for you later. We can go riding.'

She was smiling when she turned back to him. 'Good day, my lord.' She gave a small curtsy and left his chambers with her chest bursting.

∽

TYRON GOT OUT OF BED, washed, and went in search of his mother, who according to his squire, had grown impatient with his absence and fed up with his excuses. He found her seated in the solar with Cora, reading. He would have normally turned around and left upon seeing his sister, but he had already been announced. The two women studied him.

'Where on earth have you been?' Eldoris asked. 'I had people out searching for you yesterday.'

He walked in and sat in the spare chair near them. 'Am I the only member of this family who does not have spies running about the castle?'

Cora looked back at her book. 'Well, they cannot have been

very clever, Mother. He spent the entire day in his chambers with *her*.'

Ah. Just what he was trying to avoid. He looked at Cora. 'I see nothing escapes *your* spies, sister. Should I be checking under my bed for little people hiding there?'

She closed her book and smiled at him. 'Wouldn't they have gotten a show? Tell me, brother, did her goat milking experience come in handy?'

Eldoris's book snapped shut. 'Really, Cora, you would have to be the most vulgar princess this kingdom has ever lived through. I did not raise you to speak that way. Continue your reading elsewhere.'

Cora stood gracefully and walked past them, head high. Eldoris waited for the door to shut before she spoke.

'Please tell me I worry for nothing.'

'My queen, my mother, you worry for nothing.'

She placed the book next to her and folded her hands in her lap. 'You are happy. It appears there is cause for concern.'

Tyron laughed, which was very out of character. 'My happiness should surely be cause for celebration, not concern.'

Eldoris did not smile. 'It is the source from which this happiness stems that worries me. It is not long-term happiness that feeds your soul, my son. This union will come to a destructive end for both of you.'

Tyron stood up. He did not want his good mood ruined. 'I am meeting with Father now. Am I to expect a similar speech from him?'

Worry tugged at her face. 'No, my love. I believe there is news regarding Corneo. Judging by the urgency of the message delivered, my guess is it is not good news.'

∼

TYRON SAT in his father's chambers alongside Pandarus. There were reports of attacks in the North of Syrasan. Two women and four young girls had been taken from a small village on the Lotheng River. Two male family members had died trying to stop them. No one knew who the riders were as they had been unmarked, storming through the village under the cover of night. No flag, no claim.

'I do not believe they were Corneon,' Tyron said.

'Of course they were Corneon,' Pandarus snapped. 'This is exactly the type of cowardly behaviour we expect from them.'

Tyron was not convinced. 'What on earth would they want with a few women and children?'

'What do you think? They did not take the old women.'

Tyron shook his head. 'The Corneon people are not rapists. They have morals.'

'Corneo doesn't have rapists?'

It was clear Pandarus would disagree with whatever Tyron said. The king, who had been silent until that point, spoke up.

'Right now it is an isolated incident. The act of a few desperate men.'

Tyron was surprised by the comment. 'They came from somewhere. Given the location and the nature of the offence, I would say they are likely to be Zoelin.'

Pandarus made an exasperated gesture. 'Yes, let's label our new allies as criminal rapists because two of them spent one night with your Companion.'

'Enough,' Zenas said. 'Get more information. For all we know they are Syrasan men. We will act when we have something to act upon. At the moment we have only suspicion.'

Tyron raised his eyebrows. 'Really? Who are you suspicious of? Because I am at a complete loss as to where we are pointing the finger.'

Zenas and Pandarus exchanged a look that was not lost on Tyron.

'We need to gather the facts,' Zenas said. 'Pandarus is scheduled to travel to Zoelin in two days to meet with King Jayr regarding trade. He can discuss the matter with them then.'

'That's an awfully diplomatic approach. What do you expect King Jayr to say, "Oh, sorry, that was us"?'

Pandarus stood up. He had heard enough. 'Stop whining, I'll take care of it.'

He left without bowing. Tyron looked at his father, who would not meet his eyes. 'Shall I travel to the Lotheng and gather more information?'

Zenas kept his eyes on the table in front of him. 'Yes. Travel with Pandarus in two days' time. See him over the border and then look for likely breaches. I want to know where the men came from.'

CHAPTER 23

Tyron kept his word to Aldara and requested her company for a leisure ride that afternoon. They refused an escort and headed for quiet outside of the castle walls. Tyron's mind was on the attack. He was also suspicious of the unspoken exchange between Pandarus and his father. There was more to the story, but he could not fathom what it might be. Aldara could see his mind was elsewhere.

'Did everything go all right at your meetings earlier?'

He looked across at her, realising what bad company he must seem. She was wearing a peach coloured long-sleeved dress that matched the shade of her cheeks. Her hair was in a tight braid that seemed as though it was causing her discomfort. Her question hung there unanswered.

'Sorry, what did you ask me?'

'My lord, if there is something you need to do or if you would prefer to have a quiet afternoon, I understand. Please don't feel as though you need to keep *me* entertained.'

'Don't,' he said, shaking his head. His tone was more abrupt than he had intended. 'Don't address me formally in private. It isn't necessary.'

His tone only confirmed her suspicion. 'I hope you know nothing you say to me will go any further. I'm not required to relay personal conversations to Fedora. She believes this builds trust. Perhaps I can help you by listening.'

'What sort of confession are you hoping to get out of me?'

'I have heard rumours of some very bad behaviour over the last few days.'

There was something about her sitting in that impractical dress on that temperamental mare that made his pulse quicken. Or perhaps it was her old boots, which peaked out from the bottom of her dress, boots that most certainly would not have been approved by Fedora. Maybe it was the way the dress spilled down Loda's rump, inviting his hands to roam beneath it.

Aldara followed his gaze down to her boots. 'Ah,' she said. 'The only thing I saved from the fireplace. Far too comfortable to give up. I guess Hali was right, the dress was not long enough after all.' She shrugged and smiled at him.

'What else have you got hidden under that dress?' he asked her.

'A crossbow,' she replied. 'You are in good hands.'

Neither of them spoke for a moment. They just watched each other. Their horses eased together as though they were being tethered that way. As soon as Aldara was within reach, Tyron pulled her from her saddle in one swift motion, so she was seated in front of him with her legs draped to one side. He kissed her then, and the heat of it surprised them both. It did not take long for his hands to find their way inside her dress. He pulled one of her legs around so she wrapped him. The urgency of the situation became too much. There was barely time for them to get off the horse let alone off the open track they had been following.

Two confused horses stood by in the tall grass.

'Well, that was unplanned,' Aldara said, as she lay on her back next to him.

The skirt of her dress was bunched at her hips, and her tight braid had come undone. Tyron was observing her as she watched the horses graze.

'Speak for yourself. I had the entire thing planned out.'

She looked at him and smiled. 'Next time you should plan for a place where the grass is not so coarse.'

He reached over and ran a finger across her lip. 'And I didn't find the crossbow.'

She pressed her lips together. 'Perhaps you should search me again.'

His expression turned serious then. 'I think there might be another fight soon.'

The humour left her face. 'Corneo?'

'We're not sure.'

She rolled onto her side to be closer to him. 'There is going to be a war but you are not sure who with?'

'Someone is already here,' he said, turning away. 'We just don't know who it is.'

They were silent for a moment

'Where are they?'

'In the North, for now. They took women and children. Two men were killed trying to stop them. And no one knows why.'

'What on earth do they want with children?'

He shook his head. 'I wish I knew. I leave in two days to get some answers.'

He turned and watched her chest rise and fall for a moment. Then he reached out and placed a hand on it. 'The only thing more difficult than fighting is waiting for it to begin. Sitting about, anticipating the loss. Wondering which friends will return with you, which ones will get a burial, and which ones will be buried only by the snow that falls on them.'

Aldara understood grief, and she knew it extinguished everything around it, even the myth of glory that came from winning a war. She thought how odd it must be to return home a hero and be confronted with celebration while grieving. Her hand went over his.

'How ludicrous you must find the feasting as you count the empty chairs before you. There really is no win for you,' she said, speaking his thoughts aloud.

That evening, Tyron sent for her. She had barely had time to wash after their ride together when Pero appeared with a message for Fedora.

Hali helped her dress, pinned her hair, and painted her lips. She then offered to escort Aldara to his chambers, which meant she wanted to talk privately. As soon as they were out in the corridor and out of Fedora's hearing range, Aldara turned to her.

'What is it?'

'Pandarus departs tomorrow for Zoelin,' Hali said.

One look at Hali's face told her things were not going well between them. 'Has he requested you for the evening?'

'No.'

Aldara stopped walking to buy them more time. 'Well he has not acquired a new Companion, so that is positive.'

'Probably because he is embarrassed by how quickly he churns through them. He rarely sends for *one* anymore,' Hali said, eyes going to the floor. 'He prefers a more *social* evening. He likes to rekindle with some of his former flames. Except Astra of course; she is far too pure for such things, apparently.' She looked up then and shook her head. 'I am nothing to him, you know. Just another warm body in his bed.'

Aldara touched her arm. 'You are something to those who truly know you. You are most certainly something to Lord Yuri.'

Colour flushed Hali's face. 'Well, nothing can come of that.'

'If you were to become a Noble Companion—'

'If I were to become a Noble Companion I may as well be a prostitute. I will be with whatever men they want me to be with. Do you think Lord Yuri will want a used-up whore who has slept with most of his acquaintances?'

'He understands your situation.'

Hali shook her head. 'We are so far past fairy tales now. And I am terrified.'

Aldara wrapped her arms around Hali and pressed her lips into her hair. 'We're all afraid. But you have my love and friendship forever.'

A few tears ran down Hali's face, and she brushed them away. 'For as long as they let us.'

A guard passed them then, so they continued walking.

When Aldara arrived at Tyron's chambers she went straight to him. Into his hands, his mouth. All of Hali's work undone within moments. Hair unpinned, lips kissed clean, and a freshly pressed dress lay crumpled on the floor. They lay in the dark, protected by it. Time may have even stopped momentarily.

'Can I ask you something?' Aldara inquired.

'Anything.'

She had broken so many rules she had almost forgotten they were not permitted to speak about the other Companions unless asked directly.

'Will Pandarus send Hali away? Sell her?'

Tyron thought for a moment. 'I don't know. We don't speak about those things.'

'The novelty has worn off.'

'The novelty always wears off.'

She suspected that was a general statement not specific to Hali. She could not imagine a time when the novelty of him would pass. But what did she know about those things?

'Will you tell me when the novelty of me wears off? So I don't have to guess on the subject?'

He did not speak. Only even, sleepy breaths came from his mouth. She closed her eyes and tried to follow him.

A gentle glow filled the room when she woke. Tyron's arm was heavy and familiar around her. She could tell by his breathing he was awake.

'I will not sneak away,' she said, kissing the top of his chest where her face was pressed. 'I will remain here until you tell me to go. That's how it works.'

His eyes were closed, but he responded to her with his hands and then his lips. 'You left yesterday.'

'Yes, after two days. Be reasonable,' she laughed.

He shifted so he could her better. 'What will you do if I have to leave to fight another war?'

She looked up at him. His eyes were open, staring at the wall. 'I will be here praying to that God of yours, waiting for you. All you have to do is stay alive and return when it is done.'

His eyes went to her then. 'Is that all?'

She smiled at him. 'And there are a few things you need to do before you leave,' she said, tilting her hips forward.

The conversation was over.

The next time Aldara woke, blinding light poured through the window. Tyron sat at the table, washed, dressed, and watching her.

'I didn't have the heart to wake you.'

She sat up, holding the sheet around her. 'What time is it? Why are you dressed?'

He eyes swept over her. 'It's noon. I'm dressed to take you riding once you have eaten.'

She wrapped her arms around her knees and looked at him. He was about to spend days in the saddle. Taking her riding was probably the last thing he wanted to do. The gesture warmed her though.

'Isn't there something else you would rather do with your remaining time?'

His eyes went to her naked back. 'Yes, but I thought we could do both.'

Her eyes shone at him. She had never experienced that kind of energy with someone before. She was not in control of herself, and it was terrifying.

An hour later they were riding side by side through the forest. It was alive with chatty birds, nervous hares, and long-tailed green lizards lazing in the sun.

'Why do some of the lizards have more purple on their throats do you suppose?'

Tyron watched them scamper away from the horses. 'The more colourful ones are male.'

Aldara narrowed her eyes on him. 'And how do you know that?'

'We had excellent teachers. I thought Fedora was supposed to be educating you. Do I need to have a word to her? I would expect you to know about lizards,' he teased.

'She will teach us all about lizards the moment a nobleman admits to finding the topic interesting.'

Tyron pointed ahead of them. 'Here it is.'

She followed his hand and saw an opening in the trees. Through the gap, she could see sweeping grasses littered with vibrant, purple echinacea. It was a haven of light in the densest part of the forest.

'What is this place?' she asked, stopping Loda at the edge of the grass.

'A childhood discovery. We used to play here a lot,' he said, dismounting.

He tied the reigns around Otus's neck and tapped his rump so he would wander off to feed.

Aldara slipped off Loda and did the same. 'Don't you run off,' she whispered to the mare before reluctantly letting go of the bridle. The mare trotted after Otus, and the two horses grazed together. When Aldara turned back to Tyron he produced a blanket from behind his back.

'See, everybody wins today.'

She laughed as she took his hand and pulled him into the sunlight. It was a glorious feeling amid darkness to be showered by the sun's warmth. The dense trees did not even permit a breeze. Aldara let go of Tyron's hand and looked at him.

'Do you want to race me to the middle?'

He frowned down at her, a smile tugging at his lips. 'Race you? To see who is fastest?'

'Yes. That's the purpose of a race,' she said, lifting the skirt of her dress and knotting it around her hips. 'I can carry the blanket if you are worried about being disadvantaged.'

He glanced down at her bare legs and shook his head. 'All right. Go.'

Aldara squealed and took off after him. His height advantage meant his legs covered more distance with each stride, but her own legs were fast. She tried to close the distance between them, but it was no good.

'Watch out for grass snakes,' he called back to her.

She laughed. 'You're in front. They will bite you first.'

He grinned and stopped running, marking his triumphant win by throwing the blanket down in the centre of the meadow. She stopped next to him, out of breath from exertion and laughter.

'You are faster than Kadmus,' she said, collapsing on top of the grass.

He sat down next to and pulled her on top of him. He moved her legs so that they tightened around him. They were panting.

'You appear to be hot. Take off your dress,' he said.

Her face was inches from his.

'What about the blanket?'

He kissed her collarbone while his hands roamed beneath her dress. 'I'll be your blanket.'

∼

AT SOME POINT in the afternoon they retrieved the blanket. And at some point in the afternoon they both feel asleep wrapped only in the blanket and sweaty limbs.

The sound of something in the grass nearby woke Aldara. When she opened her eyes, still groggy from sleep, she saw Tyron looking at her, a finger across his lips instructing her to remain silent. She recognised the sound of footsteps slashing through the long grass. They were moving towards them. She lay still, watching Tyron mentally calculate the distance. When they were a few yards away, he reached across her and took hold of his sword. Just as the footsteps landed near them, he pulled the sword from its sheath, swinging it low across Aldara's body. He pushed himself up with his free hand and turned so his torso remained a shield for her. His sword came to a stop at the throat of a terrified Pero, who stood palms out, looking at Tyron.

Tyron lowered the sword and moved off Aldara. 'Are you all right?' he asked her.

She sat up, holding the blanket around her while her heart pounded away in her chest. 'Yes,' she said, swallowing down her fear.

He turned back to Pero. 'Are you trying to get yourself killed? What on earth are you doing here?'

'I am sorry, my lord. The king needs to see you at once. This was the only place I could think of to search for you.'

Tyron put his sword away. 'Fetch the horses.'

'Yes, my lord,' Pero said, before leaving them.

Aldara reached for her clothes and dressed as quickly as she could. 'He could have called out,' she whispered.

Tyron smiled at her. 'Squires do not call their masters.'

'Another rule I suppose.'

He finished doing his belt up and leaned over to kiss her head. 'Yes, another rule. Some people follow them you know?'

'I prefer to keep you guessing.'

He shook his head and raised his eyebrows. 'I know.' He

slipped his tunic on and sat down next to her again. 'I will send for you tonight.'

She kissed his mouth and then pressed her face into his neck. 'And I will do as I am told.'

CHAPTER 24

Their informer stood with his body slumped. His arms were as lifeless as his eyes. He was waiting for their response. They all stood around him, silent and thinking. King Zenas was holding the back of his chair, staring across the empty table in front of him. Tyron began to pace, trying to process what he had just been told. Zenas lifted his chair a short distance off the ground and slammed it back down.

'How many dead?' he asked the informer.

The man straightened a little, but the effort was too much and his shoulders fell forward once again. 'Fourteen men, Your Majesty. There are eight women and girls unaccounted for. My daughter one of them. She is only thirteen.' He stopped speaking for a moment. 'They left the older ones.'

Zenas tightened his hold on the chair. He turned his head sideways to look at the man, wanting more, but there was no more. 'And no one has seen them since?' he yelled. He was looking at his sons, wanting a different answer. 'Armed men slaughter fourteen Syrasan men and ride off with eight women, some of them children, never to be seen again?'

No one spoke.

'We have men all along the Corneo border. Where are they getting in?'

Tyron spoke up then. 'They are not Corneon.'

Another slam of the king's chair. 'That much is becoming clear. So who are they? Are they Zoelin?' He was looking at Pandarus.

Tyron walked over to the informant and placed his hands on his shoulders. 'Thank you,' he said. 'I pray that your daughter is returned to you. You can tell the people of Albus that we will be doing all we can to help.'

The man nodded. 'So you will find them? Find my daughter?'

'We will try to. I promise you that.'

The man turned as though burdened with sacks of flour and left without another word. He had been away, delivering wheat. His eldest son had tried to defend his sister with a shovel, and now he was dead.

'The attacks are calculated, not impulsive,' Tyron said once they were alone. 'We are not searching for rapists here. The girls are being collected for a reason. To be sold perhaps. Syrasan girls are easy prey in remote areas where the men have no fighting skills to defend their families.'

Zenas finally had to take a seat. His eyes remained on Pandarus, and his sword rested on the table in front of him. He scratched at his beard where sweat was gathering beneath it. 'We will need to send men to the larger villages to protect the people.'

Pandarus shook his head. 'We haven't enough men to protect all the villages in the North, and it would leave the castle vulnerable.'

Tyron was not surprised by Pandarus's response. His first concern was always himself. 'And what of the smaller villages?' he asked. 'Who decides which ones are worth protecting? The attackers will simply move on to the next village if they see our soldiers.' He was silent for a moment. 'That man's son defended his sister with a shovel.'

Zenas exhaled loudly. 'Well, these people live simple lives. Most of them are grain farmers with no weapons or training. Many do not even hunt as they survive on fish from the Lotheng. There has never been a need for them to learn to fight if they are not volunteering to.'

'Until now,' Tyron said. His mind was racing. 'The answer is not to disperse our men among them. Instead, we empower them so they can defend themselves.' He nodded as the idea took flight in his head.

Pandarus laughed. He took a seat opposite his father and crossed his arms. 'Great idea, brother. Let's give the peasants a sword each and let them fight our war. Some of these men are barely adequate farmers, but you expect them to become soldiers?'

Zenas was not laughing. He waited for Tyron's response.

'No, we have soldiers. What we need is a kingdom that is reasonably equipped to defend themselves and their families if the need arises.'

'What exactly are you suggesting?' Zenas asked, growing impatient.

Tyron sat down next to his father. 'The provision of weapons and some basic training to every village. Manors will be responsible for weapons and training on their land.'

'This is ludicrous,' Pandarus said, standing up. 'They will be fighting trained soldiers and die anyway.'

Tyron looked at him. 'How do you know they are trained soldiers?'

'Because they are not fighting with shovels,' Pandarus snapped.

'If our people are going to be slaughtered, at least let them die with a sword in their hand.' He looked at his father. 'We have nothing better to offer them at this point until we find out who is behind the attacks.'

Zenas was silent for a moment while he thought. The princes

waited, each hoping for a different response. He stood with great effort and scratched at his beard again with both hands. 'So be it,' he said, picking up his sword. 'Get it done.'

Pandarus threw his hands up. 'We are giving them false hope.'

Zenas leaned over the table, finger pointed like a small sword. 'We are giving them a chance,' he shouted. 'A chance to protect the people they love because we cannot do it!' He lowered his hand and looked at Pandarus. 'Get me some facts. Find out who is behind the attacks,' he hissed. 'And somebody tell Stamitos that the next time I ask my sons to meet with me, he better be here.'

Zenas stormed from the room and Tyron and Pandarus remained seated, looking at one another.

'This is not enough, and you know it,' Pandarus said.

Tyron nodded. 'You are right. It will not be enough. Pray that we find answers and can offer them something more, soon.'

∼

TYRON PACED OUTSIDE OF THE COMPANIONS' quarters. Aldara was no doubt being forced to change into a more suitable dress before seeing him. When she stepped out into the corridor, she seemed to know he was leaving. Her eyes studied him as she approached. He was having difficulty looking back at her, so he shifted his gaze down to the embroidery on the bodice of her purple silk dress, then to her bare arms that showed signs of being cold. When she stopped in front of him he reached out and touched her bare skin.

'I hope you are not dressed in this for me. I would rather just see you warm.'

Aldara glanced at her arms. 'You know I wear what I am told to wear.'

She looked behind her, nervous Fedora could hear them.

'Let's take a walk,' he said, his hand returning to his side.

They went outside where the day was already coming to an

end, strolling down to the stables where they fed old carrots to the horses. Tyron was silent for the longest time as they fed Otus. He could feel her eyes on him.

'It's as if the two of you are making plans,' Aldara said. 'Are you leaving tonight?'

He did not face her straight away. 'Yes.'

'Where are you going?'

He turned to her. 'I'll be gone for a while. It's nothing for you to worry about.' He leant forward and kissed her forehead.

She drew her eyebrows together. 'Don't do that.'

'Do what?' he said, pretending not to understand.

'Treat me like a child and keep your adult worries from me.'

She was pouting, which was not helping her argument. He tried not to smile. There was no dismissing her.

'There has been another attack in the North. We need to act as soon as possible.'

He told her as much as he knew, and she listened without interrupting. He told her of the plan—the sword smiths and artillators who would work day and night to produce what they needed for each village.

'I have assembled a group of men to help with the training. We leave in a few hours.'

She bit down on her lower lip. 'Can I come with you?'

He laughed, but there was no humour in it. 'No, you cannot. The safest place for you right now is here within these walls.'

'I disagree. The safest place for me is with you. I can help you,' she said, reaching out and taking his hand.

He pulled away. 'With what? This is not some pleasant trip to the country. This is a fight.' He surprised himself by raising his voice. 'Do you think we are going to saddle Loda and just ride off to save the kingdom together?' He felt too tall for her all of a sudden. Or she seemed smaller.

'No—'

'What is it you think you can help with? Your archery is

average at best, and these people already know how to ride a horse.'

She flinched when he said that. Just a little, but he noticed. He immediately regretted speaking the words. He was not angry at her, he was angry at what was ahead of him. The only thing he wanted for himself was to know she was safe, and she was threatening that. But he said none of those things out loud.

When he could no longer look at her hurt face, he turned back to Otus. She remained still, no doubt trying to imagine what a good Companion would say.

'I apologise,' she said. 'I did not think through the practicalities before I spoke.'

He hated himself at that moment. He was trying to make it easier to leave her, but it was not working. She placed a hand on the back of his head and felt his hair with her fingers. He turned into her hand, and the quarrel was over.

They went back to his quarters and removed their clothes in complete silence. His hands and mouth said everything he could not. Afterwards, he sat on the chair by the window, watching her doze while he forced down some bread with large gulps of water. Everything stuck in his throat. She opened her eyes and looked across at him, her lips spreading into a smile.

He watched as she dressed and sat on the edge of the bed, unsure of what to do next.

When it was time for him to leave, they did not touch. Could not touch. His gaze swept the room before settling on her. Her hair was out—a tousled mess. He wanted to weave his hands through it again, but then he would never leave.

'Well,' she sighed. 'You should go and teach your people all of your tricks.' She tried to smile. 'They are in good hands, my lord.'

He watched her, trying to find some words of his own, when Pero entered to tell him Queen Eldoris was waiting outside. He looked at her for a moment. No words came.

Aldara stood up. 'Good day, my lord,' she said, curtsying. She smiled at Pero as she passed him. Outside Queen Eldoris stood waiting. They stood a few feet from each other, both already missing him. Aldara dropped into a low curtsy. 'Your Majesty,' she said.

Eldoris nodded and walked past her into Tyron's quarters. The door shut and the echo of it sounded up the empty corridor.

CHAPTER 25

The women sat under the cherry trees with blankets beneath them and on top of them. They were stretched out, books open in front of them, practising the language of Braul. It was a rare day of sunshine, a parting gift from the warm season. Aldara lay between Hali, who talked incessantly, and Sapphira, who was so far removed from the conversation she had not contributed one word. Idalia sat in front of them, one blanket over her legs and another wrapped around her shoulders. She was supposed to be helping the others but had long given up trying to teach them anything. Her book sat closed in her lap.

'When can we expect to use Braul, anyway?' Hali complained. 'I have not met a man from Braul in the entire time I have been here.'

'That's because they are too poor to travel,' said Rhea, smiling at her own wit.

Idalia had been ill with a persistent fever for almost a week, and Aldara could see her face was still flushed with it. Fedora thought fresh air might aid her recovery.

'I met a Braulian man once,' Idalia said. 'And he was most

impressed when I spoke to him in his own language.' Her head was tilted back against the trunk of the tree. Her eyes had closed. 'The day is cooling quickly,' she complained.

'No, the air is still warm,' Aldara said, sitting up. She leant across and placed a hand on Idalia's face. 'You are burning hot. Perhaps you should return to bed.'

Idalia opened her eyes and glanced down at her clammy hands. 'Perhaps I should,' she agreed.

Aldara stood up and helped her to her feet, but she collapsed back to the ground with Aldara just managing to catch her. 'Hali, go and tell Fedora we need the physician.'

Sapphira stood up and took Idalia's other arm. Astra stood up also but did not move towards her. She looked afraid.

'Is she really that ill?'

'Seems that way,' Sapphira said, glancing at Aldara and rolling her eyes.

They put Idalia straight into her bed. Aldara got a cloth and some cool water. She sat beside her, wiping her face and hair. Sweat beads reappeared within moments. They stripped her down to her undergarments in an attempt to cool her. Idalia shivered and complained of the cold before falling into a fevered sleep. They covered her with a blanket and waited for the physician to arrive. Astra sat like a clenched fist on the next bed, her normally smooth face creased with worry.

Fedora finally arrived with the physician trailing behind her. They all watched silently as he prepared to examine Idalia. He pulled the blanket back and Astra gasped. All eyes went to the blood-soaked sheet beneath Idalia.

The physician looked at Fedora. 'Is she with child?' he asked, his tone matter-of-fact.

Fedora shook her head, confused. 'I am not aware of a pregnancy.'

Aldara knelt beside the bed and brought her face close to

Idalia's so she would hear. 'It is really important you tell the physician everything so he can help you.'

Her eyes were closed, and she did not respond.

'Yes, she was with child,' Astra said suddenly. All eyes went to her. 'She lost the baby a few days ago.'

Fedora stepped forward, forcing Aldara to move aside. 'You lost the baby, or you ended the pregnancy?' Her tone was firm.

Idalia opened her eyes for a moment. 'I ended it. I had to. You know I had to.'

The physician shook his head. 'What method did you use?'

She tried to focus on him, but she was too tired and her eyes closed again. 'Pennyroyal and hot water did not work. I had to do it internally.' Tears blended with the beads of sweat on her face.

'My guess is the termination was incomplete. Now there is an infection,' the physician said to Fedora. 'I will send you some silphium, which may or may not help. It would have helped more a few days ago,' he added. 'I will return in the morning. There is little more I can offer at this point.'

Fedora nodded and thanked him. Once the physician had gone, she instructed Hali and Sapphira to help Idalia onto another bed so they could change the linen. They could not risk the maids knowing anything. She sent Astra to get clean undergarments for her.

'Say nothing of this to anyone,' she instructed.

'Will she recover?' Astra whispered.

Fedora looked at her. 'You should have come to me about this.' She was not angry—she was at a loss. 'I would have helped her. Now we must wait and see what the physician says in the morning.'

Astra swallowed. 'There is one more thing you should know.'

'What is it?'

Astra glanced around to make sure the others were not listening. 'This was her second pregnancy this year. The first termination was successful.'

Fedora said nothing as she processed the new information. They all knew Idalia had been ill a number of times in the previous months. She nodded. 'Thank you. Now go get the undergarments.'

It was late in the night when Aldara eventually fell asleep next to Idalia, but she was woken a few hours later by the sound of her vomiting. Idalia lay covered in her own sick. She seemed completely unaware. Aldara cleaned her up as best she could without changing her clothes and then felt her head. It was cold despite a covering of sweat. She went to fetch Fedora, who rushed in and tried to rouse Idalia. Her breathing had become shallow, and she could not be woken. The other women began to wake, wondering what was happening.

'What's wrong with her?' Aldara asked.

Fedora shook her head. 'I think she is dying,' she said, her voice cracking. 'I will send for the physician. And inform the king.'

Aldara climbed back into bed with Idalia and tried to warm up her cold body. Astra came over to the bed and sat at the foot of it, crying. The others stood mutely, watching. Idalia's breathing became sporadic. Soon they could not hear her at all. Aldara sat up, took hold of her shoulders and shook her.

'Idalia, you need to breathe,' she said.

Her colour was changing, and her mouth was open in a way that made her unrecognisable.

Fedora walked in at that moment with King Zenas behind her. The women dispersed to the darker corners of the room. Aldara stood next to Fedora, against the wall, watching the life bleed from Idalia. Zenas stared at the still body, her skin grey, chest no longer rising. Fedora stepped forward and placed a comforting hand on his arm. He stood motionless.

By the time the physician arrived they already knew she was dead, but they all waited for him to examine her and hoped for a different outcome. A few hours earlier they had been learning

Braul. She was the only one of them to have ever met a Braulian man. Now her clammy body lay dead in front of them. They would never again see her dance or watch in awe as she entered a room, claiming everybody's attention.

Zenas did not look up when the physician spoke quietly with Fedora. She removed her hand from his arm and it covered her face for a moment. It would be the only time Aldara would see her cry. It was silent and uncomfortable for everyone present. The king did not have that luxury; his grieving would need to be done privately.

'I will have the priest come,' Zenas said, barely composed.

Fedora removed her hands from her face and took a slow inward breath. 'That is very kind, Your Majesty.'

She gave a small curtsy as he fled the room. Then she looked around at the women, who were all in shock. 'Pay your respects,' she instructed. 'Before the priest comes. And before they take her away.'

The rest of the night seemed to occur in short bursts for Aldara. The sound of Astra's violent sobs. The stunned faces of Rhea, Panthea, and Violeta, standing over the corpse. The sight of Sapphira's back shut off from it all. Hali trying to mother everybody. And finally, the arrival of the priest, who prayed for her soul while masked with nothing but disapproval. He covered her face, and then two men Aldara had never seen before arrived and carried Idalia's limp body from the room.

'Where will they take her?' Aldara asked.

Fedora was staring at the empty doorway. 'King Zenus is sending her back to her family. A burial here would not be appropriate.' Her voice was a whisper. 'The herbs do not always work.'

Aldara was not sure whether she was commenting to herself or directing the words at the women as a warning. Some of them were now asleep. Some of them were just still, like the dead. Astra had gone to bathe, trying to wash away the stench of her friend. She would not be consoled. No one knew how to help her.

Aldara lay down in her own bed, where the sheets were cool and clean. Hali climbed in next to her, saying nothing. They did not talk or touch. Eventually they slept. Because that is what the living do.

CHAPTER 26

The warmth slipped away. It left with Tyron or it died with Idalia. Aldara was not sure which. The sun just stopped trying. Idalia's absence was felt by everyone. It was as though dancing had died with her.

Tyron remained away. Pandarus returned occasionally, holding hushed meetings with the king and then disappearing again. No one knew where he went each time he left. Hali dreaded his returns. She complained of the way he spoke to her, his abrupt manner in bed. He would keep her out for days on drunken escapades, sometimes offering her up to acquaintances she had not met before.

'I am the one thing that man does not mind sharing,' Hali said one morning. Her breath smelled of wine. 'I have had more of his friends inside me in the past two days than hot meals. Only some of them of noble birth.'

Aldara hated that she could do nothing to help. 'How do the other men treat you?'

They were lying on her bed, trying not to disturb Sapphira, who was in the bed next to them with a blanket over her head, an attempt to block the noise of their voices as she tried to sleep.

'Better than Pandarus,' Hali said. 'Doesn't stop me from feeling like a cheap prostitute though. I cannot even use that term as they are not required to pay. That makes me something else I suppose.'

Aldara closed her eyes against the words. It broke her heart to hear her speak that way. She would talk to Tyron about it when he returned. Yes, *when* he returned.

The women were idle and felt suddenly misplaced at Archdale. They expected King Zenas to acquire a new Companion, but the silent war kept him too busy. Or perhaps Idalia could not be replaced.

The king sent Stamitos south to the Braul border, knowing the only fight that far south was the fight to keep the starving alive. They barely had an army. The Braulian king had been on the throne for over sixty years, and his people were politely waiting for him to die so they could try again. Those circumstances meant Sapphira and Aldara were mostly left alone. They spent many hours at the butts, practising. Many of the knights were away, so it was a quiet part of the castle, particularly as the weather grew cold.

'I should be with him,' Sapphira said one day. She was replacing the hemp on her longbow and ignoring the fact it was almost evening. She normally resented women who pined for their men, but she had become one of them. 'I am a better archer than the men with him. And I am a better teacher than all of them.'

Aldara was staring at the same target she had been staring at all afternoon, having the same conversation with Sapphira they had had all afternoon. 'Women have no place in war except to nurse the wounded…you know the rest of the boring speech. Don't make me repeat it again.'

She was sick of the sound of her voice, and she did not believe a word that came out of her own mouth anyway. She had not received one word from Tyron since his departure. She had heard however that there had been further attacks. More women and children taken, and more men killed trying to stop them. It seemed progress was not quick enough, or perhaps ineffective.

She checked in regularly with the maids, the kitchen hands, and the servants, seeing if they had any news of him. She had even worked up the courage to ask Fedora. No one seemed to know anything.

'Probably a good thing we are here. There is no one about to defend Archdale,' Sapphira said, only partly joking.

Aldara looked down the arrow, adjusted her aim slightly and released it, piercing the bullseye. There was no one around to care. Sapphira had ceased to be impressed by it days ago. She put down the longbow, took off her glove, and rubbed her tired hands together. 'Well, we will give them a good fight when they get here. The maids can join us with their fire stokers.'

'And Cora with her broomstick,' Sapphira said.

Aldara could see Fedora walking across the grass towards them. A guard escorted her.

'Bet she heard that,' Sapphira said, bracing.

'Would that be Princess Cora?' Fedora asked, stopping in front of them. 'The princess whose house you reside in?'

Aldara was impressed with that impossible hearing distance.

'I apologise,' Sapphira said, packing up. 'I meant to say *Princess* Cora with her broomstick.'

Just when Aldara thought the evening could not get any colder.

'I have a number of chores waiting for you which may help remind you of your manners in the future.' Fedora said, her tone sharp.

Sapphira turned and looked at her. 'Yes, my lady.'

∼

TYRON and his three men were staying in Lirald, a village two hours east of the Corneo border that produced modest amounts of wheat, most of which now went to Corneo. They had spent the day training the local men with crossbows, using haystacks as targets. Very few of them hit the haystacks. Next they would be travelling east to Nuwien, a village that had ideal growing conditions for root vegetables but was better known for its prostitutes. Noblemen from Veanor preferred to travel to Nuwien for women and drink in an attempt to protect their business reputations.

Tyron had been pleased with their progress until he had heard the village of Agrissi had been burned down during an attack. They had been there only five days earlier. The men had all been fantastic fishermen and terrible fighters. He had trained them hard during the day and shared meals with their families in the evenings. Their faceless enemy had responded to their newly obtained arms with fire. Three girls under the age of sixteen had been tied up and thrown onto the back of the men's horses. The kidnappers were spotted riding north.

He sat eating bland soup prepared by a local woman who had made it especially for him. The woman had also offered him accommodation in their family's home for the duration of their stay—and her eldest daughter. He had taken only the soup and made camp in a field behind the main road. He put down the bowl and threw another piece of wood onto the small fire before picking up his blackened map once again. He was trying to predict where their enemy would appear next. Somewhere in the North, always in the North. They had to be Zoelin, or at least Zoelin allies to have access to that long stretch of border.

Leksi appeared out of darkness and joined him by the fire.

'Supplies await us in Nuwien. We should leave early to maximise our time there.' He poured some soup for himself and then moved closer to the flames for warmth. 'Have you noticed there are a lot of really *big* men here? Most are well over six foot and have necks like tree trunks. And most of the women match me in size. I have mistaken them for men countless times. They are far too intimidating to sleep with. I'm confident our enemy will take one look at the locals and bypass this place.'

'What is the likelihood they will volunteer as footmen when we call on our people to fight alongside us?' Tyron asked, only partly joking. He put down the map and looked at Leksi. 'How many men do we have along the Zoelin border?'

'None as far as I am aware. Our instructions were to place more men along the Corneo border. Do we have any reason to suspect the attackers to be Zoelin? Pandarus is floating across the border almost weekly.'

'Where else can they be disappearing to? Unless they are travelling underground or flying over our heads, they are coming from the North.'

Leksi began eating his soup, but after tasting it, he changed his mind and put it down. 'Even the children are man sized in this place. We should take a few of them for our own protection.' Tyron did not laugh, and Leksi did not mind. His humour was often under-appreciated. He glanced at Tyron, realising he needed something more than a joke. 'They are Zoelin,' he agreed. 'The river is low this time of year, and the water can be crossed without risk of death from low temperatures. Proof will surface soon enough.'

'I would love to know how much Pandarus actually knows about the whole thing.'

'My guess? More than we do.' He picked up the soup again and smelled it. 'Do we have any food that does not taste like a dog's arse?'

Tyron looked at him. 'I'm not sure. What does a dog's arse taste like?'

Leksi waved a finger. 'Ah, there's the hilarious prince I know is in there.' He stood up. 'Bugger it. If I can't eat, maybe I will find myself a big Lirald woman after all. It's going to get cold, and I refuse to spend the night curled up next to you.'

Tyron watched him disappear into the dark and then made himself comfortable against the large tree that reached out over their tents, listening to the banter of the other men a few yards away. He watched the flames of the fire and tried not to think of anything outside of the strategy. Evenings were the main time she found her way into his mind, so each night he fought to keep her out. His eyes were heavy with sleep, and as they closed, he saw her face—hair sweeping across it as they rode with the wind behind them, teeth flashing with open-mouthed laughter. A playful expression that invited him to put his hands on her. His eyes opened again, and only the softly lit village was before him.

It may have been moments later, or it may have been hours. The piercing scream of a woman pulled him from sleep. His eyes snapped open, and his hand immediately reached for his sword. He could hear the collective pounding of hooves. A lit arrow caught his vision in the distance and he was on his feet in an instant, kicking the cold pot of soup over the fire before taking cover behind the large tree. Where were his men? He peered around the thick trunk and saw a house alight with flames. He could make out six men on horseback thirty yards away. Returning his sword to its sheath, he reached for his bow. Two of the horses separated from the group, and the men rode away from the village. Soon they would pass him. He waited until he could identify the riders a little better. The moment he saw reflection from their armour he took aim and shot the first rider through the neck. Before he had even heard the thud of the body hitting the ground, he reloaded his bow and shot the second rider. He missed the neck, but the arrow pierced his armour through the chest. The Corneon armies had some of the strongest armour he had ever encountered, and there would have been no way to pierce it from that distance. The only way to kill using a bow was to aim for exposed areas such as the neck or lower abdomen. These were not Corneon soldiers.

He slipped back behind the tree as the two horses trotted past him. He looked for royal symbols on the saddles, but they were unmarked. Crouching low, he crept to where Otus was tethered. Two of his men had emerged from their tents and stood by their horses waiting for instructions. Leksi was not with them.

'Go east and enter the village from the north,' Tyron said. 'We leave no opportunity for them to escape. I expect us to meet in the middle with a living and breathing Leksi in tow.'

They nodded and left on horseback.

Otus was never more alive than in the moment before battle. He did not have to be told his role. When Tyron mounted, the horse lunged into a canter and headed straight for the fire. As they neared the houses, Tyron could hear children crying and men shouting. He dug his heels into Otus and the horse stretched out beneath him. The four remaining horses he had seen earlier stood amid the shadows. Except there were not four men; he counted six, four on the ground and two on horseback. He took aim but did not release one arrow until he was close enough to see why the number of people did not match the number of horses. He realised two of the people on foot were in fact women. The men were binding their hands with strips of cotton. They did not hear Tyron approaching over the whimpering. He took care of the mounted riders first, shooting one in the back and the second through the chest. The two on the ground made the mistake of letting go of the women as they retrieved their bows and were immediately attacked with bare fists. Tyron took out his sword and cut the throat of one of them before driving the sword through the chest of the remaining man. He was surprised to discover the women were in fact young girls. Leksi had been right about their size. He carefully cut the cotton around their wrists with his sword. 'Hide,' he said to them. 'Run away from the fires and do not come out until someone comes to find you.'

Their panicked faces took in the sight of the four bodies lying about their feet. They nodded and then fled. Tyron rode along the main road that divided the village, which was lit up by the fire. Families were spilling out onto the smoke-filled road, the men clutching their new swords and the mothers clutching their children. He tried to spot his own men among the chaos, but it was a mess of shadows. A woman was crouched on the road, her hands wrapped her head as she screamed in short bursts. He kept hold of his sword as he dismounted. Otus remained where he was left, fire hissing behind him. As Tyron reached the woman, two men appeared through the haze of smoke, their swords hurtling towards him. His body moved automatically to avoid the blades, his balance steady as his sword sliced the smoke-filled air. He had the advantage of traditional Syrasan training where soldiers were blindfolded in order to enhance their senses and improve their balance. As the bodies collapsed next to the hysterical woman, Tyron felt tremendous gratitude for the unconventional methods, but the smoke was clawing at his eyes and throat, and soon he would be unable to think past it.

He pulled the screaming woman to her feet. 'Run,' he shouted at her. She backed away from him and then took off at a sprint.

The fire was now leaping between the houses, and his throat was closing against the thick smoke. He walked on, stopping only when he tripped on a dead body. He looked down at the armoured man, not from Lirald. He reached down and pulled the helmet off his head. The first thing he noticed was the black ink marked along the man's dark neck. There was an arrow wedged in his leg and blood pouring from a stomach wound. He was still crouched over the body when he saw a reflection from a sword above his head. He had just enough time to raise his own sword, block the blow, and push the attacker back. His attacker stumbled, and the sword fell to the ground between them. It was a Lirald woman. She was cowering in front of him, hands trembling. When she recognised him, she immediately fell forward onto her knees.

'Forgive me, my lord. Please. I could not see through all the smoke.'

Her dress was soaked with blood. Tyron picked up her sword and pulled her off the road, away from the smoke. He led her behind a house that was safe from the flames and handed her back the sword.

'Are you injured?' he asked, looking again at her dress.

Tears poured down her cheeks then, and she dropped the sword. 'It is my husband's blood. He was trying to stop them. They took our daughter.'

She took in a huge sobbing breath and began to cough. Once again, he picked her sword up and closed her hand around it.

'Don't cry for your daughter yet. And don't let this go or hesitate to use it again.'

He ran back into the thickening smoke, unable to see past his own hand. He listened through the crackle of fire. He could hear a woman wailing but could not tell what direction it came from. Another flash of a sword stilled him. He stopped breathing, his sword hot in hand. Leksi appeared through the smoke, his face blackened with soot. Tyron felt a rush of relief at seeing him unharmed.

'They are definitely Zoelin,' Leksi said. 'There are four dead behind me.'

'And seven dead in front of you,' Tyron said.

They lowered their swords but remained alert, continuing back down the road together, sleeves pressed over their mouths in an attempt to filter the smoke. Tyron spotted Otus, bewildered as people rushed past him with pales of water. His other men were already helping to extinguish and contain the flames. Some of the houses were beyond saving, and their occupants stood frozen in front of them, ash blowing about them as they watched. A young boy ran up to Tyron and offered to take Otus so they could join the effort.

They worked tirelessly with every other able-bodied person until they had salvaged all that could be salvaged. When all the fires were extinguished, people collapsed with exhaustion onto the blackened earth and sobbed into their hands. Some went and sat by the dead. Children wrapped in blankets were asleep on the ground or in someone's arms. Away from the smoke and the grief, Tyron and Leksi stood with their hands on their knees, coughing up black phlegm. The same boy who had taken Tyron's horse brought them water in a filthy cup. They drank it greedily, ignoring the pieces of ash floating in it. Tyron thanked the boy and asked him to fetch water for the horses.

'We should pay our respects to the dead and their families,' Leksi said, his voice hoarse.

Tyron nodded.

They wandered along the road in the hazy light of morning until they stood before the dead. Eleven Zoelin men. Four Liralds. One of them a four-year-old boy who had gotten swept up in the flames. Tyron felt his stomach heave as he looked at the small, chubby hand poking out from beneath a horse blanket. The boy's mother was kneeling next to the body, silent and unblinking. Tyron could not even manage one word to her, and he doubted she would have heard him anyway. He turned around and walked up the small hill, away from the blood soaked and burned. When he reached the top of the hill, he leant on his knees, expecting to be sick. When nothing came, he stood upright and looked at Leksi, who had followed him.

'Zoelins,' said Leksi.

'Zoelins,' Tyron echoed, wiping the sweat from his face. 'So much for allies.'

The horses of their enemy had been collected and were being tethered nearby. Leksi pointed to the shoulder of one of them. 'The horses are branded Syrasan. Bred by us, trained by us, and then used against us.'

Tyron's mind was still clouded from the smoke. 'We need to send word immediately to the king.' He linked his hands behind his head. 'At least now we understand the war we are fighting. You are the only one I trust to have this conversation on my behalf. I need you to find out what Pandarus knows. We will need men placed along the Lotheng River. Pull them from the Corneo border if necessary. And no Zoelins are to enter Syrasan.'

'That will be difficult to enforce.'

'I agree. If they want to get across, they'll find a way, but let's not make it easy for them.'

Leksi nodded and placed a blackened hand on Tyron's shoulder. 'I will leave as soon as I have cleaned up a little. Any other messages?' he asked. 'I will assure your mother you are eating. That's always her first question.'

Tyron could not smile. 'Thank you.'

Leksi removed the hand and waited. 'Anyone else?' he asked pointedly. 'Anyone else at Archdale I should send word to?'

Tyron swallowed, and it was painful. His swollen eyes blinked. 'Yes,' he replied. 'Tell her I am alive. As per the plan.'

Leksi waited for more, but nothing came. 'Oh. Well, don't bore her with detail.'

'I don't want her to know the details.'

Leksi began to cough and bent over to spit out his efforts. 'I hope I don't give anything away,' he said, returning upright. He gave a small bow before turning to leave.

'Leksi,' Tyron called after him. He stopped and turned around. 'Tell her Otus misses her. Every day.'

Leksi nodded.

CHAPTER 27

Aldara's heart quickened as she took in the sight of Leksi. There were traces of soot on his hands and face. The stench of smoke clung to his clothes. They stood in front of a large stained-glass window in the corridor just outside the Companions' quarters. The window depicted three women praying, a subtle reminder to ask God for forgiveness for their daily sins. Leksi was not interested in the images. He was watching the young maids hang laundry through the clear panel of the window.

'I could put in a good word for you if you like,' she said, trying to lighten the mood and encourage the conversation.

He turned to her and smiled, taking in her simple cotton dress and messy braid.

'You joke, but I will keep that in mind for my return. The women that do my laundry at the manor look quite different. I am afraid I do not have a lot of time. I return North this afternoon. Quick trip to update the king.'

'I understand,' she said, glancing down at the blood on his sleeves. 'Is Prince Tyron keeping well, my lord?'

He followed her eyes down to his sleeve. 'I apologise for my appearance. Not much time to clean up. This is actually an improvement on earlier.'

Aldara looked up. 'You don't need to apologise to me. I'm grateful for all you are doing. I cannot imagine what you are enduring in order to keep those people safe.'

He put his hands behind his back. 'He's alive. As per your plan, apparently.'

She swallowed hard, and her eyes did not leave him. 'We tried to keep the plan simple.'

He laughed, but he could hear the relief in her voice.

'Did he say anything else?'

He was tempted to add some colour to the message but decided to keep it honest. 'He said to tell you Otus misses you. Otus is the horse,' he added.

'Yes,' she said, eyes shining. 'I have heard the stables are not the same without him.' She blinked, and a small tear escaped. 'Thank you for keeping them both safe.'

He smiled and gave a small bow. 'I should be going. I have lots to do before leaving here.'

'I hope those things include a bath.' She wanted him to stay longer. She wanted him to talk about Tyron. She wanted to ask questions and hear his name spoken out loud. She curtsied instead. 'Thank you for taking the time to find me.'

'Thank you for not making me go all the way down to the butts. Good day, Aldara,' he said, turning to leave.

'My lord,' she called. He turned back to her. 'Tell him I pray for him every day, just in case there is a God, and on the small chance he is listening to me,' she added.

He nodded. 'Otus will be pleased to hear it.'

She smiled and watched him leave. When he was out of sight, the vision of Tyron in blood-soaked clothing, skin blackened by fire, remained with her.

That evening she lay in bed with Hali. Pandarus had once

again left for Zoelin, so the women were mentally preparing themselves for another spell of boredom.

'It makes no difference whether he is here or not nowadays,' Hali complained. 'He didn't request my company during his last visit.'

'To be fair, he was only here two days. And let's not forget about the war going on.'

'Why are you defending him? You hate him.'

Aldara was not defending him, she was trying to make Hali feel a little less frightened by her situation. Not only had Pandarus stopped requesting her company, but he had also stopped greeting her at social gatherings.

'I am just as bored with him as he is of me,' she said. 'But of course I don't get to show it like he does. I have to smile when he speaks, laugh at his terrible jokes, and cry out in his bed even when he is so drunk I can barely stand to touch him.' She went silent for a moment. 'I wish *I* had the luxury of choosing my own Companion.'

Aldara smiled. 'And who would you choose?'

'You know who I would choose—Lord Yuri. That man pours my wine and watches me eat. I have never met anyone who matches my love of food. But there is no acceptable reason for him to make an offer for me if I am sold. His children are grown. If I were to reside there, I would bring him only disgrace.'

Lord Yuri had given Hali a ruby pin during their last encounter, and Aldara noticed she had worn it every day since. 'Perhaps you are worth the disgrace.'

They were lying with their shoulders pressed together, looking up into the darkness.

'He will come back you know,' Hali said, taking Aldara's hand under the blanket.

Aldara knew who she was referring to. 'I know. But we will be like strangers again.'

Hali squeezed her hand. 'Then you will have the thrill of falling in love twice.'

She felt cold suddenly. 'There is no love between a prince and his Companion.'

'Yes, only Companionship,' Hali said, letting go of her hand and rolling onto her side. Her eyes closed. 'You sound like Fedora. Don't preach her rules to me. You have done nothing but break them since you arrived here.'

Aldara's eyes were getting heavy also. 'That particular rule protects us.'

Hali gave a soft, sleepy laugh. 'You risk everything for your horse, but not for your prince.'

They fell asleep, and when Aldara woke the next morning, on her eighteenth birthday, the bed was cold beside her.

CHAPTER 28

Tyron welcomed the snow. The Zoelins could not burn down houses in the constant damp of the cold season. If they wanted to take women, they would have to do so without the distraction of fire.

It had been six weeks since he had seen Pandarus over the border. His stern-faced brother had arrived with Leksi at their camp in Nuwien, vague with details and covering his embarrassment at the state of things with a vile tone and short fuse. Managing relations with neighbouring kingdoms was Pandarus's sole responsibility. It was not only that he had failed in that role, but that he refused to communicate on the matter. Tyron had tried to push him for details, determined to find out why the events were happening.

'Just give me two weeks to sort out the mess, and I will tell you everything.'

He had at least called it a mess, which was a start. Tyron had stared at his royal tunic, pressed trousers, and decorative sword that never left its sheath. 'Just tell me this, did you know they were Zoelin? When we were placing more of our men at the Corneo border, did you know?'

Pandarus had seemed angry. At whom, Tyron had no idea.

'I knew nothing for certain until your message yesterday.'

Tyron had hated him in that moment. 'But you suspected. This is your fourth visit to Zoelin since this fight began. Something made you return again and again. It looks suspiciously like a negotiation from where I'm standing.'

'Just give me two weeks,' Pandarus had repeated.

Tyron's eyes flicked to Leksi, who had a knack for appearing neutral. 'What do I do if you are not back in two weeks?'

Pandarus had shaken his head. 'The same thing our father and brother did when we did not return from Corneo within the estimated time frame. Wait longer.'

After Pandarus crossed the Lotheng River and slipped into the Zoelin woods, Tyron took his men to its icy banks and set up camp under the cover of tall pines. He ordered eighty men off the Corneo border and dispatched them along the river. But the river was long, and a week later two girls were snatched from the side of a road just outside of Soarid. They were just thirteen and fourteen years of age. There were no deaths this time, but there were also no witnesses. When Tyron heard the news, he gathered fifteen men and fifteen iron hammers and travelled along the river knocking down every adjoining bridge they came across, one stone at a time, until they collapsed into the icy water. The destruction of crossing points was not his most effective strategy, but he liked the idea of their enemy submerged in freezing water, fighting a strong current. He worked tirelessly alongside his men, channelling his anger into each blow of the hammer. He rested only when Leksi insisted on it, often having tools physically removed from his blistered hands. He left only one bridge standing, the bridge Pandarus had crossed a few weeks earlier. It was the bridge that Pandarus would return to, and it was also the entry point Tyron planned to use if the fight moved over the river and into Zoelin. Every day Pandarus did not return, he readied himself more and more for that fight.

When there were no more bridges to knock down, Tyron and his men rode through light snowfall to the only standing bridge and set up camp at its entrance. Tyron sent a messenger to King Zenas, updating him on their progress and location. A messenger returned with a letter telling him Stamitos had returned to Archdale and asking for news on Pandarus, but there was no news. No one crossed the lone bridge.

'In hindsight, perhaps it would have been easier to build a large wall,' Leksi said.

They were sitting on small stools in Tyron's tent, boots off, feet drying next to the fire.

'We would probably be trapping the enemy in,' Tyron said, fanning his toes closer to the flames.

Leksi stared at him. 'That is the problem you have with the idea?'

Subtle humour was wasted on Tyron those days.

'That and the lack of materials,' he said, after a long pause. He was about to add something further when one of his men peered through the gap in the tent.

'It is Prince Pandarus, my lord. He is coming across the bridge with two men.'

Tyron and Leksi glanced at each other.

'Zoelin men or Syrasan men?' Leksi said, grabbing his boots and throwing Tyron's at him.

'I believe them to be Syrasan, my lord.'

Tyron shoved his feet into his damp boots. 'Have every man armed and watching the other side of the river. No one else comes across that bridge,' he said to Leksi.

Leksi nodded and slipped through the flap of the tent. Tyron was about to follow after him when Pandarus stepped inside. They stood studying one another for a moment.

'You don't seem very pleased to see me,' Pandarus said. He turned, watching Leksi shout orders at the men. 'Where is Leksi fleeing to?'

Tyron's eyes moved over him, checking for injury, weight loss, anything that suggested it had been a difficult six weeks for him. Dark circles did not seem sufficient. 'He is securing the bridge. Now is not the time for complacency.'

Pandarus nodded. He walked past Tyron and fell onto one of the stools, feigning exhaustion. 'Do you have anything to drink?' he asked, removing his boots.

Tyron bent over and picked up his flask sitting by the entrance and handed it to Pandarus. He stood over him, waiting.

'You have nothing else?' Pandarus said, peering into it. 'Has this even been boiled? The last thing I need is to arrive at Archdale ill and have everyone suspecting some form of Zoelin plague.'

Tyron had to walk away from him. 'We have waited for you, just as you asked us to. Now, what news do you have for me?'

Pandarus placed the flask at his feet and looked at him. Tyron could see him considering his words, which made him uneasy.

'I bring confirmation the men responsible for the attacks were Zoelin.'

Tyron waited for something else. Something new. But nothing more was offered. 'Actually, I brought you that confirmation almost two months ago, when we killed seven Zoelin men in Lirald who were responsible for the death of four locals during an attempted abduction, including a young boy who died in the fires they started.'

Pandarus appeared untouched by the story, maintaining his neutral expression. 'As you are aware, we recently entered into an alliance with Zoelin, so we needed to ensure we had all the facts before laying accusations.'

Tyron could hardly believe what he was hearing. 'All right, we will have this conversation your way. What else do you have for me?'

Pandarus crossed his arms in front of him. 'Time for you to return to Archdale, brother. You are becoming cynical.'

Tyron stared at him. 'I would have preferred not to be fighting this blind war, but there would be no one left alive in the North if I had trusted your judgement.' He took a breath before continuing. 'So your friend, King Jayr, will he be returning the Syrasan women and children he has taken?'

Pandarus laughed. 'It's a little more complicated than that.'

'I'm certain I can keep up if you would just share the story with me.'

Pandarus nodded. 'All right. What would you like to know?'

'Start with why you were able to just trot off over the bridge and be welcomed at Drake Castle while I remained here killing their men? We both know you are not one for putting yourself in danger. You knew something I did not from the beginning of all this.'

'I have a good relationship with King Jayr. I did not believe he was behind these acts. We suspected our enemy to be Nydoen rebels.'

Tyron could not take in the insanity quickly enough. 'Zoelin mountain rebels? You honestly thought a handful of mountain rebels were responsible for these planned attacks? What on earth would they want with women and children?'

'They are lawless men...'

'But not moral-less. They reject their new king's politics and choose to live as their ancestors have done for centuries. That does not make them criminals.'

Pandarus leant forward and signalled for his brother to come closer. 'If you keep your voice down, I will explain.' He waited for Tyron to step closer before speaking. 'King Jayr's advisor proposed a trade during his last visit. I thought the decision was straightforward, sensible, and profitable for Syrasan. An agreement was written up and signed by both parties.' He hesitated for a moment. 'After the men departed from Archdale, our king and father decided not to honour the agreement.'

That did not make sense to Tyron. His father never went back on his word once it was given. He shook his head as he tried to process it. 'There must have been a good reason for him to break such an agreement. What was the trade? Surely not weapons...'

Pandarus shifted in his seat. 'Women.'

Tyron shook his head, confused. 'Women?'

'Yes. You remember those, don't you?'

Tyron paced, the pieces falling into place. 'What were the women for?' he asked, already knowing the answer.

'What do you think?'

'Companions. But Companions for whom? King Jayr?'

Pandarus rested his elbows on the tops of his knees. 'Maybe a handful, yes, but Syrasan women are considered exotic and beautiful in the far North. The novelty of their fair complexion I suppose. It was a well-researched and sensible trade decision.'

Tyron's mind raced. 'Asigow? King Jayr is selling women and children to savages in Asigow?'

'Savages? Honestly, brother, it's a good thing I am in charge of relations.'

'Asigow babies born with minor defects are drowned by their fathers at birth.'

Pandarus was silent.

'What was your plan?' Tyron continued. 'Travel through the kingdom, throwing a few coins at the poor in return for their daughters?'

'That is precisely what we do now!' Pandarus shouted. 'Your Companion cost less than my boots. The poor need ways to survive.'

The mention of her jolted him. He had to mentally block her before he was able to continue. 'The difference is our poor sell to their king, a king whom they trust and respect. They hand over their loved ones knowing they will have a better life in which they will never be hungry. We cannot take children from their parents without any regard as to where they will end up.'

'You can save the speech. I already had it from our father.'

'And rightfully so. You should never have signed such an agreement.'

Pandarus waved him off. 'They will not be sold off as street prostitutes! They will receive the same opportunities as our own Companions—expensive dresses, food, education. They will live among the elite and rich and possibly share a bed with the Asigow king himself.'

Tyron was still shaking his head. 'This advisor from Zoelin, was this the man you handed her over to?' He could not say her name aloud.

Pandarus said nothing.

'No wonder our father dishonoured the agreement. He saw first-hand how they treat Companions. Imagine handing young Syrasan women over to rapists. Thank God he saw sense when you could not.'

Pandarus stood, fed up with the conversation. 'I believe the current situation alters our moral compass a little, don't you?'

'No, I don't. King Jayr's men have stolen and murdered our people. We cannot reward their crimes by negotiating with them.'

Pandarus raised a finger to him. 'They have already proven they can take what they want.' He put his hand down in an attempt to calm himself. 'We cannot afford to have them as enemies. They are strong and unpredictable. As allies they will fight alongside us when the need arises. Corneo could not win against such an army, which means they may not attempt such fights in the future. You must trust that I know what I am doing.' When Tyron said nothing he added, 'We cannot fight everybody.'

Tyron stared at the ground in front of him. 'You never suspected Nydoen rebels. And you never suspected Corneo. You have known King Jayr was behind these attacks the whole time. He was simply upholding the agreement that you signed.'

Pandarus opened his hands. 'When I went to him after the first attack, he admitted to nothing. He simply asked if we were prepared to honour the trade agreement. I told him the decision was not mine to make. He said he wished there was more he could do to help.' He shook his head, almost pleading. 'Every time it was the same. He just kept asking about the agreement.'

Tyron looked at him. 'You knew. And father knew. Neither of you told me anything. Instead, you sent me off blind and wasted our men at the Corneon border.'

'How would it have appeared if we had sent men to the Zoelin border?'

'Like a fair war!' Tyron shouted.

Pandarus blinked and turned away. 'All we knew for certain was that we needed King Jayr as an ally. We could not have predicted the extent of his actions. He was having a tantrum, and we were waiting for it to pass.'

Tyron shook his head again. 'I could have predicted his actions had I been informed.'

'You were already angry. We needed rational minds to make rational decisions.'

He could not argue that point. 'If you honour the agreement, you will be endangering our people. Their respect will leave with the women you sell.'

Pandarus sat back down, picked up the flask, and drank it without further complaint. When he had emptied it, he threw it at the wall of the tent. Both men watched it roll along the ground before coming to a stop between them.

'So what now?' Tyron asked.

Pandarus watched the fire. 'We will honour the trade agreement, and the attacks will stop.'

'And what of the women and children they have already taken?'

Pandarus looked up, and Tyron glimpsed something that resembled shame in his expression. 'They will be returned. And we will credit King Jayr for it.'

Tyron nodded, already understanding. 'You will lay blame on the Nydoen rebels, and our people will sing King Jayr's praises. Clever. Though I am surprised he was willing to cooperate.'

'He wanted something in exchange of course.'

'Of course. What does he want?'

Pandarus had difficulty meeting Tyron's eyes. 'A mentor. A mentor to prepare the women for their roles. We have one housed outside of Veanor, ready for transport.'

Tyron shook his head, confused. 'What mentor?'

'Hali,' Pandarus said, trying to sound businesslike. 'She was sent to Veanor weeks ago in preparation. She departs for Onuric tomorrow.'

'Hali,' Tyron repeated.

'Yes, Hali.'

Tyron had made a point of not contacting Aldara. Not one letter had been exchanged between them. He had wanted to keep her out of the war, but in trying to protect her, he had in many ways abandoned her.

A gust of cold air pushed through the flap of the tent. It whispered along the ground to him. And the girl he had locked from his mind suddenly poured in like sunshine.

CHAPTER 29

Fedora wished she had never been told the plan. Previously when Companions had been sold, she would gently wake them during the night and hand them over to the guard waiting outside of their quarters. She was never told the details, though she had never pushed the matter either. This time, however, when Pandarus had told her Hali would be leaving, temporarily housed at a manor outside of Veanor, she had found herself asking why the housing was temporary. Much to her surprise, and later distress, Pandarus had told her his entire strategy, speaking as though he were in a confessional. Hali would be sent to Onuric Castle in the East of Zoelin to mentor the Syrasan women who were sold into the trade. Why? Why had she asked?

The following morning, after she had pulled Hali from Aldara's bed, where they had slept like sisters, she had been forced to look at Aldara and pretend she did not have answers. But she did have them, and Aldara knew it. Not much escaped that girl. She had intuition well beyond her years. The only way to maintain the dwindling trust between them was to tell her enough. Aldara had stood in front of her, eyes pleading, unable to fathom Prince Pandarus's plan. And then she had done as she always did, let her feelings get in the way of her good sense.

Later that morning Fedora had been called to the stables where Aldara had screamed at a groom who refused to let her saddle her horse. The incident saw her confined to the Companion's quarters for two days, where she remained in bed, thinking and not eating. When she was eventually permitted to leave their quarters, Fedora was called to the main gate where Aldara was being held by the guards after a physical fight to pass them. Her conduct saw her placed in the tower for the night.

When Fedora went to collect her the following morning, she went prepared for a stern talk. She looked at Aldara through the heavy, iron door, seated on the floor with her back against the icy wall, despite a perfectly good chair having been placed in her cell. Then she looked at the untouched food on the tray next to her, which was the same food she would have received in the comfort of their quarters. Fedora had just been trying to make a point, not a prisoner.

'You are a smart girl, Aldara. But you are not being very smart about this situation.'

Aldara was staring at the wall opposite her. She rolled her head back to look at Fedora. 'And where has smart gotten me?'

'You are still here at Archdale. You made it work.'

Aldara pulled her legs up and rested her chin on her knees. 'Well, I cannot make it work anymore.'

Fedora exhaled. 'Do not play defeatist. It does not suit you.'

'I'm not playing anything anymore. That's what I'm telling you. I'm tired of the upstream swim.'

She tried a different approach. 'You have two options. You can stay here, or you can return with me. If you return with me, you will behave as you have been taught to behave. No more juvenile attempts to leave. We are all sad Hali is no longer here, but that is the life of a Companion. Taking your skill set to a new audience should not be viewed as a death sentence, but rather an opportunity.'

Aldara raised her head and fixed her burning gaze on her.

∽

Aldara stared up at her mentor, head shaking. Hali was gone, taken from her while she slept. 'Can you hear yourself? Skill set. Audience.' She stood up and ran at the iron door so fast Fedora took a step back from it. 'Hali is not a set of accomplishments. She's warm and kind, attributes that were nurtured by the large family she was taken from. She's good-humoured, loves food, and hates rodents. She likes to please people, even you. That is how *she* made it work, despite belonging to a man who exploited and abused her—'

'Enough!' Fedora said, stepping forward again. She glanced over at the guard who stood at the entrance of the stairs and then looked back at Aldara. 'Enough,' she said again, quieter this time.

Aldara stepped back, panting. Her hands went over her face as she realised her grief was making her reckless.

'Let me give you two *new* choices,' Fedora said. 'You can leave with me now, calmly, and return to our quarters, or I can send a messenger to the border to inform his lordship, Prince Tyron, that you have been imprisoned for an attempted escape.' She paused. 'What do you think Prince Tyron will do when he gets that message?'

Aldara's hands dropped to her side. She knew Tyron would return, immediately. He would ride overnight to get there as quickly as possible.

'Neither of those options brings Hali back,' Fedora continued. 'One of them disrupts a very complicated war and leaves our borders without its strongest defence.'

Aldara knew she could not do that to him. She nodded,

resigning to her decision. Her body went limp as the fight left her. 'Don't send the messenger.'

'I am tempted to send one anyway, as I have no idea if I can trust a word you say.'

Aldara pressed her lips together. 'Please, you have my word. I will not attempt to leave again.'

Fedora kept her face stern and eyes on Aldara. 'Guard,' she said, stepping back from the door.

As the women followed the guard down the cold stone steps of the tower, Aldara felt as though her submission was a betrayal to Hali. Fedora, as if reading her mind, said, 'Hali would expect you to miss her, not throw your life away on her behalf. Give yourself time to adjust to life here without her. It might not be such a terrible life.'

The stairs seemed to go on and on. For a moment Aldara wondered if they were perhaps descending into hell. Then suddenly, a door swung open in front of them and a blast of snow hit her face. She paused, took a lungful of the sharp air, and then stepped out into it.

CHAPTER 30

Aldara sat with a book on her lap, watching the flames of the fire. Fedora was not around, so her legs were tucked up next to her. That was the extent of her rebellion those days. One of the maids, Edelpha, was changing the bed linen in the next room. Aldara could hear the effort in her breath. She stood up and walked over to the doorway, peeking around the corner at the heavily pregnant maid, hunched over a bed, struggling to tuck the sheet under the heavy wool mattress.

'I am sure someone else could take over this chore if you spoke up,' Aldara said, walking over to help.

Edelpha shook her head. 'The moment I admit I cannot do my job is the moment I have to step down. I need the wage for as long as possible.'

Aldara knew the story well and immediately thought of Tia, whose family had also needed the wage. She looked across the bed at the bulging stomach. 'I would be very surprised if the seneschal has not figured out how far along you are already.'

Edelpha stood up and put her hands on her lower back as she stretched it. 'He is a kind man. He chooses not to see.'

The beds were finished, but Aldara knew the maid would

have more chores to go. 'Well, what is next? I can help you for a few hours.'

'Firewood,' Eldelpha said, letting out an exhausted breath.

Aldara had been afraid of that. 'Well, we better go before Fedora returns then.'

When they stepped outside, the wind howled about them, lifting the hood of their cloaks from their heads.

'Perhaps you should wait inside,' Aldara shouted over the wind.

'I'll be all right.'

Aldara nodded, and the two women trod carefully along the cleared path that led to the wood hut. Once inside and out of the wind, Edelpha watched as Aldara loaded herself up with large logs before handing one small piece of wood to her.

'Take this,' she said. 'You need to appear useful.'

They went back out into the icy wind, trudging through the fresh snow that was already beginning to cover the path. Aldara wondered how on earth Edelpha had been managing alone. She was grateful for the low cloud cover that blocked any prying eyes above them. A few yards from the door, Edelpha's foot slipped on a patch of ice, and Aldara immediately reached out to steady her. She thought she would lose the pile of wood that was balancing on one arm, but a pair of hands reached through the fog, one steadying the logs and the other grabbing hold of her. Her eyes flicked to the gloved hand wrapped around her arm. But it was not the glove she recognised, but rather the grip of the hand. She looked up and saw Tyron's green eyes looking back at her. Her body was trembling from the cold, or perhaps not from the cold. She glanced at Eldelpha, whose face held an expression of horror as she looked at Tyron.

'Are you all right?' Aldara asked her.

The maid nodded, hugging her single log. Aldara found the strength to look back at him. He was thinner, his hair longer and damp from the snow. Signature dark circles enclosed his eyes.

Her first impulse was to reach out and touch his tired face. Instead, she stood there, taking in the sight of him.

∼

'Let's go,' he said, taking the wood from her.

He took the small log from Edelpha also and gestured for them to walk ahead of him. He watched her walking in front of him, bent against the wind. Even from behind she was achingly beautiful. Her hair spilled out from the hood of her cloak, dusted with snowflakes. His memory had not done her justice. He was grateful to see her looking so well when the rest of the kingdom seemed to be wilting beneath the weather. He could see she was trembling, so he looked down at the path in front of him. It was too much for him to watch her shiver from the cold, and far too much for him to imagine other possibilities.

When they stepped inside, Aldara reached for the wood in his arms.

'Stop,' he said. 'I have told you before you are not to carry firewood.'

It certainly was not what he had planned to say when he first saw her. She stepped back from him as he piled the wood inside the doorway. The three of them stood together in the servants' entry. Edelpha was about to say something, but Aldara shook her head, and she excused herself, waddling off through to the kitchen as fast as she could. They remained where they were, with all that distance between them. Their presence surprised and panicked the servants, who continued to pass them.

'I will accompany you back to your quarters,' he said.

But that was not what he wanted to do.

∼

Aldara could not cope with the formalities, and she hated the distance between them, but she had also been warned by Fedora that he might require physical space when he returned, so she nodded and walked off towards the steps leading up the main corridor. When they surfaced, he reached out and helped her out of her wet cloak. She stood still, feeling every fingertip that brushed over her. After he had removed his own, they stood looking at one another.

'I'm sorry. I can't do this,' Aldara said, tearing up.

Tyron shook his head. 'What can't you do?'

She inhaled sharply. 'I cannot waste time on proper conduct and return to my quarters and wait, and hope, that you will send for me.' Some tears fell then, and she brushed them aside. 'I can't wonder when you are leaving again and if I will even be told.' Another sharp breath. 'I am actually begging you to forget propriety and just let me be with you now. Please, just while you are here. Be here with me. If you can,' she added, her voice growing quiet.

She looked down at his feet. Fedora would never forgive such a speech. His silence did nothing to ease the rising panic she felt. She was working up the courage to apologise for the outburst when he stepped forward, lifted her off the ground, and crushed her against the wall. His lips were on her. His hands went under her dress, clawing at her legs as they reached higher. Not an ounce of propriety in sight. She wrapped one leg around him and could barely suppress a moan when he pressed himself harder against her. At that moment a servant came walking along the corridor and froze when he saw them. Tyron gently lowered her back onto the ground and took a step back. The young boy rushed past them, taking the stairs next to them two at a time. Aldara wanted him to pick her up again.

'We can do better than this,' he said, panting. 'Please, let me walk you back, and I promise you I will send for you as soon as I can.'

She was still collapsed against the wall. The snow had melted in her hair, and it clung to parts of her face and neck. She did not want better, she just wanted more, and now. But the rules of decency forced her to stand upright and fix her dress. She ran her fingers through her messy hair, pulling it free from her face. It should have been up. 'Of course,' she said.

She walked beside him to the entrance of the Companions' quarters. Their manners were impeccable. When he left, she went straight to the bathing room and scrubbed her body until it was pink all over. She washed her hair, twice. She did not wait for instructions from Fedora because he had given his word. He would request her. And she wanted to be ready.

∼

'WHAT ABOUT THIS ONE?' Sapphira asked, holding up a light blue silk dress.

'No,' Aldara said. 'It's not enough.'

Sapphira suppressed a laugh. 'I have never seen you like this. I'm almost blushing from the energy coming from you right now.'

'I have no idea what you mean,' Aldara said, scanning the dresses. 'This one.' She pulled out a ruby-coloured dress that showed more flesh than it covered.

'He is going to be a very lucky prince tonight,' Sapphira said, crossing her arms in front of her and smiling at Aldara.

By the time Fedora found her to advise her of the prince's return, she was dressed, her face painted, and her hair had been smoothed into a slick knot. Fedora ran her eyes over the dress. She seemed surprised by the bold choice, but she nodded her approval. Aldara still had to wait—and the wait felt eternal. Darkness covered the castle as the evening meal was served to the women. Astra took one look at Aldara in her dress and seated herself at the other end of the table. Aldara did not notice the envious stares of the other Companions. She could not even eat.

She sat, then she stood. She watched the doorway. Finally, Pero arrived with a note for Fedora, who took her time reading it before turning to look at her.

'Prince Tyron has requested your company,' she said, visibly pleased. 'Pero will escort you.' Before she had a chance to rush off, Fedora turned her around and told her to fetch a cloak to wear for the walk. 'We do not want a scandal,' she said.

Aldara grabbed the first cloak she saw and wrapped it around her. When she turned back around, Astra was standing in the doorway, looking at her.

'I remember when Idalia wore that dress to the king's birthday feast. It was his favourite gift of the evening.'

Aldara glanced down at the dress. 'I can change if you would like.' She did not want to fight about a dress, she just wanted to leave.

Astra shook her head. 'No. She would have enjoyed seeing you look this good in it. She wanted you to succeed here.'

She swallowed, unsure what to say.

'Off you go,' Astra said, her tone hardening. 'Better go and remind that prince of yours what he has missed.'

When Pero saw Aldara he pretended he had not just glimpsed what was beneath the cloak. She said, 'Good evening,' and he nodded before walking on ahead of her, all business. When they arrived at Tyron's chambers he gave a small knock on the door before opening it and letting her through.

'Thank you,' she said to the closing door. She had some work to do in winning him over.

Tyron stood up from his chair and stood there, looking at her. She could tell by his eyes he had not slept yet, but he had washed and trimmed his hair and beard. Neither of them moved for a moment. She reached up and unfastened her cloak, keeping her eyes on him as it slid off her shoulders and dropped to the floor. His weight shifted from one foot to another as he took in the sight of her—the hair, the painted eyes, the silky lips. That dress.

The dress that showed an indecent amount of milky skin all the way down to her navel. The dress with the open back that sat just above her buttocks. The dress which he could surely remove with the slightest gust of breath.

'If you have planned for us to go riding, I might need to change,' she said, helping him.

He laughed. 'Otus has seen you in less.'

A laugh from her, his undoing. No need for more words.

Neither of them could have predicted their physical response to one another. The combination of relentless and insatiable made for a long night. It was Tyron who unwillingly surrendered to sleep just before daylight reached them. At first, Aldara was careful not to wake him, but soon she discovered he could not be woken anyway. Exhaustion had taken hold of him, so she waited beside him, occasionally checking to see if his heart was still beating. It was. She kept her head pressed against it listening to life beat inside of him.

Just before noon, Tyron woke with a start. Aldara, who had finally fallen asleep herself, jumped also. When he sat up to take in his surroundings, she could see a shine of sweat on his forehead. She took hold of his arm and gently pulled him back down to her. His body was rigid, and he did not touch her.

'Did you dream?' she asked him.

∼

For a moment, Tyron thought he could smell smoke and propped himself up on one elbow. He looked down at her concerned face and tried to remember what she had asked him. Dreams. He did not want to speak about his dreams. How could he? He had dreamed of her, crouched on a road in a blood-soaked dress. He had watched as she was dragged away by her hair through the thick smoke. Now he was sure he could smell the smoke, and he was having difficulty breathing.

Aldara, seeing that he was struggling with his breath, propped herself up next to him. 'We are both safe here,' she said, placing a hand on his face.

When he looked at her, there was frenzy in his eyes. He pulled away and sat up, trying to focus on familiar items in the room, which sometimes helped to calm him. 'I learned yesterday that Idalia passed away.'

He looked at her then, but he had to blink away the vision of a dark hand around her neck. More sweat beads formed on his face.

'She was with child. There was an infection after the loss.' When he said nothing she continued. 'Your father came to her bedside. She could not be helped. Too much time had passed. Only Astra had known about the pregnancy.'

Tyron became still suddenly, as though listening for something.

'What is it?' Aldara asked.

He raised a hand to silence her, hearing the thunder of hooves. He guessed around fifty horses. 'Can you hear that?'

Aldara sat up, slowly, holding onto the sheet. She had no idea what she was listening for, but she remained silent for a while, observing him the entire time. 'I cannot hear anything. What is it you think you can hear?'

'Horses. They are here.'

He stood up and began searching for his clothes. She reached out to take his hand, and he grabbed hold of her wrist. 'Listen,' he hissed.

She remained still and calm, her hand limp beneath his grip. 'No one is here,' she said, keeping her voice quiet. 'Give yourself a moment to wake up properly. No one is here.'

All Tyron could hear at that moment was the thud of his own heart amid the tinker of castle life. It was happening again. His demons had returned. He looked at her, naked, vulnerable, and completely unafraid of him. That angered him because he was capable of killing her with one hand and no weapon. 'I think you should leave,' he said, slipping his pants on.

Aldara pressed the sheet against her chest. 'Why?'

'You are forgetting yourself. I don't need to give a reason. Get dressed.'

She watched him, sweat dripping from his face as he wrestled with his shirt. 'No.'

He stopped still and looked at her. 'Excuse me?'

'No,' she repeated. 'I won't leave you when you are feeling like this. When I know you are all right, you can send me away.'

He stepped up to the bed, fists clenched. She remained still, looking straight at him.

'Get dressed,' he said again.

She reluctantly slipped from the bed and picked her dress up off the floor. 'I'll dress, but I am not leaving you.'

His hands wiped his face and then linked on top of his head. He had not been prepared for her defiance. He had not been prepared for any of it. 'I decide when I want to see you. You do as you are told. That is how it works.'

His words made her stop and look at him. 'What has you so afraid right now? Talk to me.'

'You need to leave.'

'No!' She walked over to him and put her hands on his face. 'Tell me what is happening.'

He pushed her hands away, harder than he had meant to, but her feet remained anchored to the floor. 'I'll have the guards remove you if I have to. Then I'll have you sent away, like Hali.'

Aldara flinched as though she had been slapped by him. 'Stop it!' she pleaded. 'I understand you are afraid right now, but don't say things to me you don't mean.'

He went still then, looking at her wounded in front of him. He had done that to her. 'I just need you to leave.' His voice cracked as he spoke.

She rushed forward and wrapped herself around him. He

remained still, looking down at her as she cried against his bare chest. After a long struggle with his shirt, he had not even managed to put it on.

'I love you,' he thought she said. His eyes closed. It was his mind playing tricks on him again.

She was looking up at him, eyes pleading.

'I am not afraid of you. Let me stay with you while you battle your demons, the way you would if they were mine.'

He opened his eyes and looked at her. The sound of hooves had disappeared. The smoke had vanished. He had pushed her away, yelled, hurt her, and still she clung to him. His hands went on her then, around her, lifted her, so he could breathe her in.

'I'm sorry,' he whispered into her skin.

He had given his physical self over to her months earlier. That afternoon, in a coil of sheets, he shared his mind, in its darkest form. She listened as he spoke, as he cried, heart bleeding for him but face poised. Pity would have destroyed him at that moment, and she wanted him to share every broken piece of himself. She felt powerless, unable to help or heal him.

He told her more than he wanted to and more than he was permitted to. When he was depleted of thought and unable to speak any longer, he slept. She did not. She watched over him, willing away dreams that might wake him. He slept for hours, unmoving, aside from the odd twitch. And she lay next him, stomach empty, heart full. At some point during the night he opened his eyes and looked at her.

'I love you,' he whispered before his eyes closed once again.

EPILOGUE

Whenever Aldara woke alone in a cold bed, her first thought was always of Hali. Grief would rumble inside her, fresh as though it had happened that very morning. She had no idea how to grieve the living. It did not ease or get better with time. The chance that she might still see her one day kept her hopes high and the affliction raw.

She sat up and looked around, already knowing the room would be empty. Where was he at this ungodly hour? She swung her legs over the edge of the bed and collected her dress from the floor. As she was slipping it on, she knew there was a good chance Pero was outside. Someone was always watching over her.

She walked barefoot across the icy floor to the door, opened it just enough to poke her head through, and saw Pero, seated at his small table, quill in hand.

'What are you writing?' she whispered.

He looked up, visibly disappointed he had not heard her sooner. 'Just thoughts,' he said, pushing them away as though they meant nothing to him.

She often found him writing. When she had asked Tyron

about it, he had told her they were stories. She had loved the idea of a knight in training preferring to write stories. 'I would like to read those thoughts one day,' she said, stepping through the door and crossing her arms in front of her.

Pero looked at her, ignoring the comment. 'His lordship is training.'

His face was *almost* sympathetic.

She nodded and looked away. 'What for is the question,' she said, eyes returning to him. 'How does he seem to you?'

'What do you mean?'

She tilted her head, like one does to a child keeping secrets. 'You know exactly what I mean. Should I be worried?'

He stood up and walked over to collect the tray of food sitting near the other door. 'My guess is you are already worried.'

She looked at the tray of food in his hands. 'Is that for me?'

'Yes,' he said, offering it up to her.

'I can source my own food. You needn't have troubled yourself.'

He pushed the tray closer to her. 'Please just eat it. His lordship wants you fed. If it were up to me I'd happily let you starve.' He almost smiled at her.

Aldara took the tray from him. His jokes indicated he might be finally warming to her. 'Very well,' she said. 'Then, I am going to the butts.'

He sighed because he was expecting her to say that. 'My orders are to keep you here.'

'Just tell him we fought it out, and I won,' she said, turning to go inside.

'He'll have my head if he thought I laid a hand on you,' he called after her.

The door clunked shut behind her. She would worry about Pero later.

THE AIR WAS SO cold Aldara felt a stabbing pain in her chest with every frosty breath she took. She padded through the fresh snow, Tyron's tracks already erased in front of her. The fog was so hazardous she found herself counting the familiar trees to navigate her way through it. For a moment she wondered if she should have told Pero the truth and brought him along. Then she remembered how much trouble he would get in and reminded herself the lie was for his protection. 'Just going to bathe. I will be back before he returns,' she had said, casually walking past his suspicious gaze. She had expected him to follow her, that is why she went into the Companions' quarters and stood inside the door until he was satisfied and left. The other women were never up that early, so she could afford to linger about until it was safe to leave.

The clapping of wooden swords stopped her feet. She listened for him. And there it was, the sound of his efforts. How they did not accidentally kill each other she had no idea.

She stepped carefully, pausing behind a tree, trying to locate him amid the eerie light. It did not take them long to step into view, two men with beaten shields and wooden swords, moving about one another as though their lives were at stake. Her chest tightened as she glimpsed him through the fog. Where were the rest of his clothes? He was stripped down to trousers, boots, and a shirt that clung to his wet body. His opponent was tiring, barely getting his shield up in time to block the blows. Tyron seemed oblivious, emitting noises that made Aldara colder than she could have imagined. When his opponent, exhausted, collapsed in the snow, she waited for him to stop. It was only training after all. But down came his sword, blow after blow, while the fallen man cowered beneath his shield. She came out from behind the tree then, walking towards him, willing him to stop. She had intended to watch him awhile and then slip away unnoticed, but now she was afraid for the man beneath the shield, and she was afraid for Tyron, who was lost in his imagined rage.

She was just a few yards away when she heard the man say, 'I am done, my lord. I yield.' But Tyron did not seem to hear him. 'My lord!' the man shouted again, clutching the shield with both hands in an effort to steady it.

Aldara broke into a run. 'Tyron,' she shouted. 'The man yields. Stop.'

Tyron stopped, went still, and looked at her. He was out of breath, his entire body covered in sweat to the point there was visible steam rising from him. He seemed confused as he glanced at the sword in his hand, as if noticing it for the first time. It fell at his feet, and he took a few wary steps back from it.

Aldara was shivering, her mind racing with fear. 'My lord,' she said. 'Help the man up and we will all go inside.'

The man lowered his shield with caution and stared up at Tyron, trying to recognise him amid the sweat and fury. Tyron was beginning to understand what had happened. Aldara could see the change in his face as he came back to them from whatever dark place he had been. He did not help the man up. He looked only at the ground and walked away from them both, straight past Aldara, who knew better than to reach out for him as he passed her. She glanced at the man in the snow who was struggling to get to his feet, depleted of all strength. Then her eyes returned to Tyron, just as the fog swallowed him.

She had handed herself over to him, willingly this time. And he had made the choice to keep her, giving of himself whatever he was able to. They were joined by their grief, demons, and love. The only two choices she had was to bring him back from his hell or slip away with him.

Printed in Great Britain
by Amazon